MW01034835

Praise for Save the Village

"Michele Herman knows Greenwich Village inside out: its gestures, its codes, the complex history behind each building facade, smile, or frown. Every village is a universe, and Herman brings this one joyously alive. With compassion and humor, she tells a gripping tale of a rupture that shakes a community into a new alignment."

—Pamela Erens, author of *Matasha*, *Eleven Hours*, and *The Virgins*

"*Save the Village* is the kind of love letter the world's most famous neighborhood deserves, written with the intimate detail and wry affection only a loving insider could conjure."

—John Strausbaugh, author of *The Village*

"*Save the Village* is an unblinking deep dive into the psyche of a self-professed 'broken girl in a broken life'; a woman alone with her aging dog in the most densely populated major U.S. city; a woman who has dug deeply into the rich history of her beloved Village but who, until now, has not studied the artifacts, accidental architecture, and ghosts of her own personal history. Herman is a skilled guide, deftly directing our gaze to the largest of questions and then zooming in on the most intimate details, all at a freewheeling tempo that would have fit right in at Caffe Reggio circa 1960. As details and relationships are revealed, Becca discovers that before she can save her village, she must first save herself."

—David Roth, author of *The Femme Fatale Hypothesis*

Save the Village

Michele Herman

Regal House Publishing

Copyright © 2022 Michele Herman. All rights reserved.

Published by
Regal House Publishing, LLC
Raleigh, NC 27612
All rights reserved

ISBN -13 (paperback): 9781646030811
ISBN -13 (epub): 9781646031061
Library of Congress Control Number: 2020951631

All efforts were made to determine the copyright holders and obtain their permissions in any circumstance where copyrighted material was used. The publisher apologizes if any errors were made during this process, or if any omissions occurred. If noted, please contact the publisher and all efforts will be made to incorporate permissions in future editions.

Interior and cover design by Lafayette & Greene
Cover design © by C.B. Royal

Regal House Publishing, LLC
https://regalhousepublishing.com

The following is a work of fiction created by the author. All names, individuals, characters, places, items, brands, events, etc. were either the product of the author or were used fictitiously. Any name, place, event, person, brand, or item, current or past, is entirely coincidental.

All rights reserved. No part of this publication may be reproduced, stored in a retrieval system, or transmitted, in any form or by any means, electronic, mechanical, photocopying, recording, or otherwise, without the prior permission of Regal House Publishing.

Printed in the United States of America

to Villagers everywhere –
the honorary, the adopted, and the natives,
especially Lee and Jeffrey Kuhn

with thanks to my students, colleagues,
and teachers at The Writers Studio

The Manhattan skyline takes a curious dip between the mountain peaks of midtown and Wall Street. There's no good toe-hold for skyscrapers in Greenwich Village; the bedrock is too deep and the water table too high. So it remains largely a village of red brick and cobblestone, a village built of the earth, one piece at a time, the way a child builds a city of blocks on the living room floor. If you build too tall the whole thing might topple. Trust a developer to find the loopholes (you can't trust him for anything else): just dig deeper into the earth (*pa-chung, pa-chung*, says the pile driver) and bail more water out of it. On a quiet night you can hear the drone of the twenty-four-hour sump pumps all along the Hudson River waterfront.

Populate this Village with Villagers, a whole cast of yentas, wisemen and wisewomen, idiots and elders, sorting themselves into the available housing stock. Charming, quirky people fill the charming, quirky buildings—where retired seamen went to die, where a builder went to town with terra-cotta tiles, where a church was decommissioned, where some old bohemians who fancied themselves Spaniards stuccoed over the brick.

Most of the townhouses by now have had all their organs extracted and new ones put in by new owners with new tastes and new money, the dozen hot plates with fraying cloth cords carted out with the lead-painted plaster, the dust made of a million roach hulls and mouse skeletons. Now the bricks are repointed and the lintels recast by Rastafarian tradesmen, the contractor's sign placed in the window.

The postwar hulks are all traceable to the zoning resolution of 1961, when they figured out how to build 'em fat, build 'em quick, and build 'em cheap, and now the tenants wonder why they're constantly under scaffolding. The cold-storage warehouses alongside the waterfront were drained of ice and converted to lofts in the eighties—co-ops, New York City's answer to condos, each one a small Middle East. And don't write off the tenements, still holding on, with the toilet tank still high on the wall with a pull cord, and the wiring from 1922. Deep inside the old-law walls still stained from gaslight, you'll still find old-law Villagers, fists raised in defiance, fingers stained from nicotine.

When the Village began to grow taller, the giants who made it began shrinking from view. A new breed arrived, hoping (like all newcomers) that the magic would rub off on them, failing to realize that magic is something you must make yourself. Who says the Village has lost its manufacturing base? It runs the most ruthless and efficient export-import business in the annals of Wall Street—the real estate industry, which exports the poor and imports the rich.

The last great wave of Village giants are unsung artists, many toiling in a field so new they had to invent it: preservation. Departed giants like Jane Jacobs and Verna Small kept the Village alive (though Lionel Trilling declared it past its prime in 1929). They pushed back the developers and the slum clearers and even Moses himself, with white-gloved hands and strength that surprised even them.

Frieda Glaberson, Chair Emeritus of all of Greenwich Village, is fighting still, with the build of a hummingbird and the voice of a jackhammer. Stand on any West Village street corner, look in any direction, and you'll see a dozen problems Frieda solved, a dozen buildings and lives she saved. And the old Communist Camille Warachovsky of the proto-feminist Ironed Curtain Theater (still hanging on by a thread, she likes to say). She rescued a generation of youth from the romance of heroin in Tompkins Square Park. Without Camille, they say, there might be no new vaudeville, no Blue Man Group, no Fringe Festival.

Frieda is retired and spending more and more time in Jersey, near the grandkids. Camille is frail and housebound in her tenement one-bedroom. Who is left to beat off the developers, to save what remains, to keep the soul of Greenwich Village alive?

MONDAY

A Tour of Greenwich Village

The six women from South Carolina looked at the tour guide and were ready to love her. On Friday they had admired the Tiffany windows at the Met, on Saturday had hummed along at the matinee of "Jersey Boys," on Sunday had made the pilgrimage to Ground Zero, and today had splurged on lunch at the Mesa Grill because who doesn't love Iron Chef Bobby Flay? It had all been perfect, they told each other.

Now it was evening, and their time here was almost up. The women had just cabbed it to the Village from their midtown hotel, where their husbands were wrapping up their big East Coast engineers' meeting. Watching all the imposing buildings they would never enter and all the purposeful people they would never meet speed past from the cab windows, they relished their one last chance for Manhattan to open up and offer them more—a new friend who wasn't just a concierge or a waiter; maybe a bolder version of themselves to take back home to Plantation Pointe.

They recognized their tour guide right away from the *TimeOut* posting on the web that ranked "25 Living Legends of New York That Should Be Experienced While They're Still Alive and Kicking." The woman wore a black cape and leaned against the Washington Square Arch as if she were holding it up all by herself. She was smaller and older and more round than she had appeared in the picture, and these facts helped set them at ease. Her mouth was cut a little on the wide side, as if to allow for the passage of big emotions.

"I'm Becca Cammeyer," she said, and then she added with a smile and a twirl, "and this is my dramatic tour-guide cape, so you won't ever lose me."

They looked up at her from their twin sets and their

drawstring-waist cropped pants and their flats. They had expected a big, nasal voice, but hers was soothing and carried just the right amount of authority. Her hair was a long, rough-textured mix of dark brown and gray, much as theirs was somewhere deep under the defrizzer and the blow-drying and the gold-hued dye.

When she asked where they were from, they all clamored to answer.

Sheryl, the one in the top with the stripes and the nautical brass buttons, got in first, as usual. "You wouldn't of heard of it. It's kind of a suburb of a suburb of Greenville, South Carolina."

Becca smiled again and asked, "How many of you have been to the Village before?"

Jackie, who'd organized the tour, said that once, many years ago, she'd come to visit a boyfriend at NYU. Laura, who tended toward shyness, volunteered that her daughter had studied ballet at the Joffrey before the birth of twins put the kibosh on that dream.

"Even for those of you who have never set foot in the Village until now," Becca continued, "I think that a tiny bit will rub off on you tonight. Who knows? Maybe by the end of the evening, a little piece of South Carolina will rub off on me, though I've never been there."

Mary Anne, who liked everyone to be happy, gave the others a discreet thumbs-up. Ever since they had sat around Jackie's blond kitchen table studying printouts of Expedia itineraries, each of them had secretly feared that New York City was a test they might fail, the kind that would go on their permanent record. What if the city cast them in an unflattering light, made them heavier than they wanted to see themselves, and at the same time less substantial? What if, upon their return south, their spacious, meticulously decorated homes looked hollow and farcical? What if their husbands—their dear, hearty, hardworking husbands—turned squat and red-faced and corny on them?

"So, let's talk about Greenwich Village," said Becca, spreading the name on an invisible marquee, "arguably the most famous neighborhood on the planet." They were mesmerized by her hands, surprisingly long and thin. Her palms caught each sentence in midair as if it were an extrusion in need of molding and crimping and polishing—talk in New York City seemed to be both an art and a skilled trade. Where they came from, speech was a more pulmonary activity, having to do with the concertina-like withholding and releasing of air into select vowels.

While a pot dealer nearby whispered "smoke, smoke" in his comforting way and a silent bubble lady dipped her loop of rope into her bucket and sent a giant bubble shimmering yellow and pink into the air, Becca looked into the eager faces of her tourists. They seemed to be saying, *Give us the secret Village, the real Village*, and she was happy to oblige, because if she handed it to them, that must mean it was still hers to give.

She had a rule about index cards—never use them. She let her tourists feed her cues and she opened her mouth and followed where it led. Suburb was her first cue tonight. Ugly word out there in the world-world, but here in the bubble it was just what she needed.

"Well, you may find it hard to believe, but the Village started out as a suburb too. Let's pretend it's 1822. The city is a little collection of wooden buildings huddled down by the Battery, not two miles south of here." She pointed past the old Italian quarter and the sneaker stores of SoHo all the way to New Amsterdam. She sketched it for them: the stepped roofs, the mad commerce conducted under the buttonwood tree that grew to become the Stock Exchange, the canals dug by the beaver-like Dutch. And then she told them about the topography of Manhattan Island; tourists were always surprised to learn that Manhattan had topography. She taught them about Lispenard Swamp and Collect Pond and the germ-breeding low ground of downtown. In the terrible year of 1822 (in an era she secretly loved and wished she could walk around in), she said, yellow fever struck hard.

"The merchants got sick and passed the sickness to their wives and the wives passed it to the children and the children passed it to the aged grandparents who shared their dark cottages, and soon the bustling little city was in quarantine. The city filled with weeping and black flags at half-mast.

"And what, you may ask, does it all have to do with you here?" Teachers hate when students ask that question, but Becca knew it was where all learning begins. If you can forge a connection, you can make a student, and if you can make a student, you can make an activist.

"Because that's how the Village you're standing in, here in 2006, got born. Before they dynamited all the hills to make landfill, this was rolling countryside," she said, fanning out a caped arm to take in the traffic and the townhouses and the dorms of NYU.

"So the lucky ones with good immune systems packed up their belongings and hiked up here and built themselves an outpost on the high ground. How many of you have heard of Bank Street?" she asked, because the moment had come to engage them. Hands went up.

"Maybe you know it from the excellent Bank Street School, which practically invented modern progressive education." Then she asked if any of them were Beatles fans, because while it was usually best to pose questions she didn't already know the answers to, sometimes it was also fun to make like a prosecutor (but benign) and ask questions whose answers were obvious.

When hands shot up again, she said, "You might like to know that John Lennon lived about a half mile from here on Bank Street. It's where he wrote 'I Am the Walrus.'" They smiled as if she had passed out a small chocolate to each one.

"So how do you think Bank Street got its name?" she asked, a warm-up question, not too easy but not too hard.

"Is it on the bank of the river?" asked one tentatively.

"Excellent guess," she said, "because Bank Street actually does run to the Hudson."

Before the woman had a chance to feel bad, another piped up. "Because it's where they built the first bank?"

"Bingo. If there's one thing you should know about New Amsterdammers, it's that they were very careful with their gilders. Practically the first thing they did was build a bank."

"Becca," asked the tall one named Jackie who'd arranged the tour on the phone and who had pressed a check discreetly into Becca's hand when they arrived, one of those strange gestures from the land of money, a check Becca had then pressed deep into her pants pocket. "Would you mind giving us a real quick orientation? I mean, we've been here a few days now, but some of us have an iffy sense of direction and we keep getting turned around." The others nodded vigorously.

"Sure," Becca said, patting herself to see if she might be able to produce any props. And then she had an idea. "This is going to require some helpers." The woman with the eager face stepped right up, grabbing her balky friend by the hand and yanking her forward.

"Power in numbers, Connie," said the eager woman, winking at the others.

"Poifect," Becca said, knowing they expected a dollop of Noo Yawk and not the milder accent of the Manhattan native. With the women on either side of her, she drew a quick line dividing the eastern half of herself from the west and called it Fifth Avenue, and a diagonal like the most unlikely of beauty-pageant banners and called it Broadway, explaining that the world's most famous street grew from paths carved by the native Lenape tribe. She looked down and shrugged as she realized that her right breast would have to serve as the Upper West Side and her left the Upper East.

"We're all girls here, right?" said Becca, and they all chuckled because she sounded just like them. "What do you know? That makes my lungs Central Park, which is great because in the more hokey guidebooks they always call Central Park the lungs of Manhattan. And my belly is midtown, and you can figure out for yourselves where the Village is," she said, watching a blush spread across their cheeks. "My thighs are SoHo, my knees Tribeca, and there's the Battery down at my feet."

She turned toward the woman on one side and said, with a bow, "May I present New Jersey, the Garden State." Then she took a gamble and grabbed the hand of Connie, the skeptical friend, and asked her to make a peace sign. Out of the corner of her eye, Becca could see her glare at the others, as if to say, I signed on for a tour, not some hippie improv class. But all Becca did was gently raise her arm until it stuck straight out.

She drew a line in the air at the woman's waist level. "Brooklyn down there, Queens up here," she said. She pointed to the woman's extended arm and said, "Long Island," then wiggled her extended fingers and added, "North Fork and South Fork."

It worked. Because everyone was having fun, because a hipster couple passing by looked up from their lattes as if they might be missing out on a burgeoning art form, she asked if two of the women wouldn't mind lending their purses for just a second, and before they had time to remember that just as you didn't take candy from a stranger you certainly didn't hand over your purse to a New Yorker you'd just met, she placed one on the ground in front of her and the other on top of her head. "Lest we forget, Staten Island and the Bronx."

The women applauded. She took a bow and a breath and handed back the purses.

One of the women called out, because now the tour belonged to them all, "Becca, I used to have this old Joan Baez album, the one where she sings about the crummy hotel over Washington Square...?"

Becca pointed to a big brick building on the west side of the Square and sang "I'll be damned," the beginning of "Diamonds and Rust" in her good clear alto, a song about a ghost coming around again. It was a song she had once sung as a student at the old High School of Music & Art, where she'd been voted most likely to land on Broadway or in jail for good cause.

"It's not so crummy anymore, but it sure was when her boyfriend Bob Dylan stayed there." She surprised even herself by knowing his room number, 305, and a list of others who had stayed there: Ernest Hemingway, Dylan Thomas, Barbra Streisand, and the Rolling Stones.

She noticed two of the women shaking their heads in amazement, maybe at the thought of such fame, maybe at her memory. And then Tick and Tack the street performers, just setting up by the fountain, called, "Yo, Becca."

"Ah, my favorite colleagues," she explained as she waved. "At every performance they line up seven squatting audience members and leap over them. But don't worry," she said, raising her plain black pants to show them her plain black walking shoes. "I didn't wear my leaping shoes tonight."

They chuckled. She made a mental note to polish her shoes. And then she showed them the concrete mounds from the 1960s, not quite play structure but not quite skateboard park. "Pity us poor Villagers who lost all our hills. This is our beloved mountain range," she said, and now she inserted just the tiniest bit of politics. She explained that the Parks Department kept trying to renovate the park and tear down the mounds, but the neighbors kept suing. "Like many things in the Village, the mounds have their own preservation group. We are trying very hard to save them. And if we do, I hope one day to play hide and seek with my grandchildren, should I be blessed with any, on these very same mounds."

Becca had a rule about doling out too much personal information, but she wanted them to know that she was a mother, just like them.

"Ready to get some exercise?" she asked.

"Lead the way," said Jackie the organizer. Becca marched them north out of the park. She waved to the district manager of the community board and to the usher of the Quad Cinema arthouse.

The woman in the big stripes called out, "Do you actually know this many people or are you really famous?"

And at just that moment Becca laughed out loud because Ed Koch, a long-ago comrade of her father's, came loping up the street.

"Did you show them my house?" he asked.

She replied, "No, sir, because I believe in protecting personal privacy, but I did discreetly genuflect as we passed." He took off his baseball cap to kiss her on the cheek, and then he turned to the group and asked in his high nasal voice how they were doin'.

She waited for the women to place this familiar stranger with the surprisingly lanky body and the wrinkled little head, like a character in a Looney Tunes cartoon, an earthworm, maybe. The shy one at the end of the row whispered to her neighbor, who passed the news along.

"This is an unusually attractive group you have tonight," he said, and she could have kissed him again. He slung his arm around Becca's shoulder and said, "Treat our Becca well; she's the best in the business." Then he put the cap back on and added, "By the way, would you ladies like a movie recommendation? I'm a celebrated movie reviewer now, you know."

She made a shooing motion and told him to run along. She felt the little thrill that passed through the group. Who knew what stars and statesmen might be headed their way on these Village streets?

She steered them onto Tenth Street and stopped. "I think you'll like this block." Three-story brick houses lined either side, some of them set back behind tiny yards. The women sighed with pleasure.

"Next best thing to Charleston, right? I'm going to give you a job now, so listen up." She told them how the Village developed pretty much the way their suburb probably had, with speculative building. "Let's go back to the 1820s for a minute, when the country was brand new and it still seemed possible to form a more perfect union, to fix the problems that had plagued humans since they stepped out of their caves. There's not a lot left in Manhattan from that era, which is known as the

Federal period. But bless their modest little hearts, there are three Federal-style houses still going strong on this block. Go find us one," she said, gingerly lowering herself onto a stoop whose owners had once told her she was welcome to use it anytime.

Just days earlier, it had been muggy and airless. In a midtown Starbucks their first afternoon, the barista had said it was like living inside your own mouth, and they had heartily agreed. But now the weather had broken. The heavy shell cracked, releasing a perfectly formed autumn.

They understood now what people meant when they talked about a charge in the atmosphere, as if it had been fortified with the more important B vitamins, or caffeine-rich vapor rising off a million lattes, or maybe (mused Wynnette, known as the earth mother of the group) just plumes of pot smoke rising from that pusher they'd passed in Washington Square. They had thought urban living meant small, drafty boxes in the sky, and taxi drivers honking and swearing and shaking their fists out their windows. They had thought it was for people made of sterner stuff. But now New York City struck them as the most civilized system for organizing human life ever devised.

Laura and Wynnette examined the ruddy hand-chiseled stones of the church on the corner, and Sheryl pointed out a periodontist's office tucked cleverly into the ground floor of a townhouse. Jackie admired the window boxes full of mums in muted shades of rust and mauve that seemed to emanate from the same earth as the bricks. Some houses, they noticed, had old window glass that shimmered as they passed and others had modern panes that did nothing at all.

They felt as if they had never really looked at a building before.

They passed a house with a sales banner. "Hey, let's sell everything and call this Melora person at Downtown Domiciles and buy us a row of houses," said Mary Anne. "And we'll let the historical society ladies troop through for their annual fundraiser. Do you think they have historical-society ladies in New York?"

"Honey, I'm sure they have historical-society ladies in Antarctica," replied Connie.

"And we'll dress in black and write inscrutable plays," said Laura.

"Forget plays, I'm working my way through the *Zagat* guide," proclaimed Sheryl.

"And on the seventh day, we will drive to the north fork or the south fork or whatever fork the Hamptons are on and throw cocktail parties with the other beautiful people," said Jackie, sipping from an imaginary glass of chardonnay. "So how much do you think it costs to park your car around here?" she asked, believing that even a fantasy deserved sound planning.

Mary Anne cleared her throat. "I believe we have a home-work assignment, ladies."

They stopped to examine the house in front of them, which happened to be particularly cute. It was made of bricks so obviously formed by hand that you could almost make out thumbprints, and it had a pair of what Wynnette called sticky-outy windows poking through the roof. In a nearby sycamore, a crowd of outspoken sparrows sang a twilight song; the birds were in no hurry to fly south either.

"What do we think?" asked Jackie. "Is this our vote?"

Even Connie nodded assent.

They watched Becca approach. She favored one hip slight-ly, making some of them feel the thin electric prod of their own sciatic nerve. They wished they could get her a hot pack, a massage, a referral for an MRI. And yet there was something beautiful about the way she walked—unafraid of taking up space, dodging obstacles as if the city's atmosphere were her birthright. Mary Anne decided to practice it the rest of the eve-ning so she could take it home along with the Jacques Torres chocolate bars and the Playbills they would all tuck into their rolling suitcases in the morning.

❧

Before long, the sun would disappear behind Hoboken, the tours would end for the winter, and the legal proofreading would have to start. But now it was autumn, Manhattan's season of rebirth. Becca inhaled the city's perfume—one part street chestnuts, one part starch from men's shirts, one part Ray's Pizza. As if the tour were being art-directed by heavenly bodies, the Earth turned a notch on its axis and western sun poured like candlelight through every opening in the street grid. The bricks glowed; the brownstone glittered like maple-sugar candy. Becca caught up to the women, standing proudly in front of the finest of the Federal-style houses. She smiled and high-fived them all and called them her budding architectural historians.

She had meant to be an actress. She had meant to be a singer. She had meant to be a history professor. She had meant to change the world. In the middle of a tour on a crisp fall evening, she was all of the above.

"So let's define the Federal style," she said. She taught them about townhouse fenestration. She showed them the pitched roof and the fan light and taught them to recognize the Flemish-bond brick pattern of alternating "headers" and "stretchers," which she said was a sign of fine workmanship. Then she snuck in a tidbit of consciousness raising, shaking her head and saying the city had long since given up the art of building on a human scale.

They shook their heads too, her knowing urbanites.

"How I admire the people who built these little houses. See this patch in the marble, where some clever mason cut a new piece and fitted it in where there must have been damage? It's called—wait for it—a Dutchman. And it's not like a new slab of stone would have been hard to come by; Westchester was full of marble, and it could be shipped right down the Hudson on barges."

"How come the railings all have those little openings at the bottom?" asked Jackie.

"Let me paint a picture for you. It's the nineteenth century, let's say pre-1842, because that's when the Croton reservoir system opened and people got their first taste of clean water from upstate. The streets aren't paved. There are two main ways to travel: by foot and by horse."

"Oh, I know," yelled one of the others. "It's a boot scraper."

Becca nodded. "New York used to be one poopy town. Right into the early twentieth century, pigs roamed these streets." Such delight on their faces—she could have told them that in Greenwich Village every pig had a pilot's license. She could have flapped her cape and taken off herself.

Becca walked them down to what she called the South Village, below Washington Square. She called it the crucible, what made the Village the Village and maybe what made the U.S. the U.S.

"I don't think we're in Charleston anymore," said Sheryl, waving her striped sleeve at what appeared to be an enormous horse poop in the gutter with hay sticking out at all angles like some ancient peasant mortar, and a paper plate translucent with orange pizza oil rolling down the sidewalk on a breeze.

They followed her down MacDougal Street, where the sixties seemed to be something of a chronic condition. Tiny falafel shops down or up half-flights of shallow steps. Bongs as grand as Murano chandeliers displayed in storefronts. They had to make way for another tour group to pass on the narrow sidewalk. The women in this other group, with their ample silhouettes and their flattering fashions, looked so familiar for a second that they thought they were watching their own lives pass by. This group had husbands along, two of them laughing so hard at an S&M display in a nearby head shop that their faces turned red and they had to stop and catch their breath.

"The poor will always be with us," Becca said, after stopping them in front of a run-down, six-story apartment building very much like its neighbors. It was formed of grimy bricks, wooden window frames reduced to flakes, and an iron railing shedding chunks of what was surely pure lead paint. The whole building appeared to be imprisoned behind crisscrossing fire escapes.

She was amazed when they all bowed their heads, church-like. "Now let's talk about the invisible buildings and the invisible people who live in them. And it's not like they're not trying to get your attention. Some forgotten Italian immigrant worked very hard carving that stone. If you step back a little, you can see the name carved above the door. You can be darned sure Olivia wasn't any wife or daughter of his."

She followed a look as it passed through the group on its way to the shy one at the end of the row. "It's my daughter," the woman said. "My daughter, the one I mentioned with the twins. Her name is Olivia. I don't think I'll take a picture for her. It would make her sad."

She had them now, she could see it in their eyes. So much was already lost, but maybe it wasn't too late to save the South Village.

"Do me one little favor," she said as she passed out golden-rod-yellow pre-addressed postcards. "Drop a postcard in the mail. Jot a little note to the Landmarks Commission and tell them about your visit. Tell them you think they should calendar the South Village—that's the language. It helps like crazy—they listen to tourists. For those who haven't used snail mail in a while, a postcard stamp costs thirty-three cents."

They said, of course, we'd be happy to, as they slipped the cards into side pockets of their purses. She could tell they meant it. They understood. It wasn't an agenda. It wasn't a quid pro quo. It was a love they shared now.

Becca could have kept on walking them all evening. There was so much to show them. She would take them west to the Hudson to watch mallards rise and fall with each passing wave where the great ocean liners were once berthed. She would tell them the story of the man who used to give pony rides in a dusty vacant lot when she was a kid. A Village populated with ghosts, the only home she had ever known.

But an Abba tune played deep in one of the women's purses. The tall one mouthed a "sorry" as she dug for her phone and

took the call, expertly cupping her free ear to block the city's
ambient noise. She conferred with the others.

"Hey, Becca," she said. "We've got an idea we want to run
by you."

"I'm all yours," she said, but it wasn't true. Tourists had
been known to ask her where she lived, what her husband did
(without first asking whether she had one), could they have her
address for their Christmas-card list? Her cousin Joycie, who
was a therapist, had told her it was a kind of transference. It
could pop the bubble.

"The men are just starting dessert and want us to meet them
in the hotel bar for a drink," said the woman. "Come uptown
and have a drink. On us. We want y'all to meet."

No, no, no, she thought as she politely demurred. She just
wanted to take her bow and make a clean exit.

But they persisted. "At least let us buy you a cupcake at that
place where Carrie and her friends used to go. That's somewhere around here, isn't it?"

She had no TV, but she knew the general idea; the *Sex in the
City* tour buses were constantly circling the neighborhood and
idling their motors, so high above the ground and long and fat
there was no getting around them.

It took all she had, but she smiled politely and thanked the
women, and said it was getting time for her to take them back
to Washington Square.

"*Ketzelah*," the voice of her dead father whispered in her ear
as it often did. "I'm proud of you. If you don't bend, you break.
Go get yourself a malted; you earned it."

She smiled—she hadn't seen a malted on a menu in decades.

It was dark now. At some point clouds had rolled in and
settled low, not much higher than the water tower on top of
Ed Koch's big white apartment building. The park had emptied
out. The breeze dried Becca's lips as fast as she could moisten
them. Her father's old class ring, tight just this morning, spun
around her finger every time she made a sweeping gesture.

She said her goodbyes and headed west.

Someone called her name. Jackie was trotting toward her on her long legs, holding out a camera.

"We got so caught up we forgot to ask. If you don't have somewhere you need to be, could we trouble you? Just a couple with us in front of the Arch, now that we're experts and all."

Becca held out her hand. The little camera was warm from the woman's pocket. She held it up and gestured for the group to gather more closely at the base of the Arch, the eastern flank below the statue of George Washington, the good soldier.

Soon they would be sipping a glass of wine in the softly lit hotel bar, telling the husbands about their triumphant evening. But first they smiled for Becca. At times they chafed at being lumped together—well, Connie more than the others. But now they slung their arms around each other and pulled in close and smiled. Jackie was already planning their next trip in her head. They would book rooms in that hotel over Washington Square. They would definitely learn the subway system. They would look up Becca and insist on that cupcake they owed her.

"Don't be stingy now," Jackie called. "It doesn't cost a penny and we don't want anyone making a goofy face. We want to show all our friends how at home we are in New York City."

Becca handed the camera back, grabbed a damp handful of cape tighter around her, and trudged home.

The Free and Independent Republic of Washington Square

On the western flank of the Washington Square Arch there is a small door. In 1917 Marcel Duchamp and five anarchist friends broke the lock, climbed to the top of the Arch on the narrow, unlit staircase inside, and, with a proclamation consisting entirely of the repeated word "whereas," declared Greenwich Village to be the Free and Independent Republic of Washington Square.

The lock had been replaced over the years but in 2006 the door remained. The parks worker in charge of all downtown parks was supposed to make the rounds in his green truck with the maple-leaf logo, locking up and turning off the lights in the comfort stations. His last stop was usually his most complicated and unruly downtown park, where he was supposed to shoo away the drug dealers and lock the doors and turn off the newly installed klieg lights aimed at the Arch, or else the next morning the parks commissioner would be barraged with complaints from the wealthy tenants on the north side of the square who had been kept up all night.

But even in 2006, the Parks Department hadn't fully bounced back from the dark years of the 1970s fiscal crisis, when all city agencies had been functioning with skeleton crews, when the whole city was held together with caution tape and Dutchmen. The parks worker was grossly underpaid because of a complicated formula having to do with budget lines. Anyway, he didn't show that night. The door in the Arch was ajar, for anyone who happened to notice its existence, anyone who might have a reason for leaving something inside and walking quickly away into the winding Village streets.

Becca stepped mechanically around a small "Law and Order" crew just finishing up for the night. The weather had lagged behind a season, as it so often did, and was playing catch up. A manic breeze slid across the Hudson, hit the Village, and ran in circles on every corner, clearing out the summer smell of dog pee. But the cold, dry air burned Becca's throat, already raw from talking, and it made her eyes water. A gust hit her full in the face, and she felt tight lines down her cheeks from where the tears had dried, as if her skin were made of seersucker. The wind kept prying her cape open.

For Manhattanites, autumn was a dose of amphetamines after the long schvitz of summer. The city's engines churned. The IRT rattled the sidewalk slabs. The 9/11 memorial tiles on Seventh Avenue clattered against their chain-link fence. A *New York Post* flapped in the trash, screaming that the Dow was fast approaching 12,000 for the first time. In the genteel Village apartment buildings with the British names—the Devonshire and the Windsor—thirteen-year-olds chanted their Torah passages with their bar mitzvah coaches and then scratched in the circles in their practice books for the dreaded specialized high school test. NYU students stubbed out their joints and waved the haze from the room to settle down for their midterms in finance. To Becca they seemed like a pack of lunatics achieving, achieving, achieving, like those sled dogs that will keep pulling until they die, too busy to ask why.

Melora Ross of Downtown Domiciles had just finished showing a West Village townhouse (25', 3 BR, 2 B, EIK w/subzero, WSHR/DR, backyd) to her most promising clients, a young couple who now stood shivering fetchingly on the stoop while she locked up.

It was the fourth house she had shown them, and it was a modest one—like beagles, nineteenth-century Village townhouses tended to come in small and medium—because this couple had arrived a decade after all the best ones had been snatched up.

Melora fumbled with the lock, her clipboard in one hand and the key in the other; for a realtor, she was inept with other people's keys. Under her breath she called the lock a mother-fucker, but she smiled sweetly at the couple, a Chilean-born furniture designer and his media-buyer fiancée from Palo Alto. She rummaged through her mind for a factoid to ease the awkward moment that always came at the end of a showing, when she always feared she came across as either too needy or too slick, too chummy or too cool.

"See that little church across the street?" she said, gesturing with her chin. "That's where they have the annual blessing of the cats and dogs. It's the sweetest thing; you'll love it."

But who, she asked herself, who will bless the realtors?

By day, many constituents fought for ownership of Washington Square, but at night it belonged to the rodents, which had been there longer and had burrowed more deeply than any humans. It was the rats who knew the park most intimately and felt its disturbances most keenly. When the Arch was being restored a year before, its surface pressure-washed and the pock-marked face of George Washington stabilized with fillers, the noise and vibrations disturbed their sleep patterns for weeks. Rats are capable of solving problems, but they prefer to work within a groove, with only small improvisations and only when necessary. Rats are social, and most of their socializing, like humans', centers on the impulse to fill their bellies and then sleep someplace warm and close.

The rats depend on the humans, of course—two of the most successful species on the planet Earth are looped together in ways too complex to sort out. The rats live peaceably enough among the strange species that lumbers upright with exposed bellies. Humans are the rats' main predators, true, but also their caterers. The formula is simple enough: the more humans, the more food. In Washington Square, nourishment washes in daily in two waves. These tides have a second, more remote pattern—lean, cold times when the tide grows weak, when the smells diminish and the harvest peters out. The rats can't say how the pattern works, but they do know this: the lean time always follows the fattest time, so it is important to stoke themselves whenever they can.

Rodents' teeth have an interesting quality: like human fingernails, they keep growing, until they begin to curl inward into jawbone and flesh. It is their job, their career, their life's work to gnaw. If they stop, they die.

The wind swirled the dead leaves of the ginkgoes and the locusts into a vortex, and the rats were torn. They sensed a danger they couldn't name, but a rat's first duty is to its gullet. The day's buffet leavings hadn't been stored safely inside them yet—a nice oily french fry discarded near the Garibaldi statue, half a strawberry yogurt embedded deep in the playground safety surfacing that was so hard for clumsy-limbed humans, their fat, flat tongues so far from the earth, to clean up. In the overflowing trash cans, cheese, noodles, bittersweet brown foam coating the side of a paper cup.

Things might have turned out different if Mary Anne and Connie hadn't gotten into an argument about the best way to get back to Midtown. They were footsore and chilled; it was glove weather now, and they just wanted to be home. But Connie, who had irritable bowels, needed a restroom and they had to hunt for a Starbucks.

"It's almost nine already," said Mary Anne. "We've been spending a small fortune on cabs. Let's just get on the subway. It's right over there, by the library."

But it wasn't on the corner where she'd remembered it, and in the end they walked in a circle and found themselves back in Washington Square.

They headed down a bench-lined path that appeared to be the quickest route back to well-lit Sixth Avenue.

"Where'd everybody go?" said Sheryl. "Was there a memo we didn't get?"

Wynnette huddled close to Laura, and Jackie grabbed Sheryl's hand.

Out of nowhere came a whispered "Smoke? Smoke?"

Wynnette shrieked and jumped straight in the air. They all laughed nervously. The floodlights on the Arch seemed to flicker.

"For heaven's sake," said Connie. "I'm running ahead and hailing a taxi. One little cab ride is not going to ruin the planet."

It was a highly articulated building with as many concavities and convexities as a very old person, and they were all encrusted with dirt. Its brick was buff colored, its trim made of sandstone, and its wooden window frames, painted park-bench green, had faded to bus-exhaust gray. Once the brick had caught sunlight and moonlight and reflected them back onto the street, but it had grown stingy with age and held on to the light. There was an old-fashioned girl's name carved in slightly rounded block letters above the lintel, or rather the space around the letters was carved away and the letters remained in high relief. It was called The Rebecca, and it was a long story.

Becca climbed the stoop, its stairs so tall and shallow that people visiting for the first time had the uneasy feeling they might fall over backward and land skull first on the old slate curb. She opened the front door with a key so old the ridges were worn smooth. The building had no foyer, no ceramic stand for an umbrella, no shelf to set your baggage down. No daylight unless someone propped open the back door, home of the gray Rubbermaid trash bins and the old refrigerator that Carlos the super couldn't seem to let go of.

Six hearty husbands, their bellies full of crème brulée, sat in the Hilton bar in Midtown getting a little buzz on while they waited for their wives. The Mets were playing the Braves on the silent TV over the bar and four innings had already come and gone. They had long since slid off their suit jackets and set them on the backs of their chairs and seesawed their ties loose, and now they flicked their wrists to check their watches. The Braves had one run, and the men all glanced up now and again to check for action, but there was none.

It was one of those bars built on a country-house-library principle, everything larger and darker and more comfy than it needed to be, a hotel designer's idea of masculinity. The chairs were on invisible casters that rolled on the slightest whim. No one in the bar knew anyone else. Successful business guys in little groups all around the room. Wedding ring on every finger, even the bartender's.

"Any minute they're going to come waltzing in with tales to tell," said James.

"And purchases to show off," added Arny.

Marc, husband of Jackie the organizer, was secretly troubled by anxiety. It had recently bloomed into two separate episodes of what might have been tiny panic attacks, but because two half panic attacks add up to only one full one at the most, and two halves do not constitute a trend, he had yet to discuss the matter with anyone. He had read up online and knew enough to recognize one sure sign: he was hoarding his breath. He was breathing as usual, but taking in more than he was letting out, which meant there was a carbon dioxide issue. He told himself to exhale, but it was like talking to a submarine from a boat. The jitters in the ribs. He couldn't say what he was anxious about, but it didn't matter; the anxiety would attach itself to any host: office politics, politics-politics, investments. At work there was a carbon monoxide issue.

He grew very cold, so cold he felt he was surely wet to the touch. He put his jacket back on, checked all the pockets: wallet, keys, trip itinerary. The hotel still used brass keys, which he liked: heavy, nonbreakable, noisy. He liked understanding how things worked. He burped and tasted the basil butter from the steak he had chewed an hour ago. He tasted garlic and wine, very insistently. He swallowed but the gases and the acids didn't want to stay down. He excused himself and speed-walked in what he hoped was the direction of the restrooms. When he got there, up came dinner in three distinct courses, much as it had gone in. The last heave brought up wilted greens and an asparagus tip. Jackie and the others were probably paying the cabbie out on the Avenue of the Americas right now. Or else they were walking up the block after exiting the subway, blisters on their ankles—they weren't used to so much walking. He gargled and splashed cold water on his yellow-white face. He got a fuzzy image of his daughter, Lexie. He went back to the bar, so woody after the fluorescents and tiles of the bathroom. He guessed that Washington Square was two miles south, but he didn't really know.

"You think they had a sudden outbreak of thrift and actually took the subway?" James was asking.

"Yeah," replied Lanny. "Maybe it's like the time they decided to compost. Remember that little adventure?"

"Hey, I'd like to remind the rest of you energy hogs that our household takes its composting seriously."

"Let's all call at once and completely freak them out," said Lanny, who, not for nothing, was the husband of Sheryl, the practical joker.

So the men fished their phones from their suit pants. Lanny counted to three and they dialed.

None of the wives picked up.

"Looks like you called it, James," said Rog. "No reception— they must be in the subway." These were Marc's best friends. Smart. Seasoned pros. If they weren't worrying, Marc told himself, why should he?

"I'll never forget the look on Sheryl's face when she opened up that compost bin the first time," said Lanny. "'It's supposed to be fresh as the forest floor, according to the girl at the farmers' market,' she said, and then she opened it, and that stuff was fresh like a different substance entirely, let me tell you."

The call came on her cell when she was just heading to the yoga studio, looking forward to emerging ninety minutes later all glowy and loose, feeling only lightly anchored to the sidewalk. She recognized the number of the client, the woman from Palo Alto.

"You've been really great and really patient with us," she

began, and Melora, already hearing the "but," felt her core sink and her shoulders fold. "And it's been terrific working with you, which is why I wanted to tell you that we changed our plans a little, or slowed them down. We're going to rent first for a year."

And Melora thought, Okay, this is manageable. I'll show them rentals.

Then the woman said a funny thing had happened. They had run into an old college friend in the East Village who was traveling to Nepal and looking for someone trustworthy to sublet her apartment for six months.

The one thing tenements weren't stingy with was heat. At the third-floor landing, where Becca stopped to rest, a steam pipe PSSSSSTed at her as if it had something new to say. The stairwell smelled of eons of old soup. She flung off her cape, which had begun to chafe her neck like a burlap sack. Her perspiration seemed to smell like old soup too.

It was here that the magical staircase had been born.

"Who invented staircases anyway?" her son, Aaron, now grown, had asked one day when he was five or six.

"Oh, that's easy," said Becca. "Guiseppe Staracasa of Ravenna, Italy. The word staircase is what we call a corruption of the original Italian. This was circa 1547." She couldn't resist slipping in a Latin lesson about the word circa, and a history lesson about the Renaissance. "Before that, everyone just slid down hills on their *tuchases*, which was terrible, because everyone's pants were dirty, and everyone had a painful condition called *tuchas*-callus."

"Who invented escalators then?"

"It's a little-known fact that they were invented by a woman named…" and here Becca paused as if trying to remember, while she waited for a good name to materialize. "Oh yes, Margaret Escalata," she explained. "Funny, her family came from Italy too; it must be because there are so many hills in Italy. But she grew up in our country, and she didn't live nearly so long ago. Maybe the post office will issue a stamp with her picture on it. The story goes that she had a little boy with very short weak legs from a condition called rickets, but don't worry because little boys never get it anymore as long as they eat lots of good food with vitamins and get enough exercise."

"I sure wish we had an escalator."

"I'll tell you something cool," said Becca, thinking fast. "Did you know that we have a magical staircase?"

Aaron got very still.

"It's just a tiny bit magical, and you know the building is old, right?"

He nodded, wide-eyed.

"That means the magic is old, and it's really slow, and sometimes it forgets things."

"How do you work it?" he asked, very quietly, as if the magic were a cardinal that had lighted on the fire escape.

"Well, first you have to make a wish, and it can only be a very small wish, like…like I wish Cole could come over after school tomorrow. Because like I said, the magic is old and we want to preserve it as long as possible."

"And then what?"

"Then you have to muster all the discipline you possibly can, which means you have to think about other things and not pester it. It hates to be pestered. Oh, there's one more really important thing. After you make the wish, you have to activate it. How do you think you do that?"

"You tap the banister three times," he said. "That sends the signal."

"How did you know? That's exactly it."

"Mom? Do I tell the wish or keep it quiet?"

"Excellent question. That's my favorite thing about the staircase magic—it's not all secretive like birthday wishes. We get to share them with each other."

"I wish for a hot fudge sundae."

Becca grinned because she happened to have a tub of Breyer's in the freezer, a couple of squares of baking chocolate in the fridge and the *Joy of Cooking* recipe committed to memory.

"One more interesting thing I forgot to mention. Most of the wishes may take—who knows?—months to come true, but you get your first wish granted the very same day."

Aaron yelled, "Woo hoo," and ran the rest of the way home.

Now, alone, she rounded the corner at the fourth floor. The steps sagged from the weight of all their footfalls and wishes. She could have wished for a windfall, or a tenure-track position. She wasn't picky anymore; a couple of classes at Borough of Manhattan Community College would do just fine. She could have wished for Aaron to come home from Costa Rica, where a month of post-college volunteering had stretched to an aimless year and a half. But the staircase magic was old and she was very tired. Please let me make the rent this month, she said, and tapped the banister three times.

At the fifth floor, a genie appeared. Becca smiled at the sight of her neighbor Ed Korn, a man in a worn white undershirt, trousers, and socks, carrying a neatly tied D'Ag bag of trash.

"You look tempest tossed," he said. "Windy out there?"

"Listen, Ed. I have to do something I hate, so I'm going to do it really fast to get it over with. Can you spare ten bucks? Just till the check clears."

Without saying a word he put his bag in the chute. The trash clanked on its way down as he fished a skinny billfold from his pocket.

By this time it was too late for the last yoga class, so Melora went back home. She dumped all her stuff and herself in the middle of the living room and then called, "You here?" Her husband, Niko, had stormed off in the morning and there was no sign of him now, nearly twelve hours later.

She was still too mad to call him so she called her son, though she didn't know his daily doings, either. She got his jumpy voicemail: "This is Cole. Talk to me." Why did no one in this family say goodbye? Cole's voice had been deep for a decade, but it still startled her. Maybe it was why men ruled the world—all that authority whenever they opened their mouths.

Maybe it was why they never admitted when they were wrong. People were constantly telling Melora she sounded like a little girl; no wonder women were more attuned to their own vulnerability. If she were an academic, she would pursue this theory. But she would have to set up a control group. Who? How? No wonder she was a realtor.

Jay Supak, the longtime reporter/photographer from *Village-Week*, was covering a community board hearing in the basement cafeteria of Our Lady of Pompeii. The schools committee was arguing about middle-school seats, and because Jay had no kids and didn't think it likely at this stage that he ever would, he was having a hard time keeping his eyes open. An argumentative mother behind him woke him up; his pencil made a thick line down the page of notes he had just taken. His phone vibrated in his vest pocket and he walked swiftly out to the hall, hoping for a reprieve.

"I need you at Washington Square this minute," said his editor, who never left the office if he could help it.

Photojay, as he secretly enjoyed being known, packed his gear, cradled his camera against his chest and zipped his parka around it, and took the stairs two at a time (and then regretted it when he had to run against the fierce wind). He caught the whole thing from across the Square in the safety of the courtyard of NYU Law School.

They all laughed a little too heartily, and Wes started to tell the story about the time Wynnette tried to make her own yogurt, so they didn't notice when the bartender reached up to unmute the TV, and when the green stadium disappeared and the anchor on NY1, a serious African-American man, pressed a finger to his ear and smoothed the furrows on his brow to offer the confused initial report.

"Reporting live. There has been an explosion in Washington Square Park. Police have cordoned off a several-block radius.

We do not yet have word on the origin of the explosion, and whether it was related to tonight's sudden and unusually high winds, gusting up to forty miles per hour. What we do know so far: the Washington Square Arch has sustained serious damage. There were not believed to be large crowds in the park due to the weather conditions. Debris is still falling. It's a scene of considerable devastation."

Someone at the bar had a bunch of single-ride MetroCards, and he pointed the men in the direction of the E train and told them to get off at West Fourth. So they finally rode the subway like ordinary New Yorkers.

It rumbled the oaken floorboards, it rattled the brass door-knobs, and the lights went out. Please, no, prayed a tenement's worth of atheists and agnostics, all connoisseurs of random disaster, as they converged in the pitch-black stairwell. It could be a water main break. A steam-pipe explosion. A sick old syca-more giving way in a tree pit outside, knocking over something big but inanimate like an SUV. Gunshots of a domestic dis-pute involving two loonies. Only a few blocks from here Joel Steinberg had killed his illegally adopted daughter Lisa while Hedda the wife looked on. And remember that Polish man who went crazy and killed his two little blond boys who used to play in the Bleecker Street playground? The mom still lived in the neighborhood; they would see her coming from work in pumps with her haunted eyes and a little bag of groceries.

Our wives are in there, they said, and it was as if they'd spoken the secret password. They were practically handed up the block. Their briefcases (for just a couple of hours before there had been a PowerPoint presentation and handouts and prepared notes) banged against their hips. And then they hit the wall, a blue wall of police barricades. There was a lady sergeant, and they said the password again, but she remained unmoved. I can't let you past the barricades, she said. We don't know enough yet.

She had a strong New York accent, a street-sounding accent. They were jostled as if they were in a crowded stadium.

"We think our wives might be in there," they said again, adding, "we're not from here," as if that were not already obvious, as if it might provide some dispensation.

They saw a flame rise in the distance.

"Okay. Now listen to me," said the cop, her hand against her side where her weaponry lived. "We don't know yet whether this was accidental or not, and we don't know if it's over. There's a whole lot we don't know and very little we do know, so we absolutely have to wait. I'm sorry."

It was noisy with sirens and bright with blinking lights bouncing off the street signs' reflective surfaces, off the window glass of a record store and a burrito place. The street and sidewalk were too narrow. They stood on their toes even though it didn't help. They plea-bargained with God. Please just let them be okay. Please, we'll get serious about mileage standards. We'll push electric cars. They pictured the phone calls to their grown children. What were the odds? It was a small explosion, nothing like the scale of the Twin Towers. Just a mini-event. Pick up the pieces in the morning and get on with it. Get on the plane and fly away home.

"Folks, we need your attention and cooperation," said a voice through a bullhorn. "We are taking extra precautions. We are going to move this barricade back a block, and we need you to turn around quietly and walk calmly over to Sixth Avenue."

Everyone resembled their wives and no one did. They were guys—what did they know from shades of polar fleece and hairstyles? They would know their wives if they saw them, that's what they knew. It was like songs on the radio—you could love them to death and sing along while they played but that didn't mean you could reproduce them on your own.

Becca felt her way to the kitchen and grabbed a flashlight from the drawer and shone it on the clay pot that lived on the counter, known affectionately as "the vessel," which Aaron had sculpted years before at Greenwich House Pottery, perhaps the heaviest pot of its size ever made. She dug through the color-coded keys—Ed's, the super's, various old friends' she wasn't on speaking terms with anymore. She grabbed the keys she grabbed most often these days, the purple ones belonging to Camille in 1G.

Ed was in the hall. Time slowed for a second, and, in the wan emergency light at the end of the hall, she got a good look at her comrade from a dozen neighborhood battles. He lived in her mind as a forty-five-year-old, relatively fit, with good bones in his face and salt-and-pepper hair. A twinkle in the eye, a slightly raffish tilt of the eyebrow. But it turned out that that Ed was long gone. The Ed in front of her still had the raffish tilt, but his skin was covered in overlapping layers of freckles from too many summers spent sunning in a Speedo on the old Hudson River piers. A slack little belly lurked under the undershirt. Even his earlobes drooped.

"Shit, Ed. Tell me that was just some little event, not the other shoe."

And then the emergency light sizzled and went out, and Ed's sibilant voice was the only thing left in the world.

"We're going to go down very carefully and calmly. It's probably just one of those steam-pipe explosions—they wreak all kinds of havoc."

Becca sent each foot out to scout for stair tread. If ever a person knew a place, Becca knew this stairwell. And if ever a person trusted her memory, it was Becca. But it turned out she didn't know a thing. She relied on the incredible luxury of her eyesight and of Con Ed to light her way. She relied on the tendency of the physical world to stay put. When the love of her life, the man she called the Viking, was about to leave all those years ago, she had run her fingers across his face and tried to memorize it like chord progressions on the guitar.

"Camille, honey," she said, poking her head in the small one-bedroom on the first floor.

"Rebecca?"

"Everyone's going down to see what's going on. Tell me—do you want to go?"

"And they're going to stand there like doofuses and stare into the dark? You go. Report back if you learn anything new."

An explosion.

A bomb.

No, not a bomb, a burst steam pipe. Ooh, those are nasty. Remember a couple of years ago, right near there, in fact? It took weeks to clean up the glop.

The crowd on the sidewalk latched onto the steam pipe explanation. Steam was just water and heat, pressure inside pipes, the most benign disaster imaginable, not even any flammable gases or noxious fumes.

But then a new ripple blew down the block: a bomb after all.

"Becca?" someone said. It was Mindy, the super's wife. "Did you work tonight?"

"I just came from there. Everything was normal. It was magical, in fact."

"My car's right in front of the building," said the single mom on the third floor. "We could listen to the radio for a little while as long as we don't run down the battery." So they all gathered around the Corolla.

The question Photojay asked himself was this: what exactly was he catching? The weather was so dramatic that the bomb went unnoticed for a beat. Trees were indeed toppling, but not from the wind. It was as if the Washington Square fountain suddenly roared to life, though it was not fountain season, and it was not water jetting into the air. Jay imagined terrorists in some cell nearby high-fiving each other. What a perfect cover the wind was! What beautiful sleight of hand! Keep 'em busy watching the left hand and you can do whatever you want with the right.

Of course, the explosion was too sudden and too confused and too dusty and yet too wet on a dark night to see clearly, to know what exactly was launched into the October sky, sailed through the openings in the chain-link fence, and splatted north onto the surrounding streets. The debris spattered "The Row" made famous by Henry James, the facades of the gracious Greek Revival homes on the north side of the Square. "Genteel" was the word often used to describe them. Edward Hopper's former studio was preserved there, alongside NYU offices and homes for senior faculty.

Things happened so fast, he thought, and then he thought, what an inane thing to think. Of course they happened fast; that was half the point of a bomb. You never knew these days when things would fly up from the ground or fall from the sky. The unspeakable is always walking right alongside us. Safety is always an illusion, as conditional as love.

The radio only got AM. Becca recognized the voice of the CBS news reporter on the car radio, one of those guys who'd been reading the news forever, with a voice comic-book-like in its depth. He was paired with a no-nonsense woman who bit off the ends of her sentences like duct tape and seemed to be the brains of the operation. They were both flustered. One minute they were reporting a windstorm and downed hundred-year-old trees, the next they were reporting an explosion. They were interrupted by a string of commercials.

"Reporting live from Greenwich Village," she said the second they returned. "The Washington Square Arch appears to have sustained some serious damage from a bomb that exploded moments ago." The steam-pipe theory turned out to be right, too, because the bomber or bombers managed to hit several strata of juncture points, knocking out a steam pipe along with the power and a fiber-optic network. They had no idea how many casualties there were, but the wind had cleared the park out, thank heaven.

Becca's brain flashed with a million snapshots of Washington Square but seemed to have room for only one word: but, but, but. She felt a pang of guilt so acute she almost fell onto the dark sidewalk.

෴

Bad things did happen, of course they did, but usually only to one person or one household at a time, and that was the point of having, of being, a support group; you provided solace to the others or the others provided it to you, and Laura baked her famous sticky buns.

The husbands could hardly remember what happened when. At some point they were in a precinct where a cop actually fed forms into a typewriter; or was that a dream? The cops sent them back to the hotel, where they waited in Marc and Jackie's room. They ran through the list in case they were called upon: Connie and Mary Anne, a.k.a. Lucy and Ethel; shy Laura; brash Sheryl; Wynnette, their Southern earth mother; and Jackie, who herded the others like a border collie. Surely Jackie had nosed them to safety in time.

"Think about it," James said. "They could be injured or in shock. If they got taken to the hospital, they could be trying to call. The cell phone service is out and the land lines are out, and there's maybe one pay phone with a huge line of people waiting to use it."

"How many hospitals are there downtown?" Marc asked. They were men used to information being readily available. Six men with secretaries and laptops and the seven habits of highly effective men. Everything in the hotel worked just fine. Their own cell phones sat slippery and silent in their pants pockets. They paced. They sat down on the edge of the soft king beds but then stood back up. Then, shortly after ten, the calls started. The news was on in South Carolina. Their grown children called, knowing their mothers' New York itinerary. "I'm sure everything's fine—" they began, and waited for the reassurance that didn't come.

"Lexie, honey—" said Marc.

"We don't know, we don't know," they said over and over. They took deep breaths to compose themselves, they ran their hands through thinning hair.

෴

They were almost home free when the Earth split open, a tornado hit, a thousand car alarms sounded, rock fell from the sky or perhaps rose up from the Earth like a geyser. Concrete and asphalt. Panic opened its six mouths and shrieked, its uvulas swinging like brass bells: danger, warning, all over this land.

No, you misunderstand! This is what Mary Anne, Connie, Jackie, Sheryl, Wynnette, and Laura would have yelled if they still had throats with vocal chords sealed inside them. If they still had tongues to moisten their mouths and lips to form the words, and lungs to power them—such strong lungs they'd had. No! We are just visiting. You have made a mistake. We have seat assignments on Delta. Hexagonal paving stones exploded into every kind of polygon. A heavy-duty rubber swing still on its chains. Pieces of a fiberglass play structure. A slab from George Washington's tri-cornered hat. Their last thoughts before New York City opened its rabid mouth and swallowed them whole: Take me back to my sturdy husband. Take me home where it's safe.

Blood of squirrels, blood of rats, blood of two NYU Steinhardt theater students heading home from a rehearsal, blood of homeless chess players, blood of the lone pot dealer who'd had the foresight to dress for winter, and blood of six tourists from South Carolina. The more radical preservationists had their prayers answered: Washington Square was saved from hostile takeover by NYU and returned to its roots as a potter's field.

Somewhere inside the smoke and the slabs of marble, six leather purses flew through the air, and inside them, six ringtones played simultaneously.

TUESDAY

CAUTION, CAUTION, CAUTION

The Arch knocked Iraq off the front page for the first time in weeks; there was that, Becca thought, as she stood at the newsstand in Sheridan Square with Carny on the leash, hands unsteady, and looked at the *Times*. They had snuck out very early, into a morning that was clear and dry, delicious even. Less breeze than 9/11, but close enough: it was bomb weather in Manhattan.

There on the front page were the smiling faces of her women, just as they had flashed in the camera's viewfinder and all night as she tossed in bed, but in this photo they were indoors and gathered around a table. She pulled out her glasses: the caption said it was a Chamber of Commerce luncheon the previous spring honoring Mary Anne Rasmussen. Becca looked closely. Mary Anne: the friendly one who had stepped right up when Becca asked for volunteers.

The last person to see them alive—what did that make her, exactly? Not a witness, because she had walked away. Not an accomplice, though she felt like one. The smell of fire was still in the air, fading to the smell of smoke. Not the crematorium smell from that other autumn. Everything would be held up to 9/11 and found wanting in scale.

All the other Village landmarks were pinned in their usual places: the Gray's Papaya hot dog joint, the basketball court, the garden that used to be the dive bar where Eugene O'Neill dreamed up "The Iceman Cometh." But all the lights were off. The streets east of Sixth were cordoned off with barricades, the ones that were usually used to block potholes and Halloween parade crowds. A cop had his finger in a roll of yellow tape and was unfurling yards of caution, caution, caution.

Inside the barricades was Becca's livelihood. Inside Becca

were questions. The last person to see them alive; what did that make her? It made her alive is all it did, same as before, maybe a little more so just by contrast.

She and Carny trudged up to the Citibank in Chelsea, where there was power, to deposit the dead woman's check. She smoothed it out on the counter. It came from the account of Marc and Jackie Kitchens of Plantation Pointe, South Carolina, and it still smelled of perfume.

Three boys blew in like a breath of bad energy. One was tall and skinny, with cornrows and big pants, another had short arms and a belly that swaggered in front of him, and the third was quiet and wary. The other customers stopped what they were doing to calculate the color of this alert: a woman with a puggle that Carny kept trying to sniff, another with a yoga mat. But Becca could see they were just theater wannabe kids hungry for an audience.

The chubby boy reached into his pocket and, much to the relief of the jumpy woman with the puggle at the next ATM, pulled out a Snicker's bar. He held it like a microphone and sang a snippet of "It Sucks to Be Me" from Avenue Q. And then the boy in the big pants grabbed the candy bar, thrust his crotch out and sang in a falsetto about humps and lovely lady lumps from a novelty hit the summer before.

The mike passed to the quiet boy. He wore hoop earrings and eyeliner above small, close-set eyes, and had a round flat face so covered with acne you couldn't be sure if he was Black or Hispanic or Asian, or maybe just enough of each that no one would ever claim him, like a calico alley cat. He was so close to being beautiful that it was painful to look at him and yet hard not to stare.

"Our talented friend here would like to sing you all a song," said the tall boy, shoving him forward.

The quiet boy took a deep breath and grabbed the Snicker's. "Now all rise for our national anthem," he said, lowering his voice so he sounded like an announcer at Shea. He started spreading the news that he was leaving today.

He had a tremulous tenor and he gave "New York New York" the pace of a dirge, dropping the g's and holding the lyrics back a beat like Sinatra, as if he were such a cool customer he could hop back on the song whenever he felt like it.

"Hey, who's got a hat?" said the boy with the big pants. "Someone got a hat? You sorry excuse for a street performer ain't got no hat."

The boy sang about wanting to be a part of it, and the same friend said, "Yeah, you'll be a part of it, when the economy crashes," and everyone, even the woman with the yoga mat, laughed, because it was 2006 and they all knew the economy was never going to crash; it hadn't crashed after 9/11, and it certainly wouldn't crash because of a small bomb almost a mile away.

"Oh yes, I'm a part of it," said the chubby boy with a flurry of gestures that was one part Brooke Astor, one part little girl on the Olympic balance beam. "I have a pied-a-terre just off the park. Oh, it's just a little place, on the museum block."

Eventually they stopped joking and let him sing. Becca dipped her card into the slot.

The boy flubbed a lyric and put a finger to his lips, and then to balance the gesture he planted his feet on the dirty tile floor as if it were an undeveloped tract somewhere in Oklahoma.

The boy snuck a sidelong glance at her, as if she might be a talent scout or an agent, one of those unprepossessing miracle workers in the crummy offices in the West Forties. And now Becca was the one who looked away, because it wasn't so easy after all to be the audience. It was a relationship as complicated and demanding as any other.

Now he plunged into the song like a sensory deprivation tank. The acoustics were surprisingly good. The boy with the big pants took one of the service phones off its hook. "Listen to this, Bangalore," he yelled.

Meanwhile, because she had kept the ATM waiting too long, it aborted her transaction and returned to the starting screen. Becca pulled out her card and started again. She fed the envelope into the slot. Tomorrow night, another tour. Then winter and the proofreading and whatever else she could scrape together.

The boy took a deep breath and began the list of heights he would reach in the city so pleased with itself that it demanded you say its name twice: king of the hill, top of the heap—all those corny phrases no self-respecting New Yorker had ever uttered, except on Broadway.

He had talent, this boy; but talent, Becca knew, was never enough. Talent with backing, talent with thick skin, talent with a stable home life, talent with a mentor.

The puggle woman said, "Whoops, just one more check, Bailey, and then cookie time," and the yoga woman, talking on her cell, slid a wad of cash into her wallet.

The boy sang, "I'll make it anywhere," and for a second his eyes fixed again on Becca's, and he knew she was no talent scout, and she knew he was a fragile, effeminate kid.

A poster on the wall showed an artfully blurred photograph of a woman with a baby on her hip. In the background were those soft apple-green accents that were all the rage. With her free hand the woman was reaching for a white ceramic coffee mug on the counter, too busy to worry about her own financial future but comforted knowing that Citibank would do it for her. The boy sang, "So long, we're through, New York, New York." And Becca stood at the screen hitting go back, go back, go back.

When she and Carny got home, there was a crowd in front of the stoop, as she imagined there would be.

"Coming through with a Bassett hound," she said, giving the New York shoulder to the group and heading for the steps. But Carny put on the brakes and squatted to poop. They assaulted her with flashes of light while microphones marched toward her face. She heard her name repeated, followed by overlapping requests: Just a word? Can you tell us about the tourists? I'm from the....

She recognized the main tabloids and the lesser ones. A kid from the *Columbia Journalism Review*, and that creepy guy from *VillageWeek* who seemed to be everywhere and nowhere at the same time. An NY1 local-cable reporter who had interviewed her when she was New Yorker of the Week, a smart young Dominican woman who was going places.

"Sorry, guys," she said. What did this attention make her? "Right now I'm just a woman walking a dog who wants his breakfast," she said. "Please clear away."

Mindy, the super's wife, came out mad, with Jamie, her youngest, on her hip looking stunned. "People live here," she said. "Don't turn us into a media circus. Becca doesn't want to talk and if she changes her mind, she'll do it when she's good and ready."

Becca scooped poop into an English muffin bag and tied a slipknot while the media outlets looked on.

"Now," she said, "I will make a brief statement and ask that you leave. The women were lovely. They enjoyed the Village greatly."

"You were the last to see them alive—what perspective can you offer us?"

"Perspective? Who has any perspective right now?"

"Do you think it was terrorists from abroad?"

"If the NYPD and the FBI don't know, why are you asking me?"

Aftershocks

From Jay Supak's first dispatch for *VillageWeek* online (unseen in the Village, where the power was still off):

Tuesday: Villagers as a rule are hungry for information, but little was forthcoming from the police department, the OEM, or the mayor's office in the aftermath of Monday's bombing of Washington Square. The bombing occurred at 9:07 p.m., coinciding with a period of high winds and low cloud cover that, experts believe, severely exacerbated the effects of the explosion.

According to the police commissioner, this much is known in the tragic incident for which no responsible party has come forward: the explosives used appear to have been ordinary dynamite, readily available. Dynamite per se is rarely used anymore but has become a generic term for a variety of explosives including slurries and Tovex, a DuPont product.

Aside from the two dozen who sustained injuries, most of them treated at nearby Beth Israel Medical Center, nine casualties have been confirmed. One was a marijuana dealer who was a regular presence around the Square. Two were New York University students believed to be on their way back to their residence hall on Washington Place after a study session. The other six were a group of female tourists from South Carolina who had taken a walking tour of the central Village given by local tour guide Rebecca Cammeyer, believed to be the last person to see them alive. Cammeyer, when reached for comment, said only that the women were "lovely" and that she had "no perspective."

Because the bomb was detonated in a residential district consisting largely of nineteenth-century structures, a large area has been cordoned off while fire, water, and police inspectors undertake a thorough examination of the buildings and the trees to determine the extent and severity of the damage and the likelihood of additional collapse. Window glass and earthen foundations are considered particularly vulnerable to aftershocks. Though most of the damage is believed to have occurred in the Square and immediately across the street on Washington Square North, residents and businesses within a two-block radius of the Square have been evacuated until further notice. The blast appears to have ruptured a water pipe, though reportedly not a main, creating the additional challenge of localized flooding immediately to the north. Power remains off until Con Edison can restore severed connections, some of which travel directly under the damaged park. As a precaution, Con Ed has turned off the gas. Cellular phone service remains spotty.

The blocks inside the barricades include a fairly eclectic mix of building types, with mostly brick townhouses dating to the mid-1800s to the north, mostly late nineteenth-century tenements to the south, large structures belonging to NYU to the east, and a mix of commercial structures to the west on Sixth Avenue. The oldest buildings appear to have withstood the impact better than newer construction.

The terrible irony is that the Washington Square Arch restoration had been completed only two and a half years before, in the spring of 2004. The monumental structure, fashioned from Tuckahoe marble in 1820–22 to commemorate Washington's inaugural (replacing a temporary wooden one erected in 1889), now lies in pieces strewn widely across the north part of the ten-acre Square. One of the two statues of George Washington, which had stood in front of the east flank, survives in large pieces, but the other was damaged, possibly beyond repair. The parks commissioner stated that his crew would work to restore the entire Arch as soon as they were given the green light.

"Washington will rise again," the parks commissioner said. "The father of the nation will not be deterred despite those who would attack the foundations and cherished symbols of this nation, this city, and this indomitable neighborhood."

The commissioner's words notwithstanding, the Village is looking desolate and sounding uncharacteristically quiet. Automobile and sidewalk traffic is sparse though the day is crisp and clear. The organizers of the annual Village Halloween parade have not yet issued a statement about whether the event will take place as usual next week. It is likely to be a sad Halloween for the children of the Village, who will either travel to other neighborhoods or sit out trick-or-treating altogether in solidarity with their fallen neighbors.

Though the scale of this disaster does not compare in any way to that of 9/11, which occurred just over five years ago about a mile and a half to the south, this tragic event, many Villagers concur, feels far more personal. "Washington Square is entirely different from the World Trade Center," said Frieda Glaberson, chair emerita of Community Board 2. "This square is beloved. It's our backyard, our playground, our dog run, our amphitheater, our meeting place. It's practically an extra room in our apartments. The worst part aside from the deaths is the not knowing."

From Jay Supak's unpublished reporter's notebook:

The mayor could not be reached for comment because he was smack in the middle of a town hall meeting on Staten Island. When finally reached during a bathroom break, he said in his usual nasal tone with its hints of impatience and superciliousness: sacred site, those we've lost, love and solidarity, will not allow terrorists to deter, build on the footprints of the past the city of the future.

The Manhattan Borough President said that his office was putting all its resources (including not one but both of his twenty-two-year-old interns) into discovering the criminal who would do harm to this beloved icon of Greenwich Village, New York City, and indeed the world.

Frieda Glaberson, chair emerita of Community Board 2, said, "I was there when the Arch was put up, and let me tell you I've been there ever since, and please, don't go to any trouble when I die—although I have high hopes of immortality—but should I die, I'm a tiny little woman, just a tiny little monument alongside Garibaldi and the two George Washingtons. And please, just one monument will do. Put me in full battle gear, mounted on a steed with a feather in my cap, and call it macaroni or whatever you like. Have you seen the latest photos of my grandson?"

And Rebecca Cammeyer, who was not reachable for a real comment because it's fucking dark out and she's sitting in her rent-controlled tenement trying to see by the light of an old yahrzeit candle dug out of her junk drawer. But had she been reached she would have said: I love this Square more than any living human. I would buy this Square to protect it in perpetuity from evil NYU if I weren't completely broke because creative artists always get the shaft in this world. Everything was better and purer and more noble in the nineteenth century, and why am I stuck with this sucky year 2006, with all these vapid, rapacious yuppies trying to suck the soul out of my neighborhood?

And then Jay filed his real report and went back out to mill around in the middle of the crowd, because this was what a photojournalist lived for. And because it was lonely at home.

Rent-controlled tenants inhabited their apartments like bugs trapped under a glass. They would never know the fresh, sweet smell of sawdust or have a say over the temperature. The air they breathed belonged to someone else and they knew they would never get out alive.

Later in the morning, Becca couldn't bear to go back out and couldn't bear to stay in, so she went down again to check in on Camille. "Camille, honey. Are you managing okay? Would you like some company?"

Becca could see her editing her reply; forming the first words of the day took effort now.

"You have a scared face," she said, seeing right through Becca as usual. "I think perhaps it is I who should be asking you how you're managing."

"I took my phone off the hook. Mindy says the reporters won't stop sniffing around in person. I don't know what more they want me to tell them."

"Mindy is a warrior," Camille said. "She is no doubt beating them off with mops and brooms, as befits the super's wife."

"Do you mind if we just sit for a while? I wish we could listen to an opera together."

"My records crackle."

"That's my favorite thing about them."

"I have an idea," Camille said. "Go in the bedroom and somewhere under the bed you will find the—what was the name for those enormous…?" and Camille, who could barely walk and whose hands trembled and dropped teaspoons, put an invisible one on her shoulder and briefly became a head-bobbing street kid.

"Boom box," said Becca. "Ghetto blaster. Camille, I hope I'm half as lucid as you if I make it to your age."

"Ah well, sometimes I'd rather grow fuzzy and remote. I believe the ghetto blaster can run on batteries, which I should have somewhere in the sideboard. And I have cassette tapes. The sweet vindication of the pack rat!"

Becca got the player in working order, pulled *Cosi fan Tutte* from a crooked stack, and kissed the top of Camille's head, her dry white hair such a thin cover for her scalp, and her skull such a hard shell for the wonders that swirled inside. "Thank you, Camille. I don't know what I would do without you."

"Well, then, we shall rehearse, because I feel logy this morning and am likely to doze off before the end of the overture. You will hardly miss me. Just tiptoe out when you're ready and leave me to dream of silly young lovers in Napoli. Tanissa will be here before long to prepare my lunch."

So they sat and listened, surrounded by the old familiar posters, the Hirschfeld caricature, the dusty puppets like childhood friends. Becca scanned the bookshelves and let herself fall headlong back into the promise of the previous century: Marianne Moore, Langston Hughes, Erich Fromm, Bruno Bettelheim, Stella Adler. And then her eye landed on Camille's own slim volume, *Stage Flight*. Her perfect little book, one part memoir and one part advice to young theater artists, a copy kept on every actor's shelf beside the Stanislavsky and the Uta Hagen. The famous cover with the black-and-white photo of a sparrow on a bare stage about to take wing from its taped mark. Or the paperback reissue with the full-color dancing marionette.

Becca had devoured it, lived by it, even before she knew Camille. She was in high school at Music and Art then, and her life wouldn't stop unraveling. First the divorce, then her mother's remarriage and move to Mamaroneck. Becca's insistence on staying behind with her father, followed by his sudden death from a massive heart attack in the middle of a community board hearing. Somehow she managed to stay on alone in the apartment upstairs; it was the seventies and seventeen-year-olds were the last thing on anyone's mind. One day she came home from school and saw movers climbing the stoop carrying marionettes and puppets and posters. And though she had never been a believer, she was convinced the universe regretted its actions and was offering up Camille, the best possible consolation.

Becca's own copy of *Stage Flight* was upstairs, signed by Camille with her soaring, slanted Fs: Fly, dear Becca, fly. She hadn't thought about it in years. Now she pulled the book off the shelf and turned to the back leaf, photo by Otto Warachovsky, showing Camille in her prime, hair already streaked with white in a dancer's bun, her long, severely angled face softened by the good joke Otto seemed to have caught her in the middle of telling.

While Mozart's lovers made a mess of things and Camille dozed, Becca read about the birth of the marionettes. Camille and Otto had made the first two on a dare when they were newlyweds with no money. They were living in a rented carriage house upstate waiting out the blacklist. They had bought out the ends of six bolts of fabric—broadcloth and velvet and bro-cade—from a yard-goods store going out of business, as well as its entire collection of trimmings. They set these on a table in the hallway between the two rooms. The house was owned by a tinkerer, so they also set up a pile of tools to share: an old staple gun, industrial-size Elmer's Glue, nails and screws, planks and pegs, wires, string, a jigsaw, sandpaper, and a rasp.

"It might have been the happiest month of my life," Becca read, "and I have been blessed with much happiness after a rath-er unpromising start. We made it all up as we went along, shar-ing our materials and our trials, humming arias as we worked. We made a vow not to emerge until each of our marionettes was finished. Only we used the word 'alive.' My marvelous Otto. It was like living with Geppetto of the Hudson Valley. On Saturdays (for blue laws were still in effect and everything was shut tight on Sundays), we rested our fingers and we explored. It turned out the Hudson Valley was a perfect home base for the study of our new land. We learned our history, the great, the silly, and the obscure, until we felt American right down to our Ichabod Crane and our nothing to fear but fear itself."

Camille shifted in her sleep, and Becca checked to be sure her skinny chest was rising and falling inside her starched white blouse. She closed the book and got up. She needed to walk Carny. She needed to face the reporters, needed to visit the shrine that had no doubt sprung up near the park. Needed to write a new resume.

But the book opened obligingly to the page where she had left off, and she read on, though she knew the stories well. "Our respective labor pains were severe," wrote Camille, "but Otto gave birth to Doña Quixota who tilted at gristmills with a rolling pin. And I was proud mother of Pinocchia whose nose grew longer when she told more truth than her listeners were ready to hear. Together we made her a small desk with a secretary chair that swiveled, and we gave her a boss named Mr. Muleton, with the face of a donkey. No one had ever set a marionette show in an office before."

She turned to her favorite chapter, the one in which Camille talked about the theater sketches they had named "amuse-ments," what would now be called performance pieces or dis-ruptions.

"Once you have marionettes," Becca read, "you disarm peo-ple and attract children. Once you put on funny costumes with plumes or pointy-toed slippers, people can't help themselves: they grow enchanted. And so we tried to change the world through enchantment, one pair of eyes at a time, to bring a smile of the sort that said, ah, yes, we foolish humans make one unholy mess after another, but I will try to remember to forgive myself and others, and to give and receive pleasure in this short life. And that, as it happens, is my best advice to actors."

Becca went to the window and peered down. Two of the reporters were camping out on the stoop with a camera and Starbucks cups between them; they knew she would appear eventually to walk the dog. When you're a famous tour guide, even one who's lost her tourists, everyone in the Village knows your routines. Becca needed to get on with it, but first she slipped onto the Amalfi Coast just after the war with Camille and Otto and their troupers.

"One Saturday evening near the open-air market, we set up our stage. Well, we had no stage but we had much colorful bunting that Otto and I had made from old linens we found in a secondhand shop. Otto had the idea to cut all of the napkins in half on the diagonal and sew them onto bright grosgrain ribbons. They were lovely pale pastels alternating with many shades of white and ivory. There was nothing in the piazza from which to hang them so we enlisted some local children and since we spoke little Italian and none of them Polish or French or Yiddish or English, we placed our hands on their shoulders and moved them into a square and gestured until they understood that they were to be our proscenium arch and wings. We were flush with *lire* from tips the night before, so we paid them well.

"It was the end of the evening *passeggiatta,* and the whole town seemed to gather round. Overlooking the calm sea, we performed our pantomimes as the sun went down and we were, as they say, a smash hit.

"We stayed that night with a family that had befriended us. The kitchen had an ingenious system whereby one could wash the dishes and put them wet in the cupboard and all the water would drain via a pipe to the sink. We talked that evening about getting a patent to bring this system to the States. We grew very excited and began to spend our fortune as we lay on the floor in the spare bedroom, not yet aware that electric dishwashers would soon become commonplace, or that all our other harebrained, get-rich-quick schemes would likewise prove unworkable in this way or that. So we wrote a new amusement about a bunch of bumblers trying to get rich quick and it grew to become 'The Schemers,' still our greatest hit."

The cassette tape had long since clicked off. Becca tore herself away from Italy and back to the tenement where she'd been conceived, here near the end of Camille's life and somewhere well past the middle of her own. She put the book back on the shelf (smiling when she realized that Camille had hidden a whole second layer of books in the back). Becca hadn't created a theater troupe. She hadn't saved the Village. She hadn't socked away savings for her old age or a down payment so that Aaron might one day come back to the city. "Oh, Camille," she whispered, "tell me before it's too late how to have a happy life."

Once Becca had been the girl with wings. She had found a store in the flower district with a bin of peacock feathers on sale. She'd bought turquoise tulle in the garment district and strings of gold sequins in the trimming district and green glass beads in the bead district and she had stretched a pair of periwinkle tights over coat hangers her father had curved into ovals for her. The makeup crew had sprinkled glitter in her hair and she had flown in from the wing of the stage and sung a song written by Comden and Green. She sparkled on the stage, far enough away that no one could hurt her and she could hurt no one, and she knew that was the real reason they called performers stars.

Becca was just tiptoeing out when Camille opened her eyes and said, "I have had my second good idea of the morning. It came to me in my dream. If you would, go into the bedroom again and dig under the things on top of the bureau until you reach the brown box."

In the bedroom, Becca waded through silk scarves. The box smelled of leather and sachet and had scalloped edges. She set it down on Camille's coffee table.

"Oh, bother," said Camille as she rummaged through a tangle of jewelry. "That will be a day worth celebrating, when they find a remedy for arthritic fingers."

"Are these all from Otto or were there lots of other suitors?"

Now Becca got a smile out of Camille. If she'd been younger, she might have blushed. "Some were my mother's that we managed to hold on to. As you can see, we had means in Europe. But you're right that most of the others are from

Otto. The man had wonderful taste." Finally, she fished out the biggest piece, a gold locket, and leaned forward to place it gently in Becca's hand. "This was supposed to be a surprise, for after, but that wouldn't be much fun for me, would it? There are strings attached, so to speak," she said, smiling. "You may have it only if you promise to enjoy it and not lock it up somewhere in a safe deposit box."

The locket was a style Becca had never seen before—not fussy and flowery like most good jewelry, but slyly modern with filigree in irregular curlicues. It was heavy, too, made to last. It hung from a gold chain with long narrow links that made a soft tink as they collapsed on themselves and puddled in her palm.

"It's magnificent," said Becca. "You should wear it."

"You will laugh, but I don't seem to have enough weight to support it; it cuts into my neck."

Camille motioned for Becca to open it. Inside was a photo, carefully cut to fit the oval, of a young Camille and Otto, with a dark Van Dyke beard and good straight legs. They stood in front of a mountain range and wore old-fashioned skis.

Becca closed her fingers around it and held on tight. She put it on, embarrassed by her gray sweatshirt.

"It may be the most beautiful piece of jewelry I've ever seen," she said.

"You have my permission to put a new photo on top of us. That is the Jungfrau behind us. I don't think it will mind."

She couldn't imagine whose smiling face she might put inside; she would leave the photo of Camille and Otto.

The closest thing Becca had to an anniversary was August 3. It was the day she had met the Viking. She had tried to celebrate it with him, but he always shrugged it off.

They had met at Garber's Hardware, and the store had lasted all these years but the Viking had not. That day she was tossing a broken hinge from one hand to the other, impatient for the line to move. She was in her unofficial uniform of the period, overalls over a tank top, no bra, huaraches that had stained her feet brown. A deep voice with an accent from someplace cool and far away said, "Don't get that kind again. It will crack in exactly the same place."

She whipped around and saw a man as long and thin and pale as a mainsail, with a face high above her made of pastel crags, pinks and blues and yellow-white hair that wouldn't stay behind his ears.

Things got complicated. The better-quality hinge was a slightly different size, which meant drilling new holes in the old kitchen cabinet. Somehow he ended up following her home and fixing it for her, and she offered to pay him and he refused, though she had no money and he couldn't afford to work for free. She stood behind him as he worked and watched his long muscles tauten and disappear back into his smooth, hairless arms below the sleeves of his white T-shirt. His hands were so big she imagined them spanning whole parts of her, maybe her entire torso. She put her own hand on her belly to see how far it would reach, but at that same moment he turned around to ask for a different drill bit. Is something wrong? he asked with great concern. All she did was smile, because she did have an ache.

He spent the night. And then gradually he moved in.

Lars, Erik, Leif she would call just to bug him, but his real name was plain, all-purpose Peter—the piper, the pumpkin-eater, the wolf boy, the hard one. Eventually he became simply the Viking, because he was always threatening to set sail for other shores.

He was a painter and his paintings were explorations of paleness. They forced the viewer to see infinite gradations. If you concentrated, the whole rainbow was in each whitish canvas. The straight lines resembled his hair combed back after a shower before it fell onto the scenic overlook of his brow bone. It had been down past his shoulders, tucked behind his ears, thick and heavy and straight, even in August. You could see past the face to the skeleton. She used to run her fingers over his brows to feel the cavity where his eyeballs lived. How she had learned him: the ridges on each of his bottom front teeth, the three tiny birthmarks just above his collarbone. "Make beads in a bowl," she would say, and he would lift his shoulder to create the hollow in his collarbone, and she would lick the beads. The hairs on his chest that gave way to the darker but still blond ones on his belly.

He had done similar things to her when she'd been too young to know how lovely she was.

Lost in the Middle

Melora woke up sometime between the bombing of the Arch and the morning with her phone still in her hand and listened for Niko sounds and felt for Niko heat, but the bed was still empty. He had prolonged his travels many times before, but he had always called or emailed to let her know.

People were dead just blocks from her, and she was all alone in an enormous house, a dark and inert house, a ridiculous house, and all she could think about was that she had driven her husband away. The fight had been bigger and uglier and stupider than usual. She remembered having a brief insight somewhere in the middle of it: fights have predictable stages, like a suntan, like grief. She told herself it would be smart to map them out so she wouldn't get so lost in the middle the next time.

"It's *your* son's law-school tuition," he had called down the stairs.

"Don't you *your son* me," she called back.

"Where's the goddamned shoe-polishing kit?"

"How the fuck should I know what you've done with your precious little kit?"

Once she had been charmed by Niko's old-world concern for his shoes. A box full of Kiwi cans and chamois cloths and separate brushes for black, brown, cordovan, oxblood. She'd never heard of a color called oxblood until she met him. He was always complaining about the shoe polish drying up, as if she'd gone in and taken all the lids off herself.

Niko was the kind of short man who compensated by meticulously tending to himself. He lifted weights, he spent as much time on his hair as she did, he sent out his shirts, the kind of shirts that said don't fuck with me. He was dark verging on swarthy, but not hairy. She had once thought his face the most beautiful thing she had ever seen, but now everything she did seemed to make it turn purple. Sometimes she just watched it the way you'd watch a hazy, darkening sky to see if a downpour was about to arrive.

They had continued yelling up and down the staircase, and she couldn't find a way to stop it. Eventually he had come down the steps. The door slammed and the brass mail slot rattled.

"Go run home to your mommy in Astoria," she had said to the door. "Go eat her greasy moussaka and have a quadruple bypass and mar your precious smooth chest."

She swung her legs out of the bed, determined to be a better person, a person she could respect. She stuck her tongue out at the giant painting on the wall, an early Alex Katz they had bought because Niko thought the woman in the painting looked like her.

She looked at her feet. Even her feet—the kind with the second toe longer than the big toe—were failures. Her toes looked like a miniature model of her and Niko standing side by side.

There used to be sounds and predictable markers of the hour in this house—the hour when she woke Cole up for school, and when Fabienne's key went in the lock and her quiet footfalls landed in the hall and the coffee maker began to sigh like an old Jewish man. And Niko would groan and sigh like a young man with burdens in the big world, and fling the covers off him (off her in the process) and march to the master bathroom, the bathroom of the master, and fluids would start to land on porcelain and swish inside his mouth. And Melora would shower and dress and make lunch for Cole. And one by one they had kissed her on the cheek, and she had taken her mug of coffee up to the office where she began a long day of trying to make people happy, because that, to her, had always been the key to her job; it was about happiness and security, but sexy security, not boring security like the kind life insurance provided. It was about being enveloped by pleasing spaces and colors and comfort in one's own home, like a very large plaster and wood embrace. And then at the end of the day her men would come back to her.

Sometimes Melora feared she was a bad realtor, and that being a realtor in the first place was bad, so either she was doubly bad or she was a good realtor, which might be worse because then there would be an implication that she took the work seriously, like a calling. The truth was that she did, or she had. When people list the basic necessities of humans, she had once told Niko, money and love don't even make the top three, but shelter does.

She had placed three increasingly hysterical calls to Cole, who was a law student at NYU and who finally picked up to say he was perfectly intact. But Niko never picked up. In between, her mother on Long Island got through and sobbed with relief at the sound of Melora's voice, and the two of them sobbed together like girlfriends, which was how Melora's mother liked it.

Now she got herself up and dressed and went downstairs. She went to turn on the radio before remembering there was no power, and then pulled out an English muffin before she remembered she couldn't toast it. She had no appetite anyway.

She eventually padded down to the basement, the only room she could bear these days, where the morning sun was coming in just enough that she could see. She made her way to the corner they used to call the plastic forest. It was a stash of Cole's old toys, the big pretend ones that were supposed to have taught Cole to be a grown-up. She took out the easel and flipped it around to the blackboard side. There was still a piece of chalk in whatever you called it—the chalk trough? She wrote 'Ms. Ross' on the board, clicking the chalk against the board with each line the way teachers did. She erased it and tried again in cursive; if she was serious about changing her life, she would need this skill. The writing trailed downward and grew small. Be big and bold, she told herself. On the third try she found her groove. She pointed to the invisible class.

"Some of you may be able to read this now. If you can't yet, don't worry. Like all big jobs, we will break it down into nice little jobs and before long you will all be able to do one of the best magic tricks in the world: read." She stopped to let her students take this in and imagined a terrified face out there—a kid who might not learn to read in her class.

She waved away the previous speech.

"Good morning, class," she said. "My name is Ms. Ross, and we're going to get to know each other very well this year." She sounded like a Romper Room lady.

"Okay, people. I'm Melora. Let's get this show on the road. Tell me one thing about yourself. It can be a thing you like or a thing that's kind of weird—whatever you feel like sharing is perfectly fine."

Olly Olly Oxen Free

Evening finally arrived, and everyone on Becca's block came out. The old Commies with the berets and the onion-roll breath, the artists in the ironically oversized polyester clothes from the Westbeth basement sale, and the young families with their titanium strollers, each the color of a different tropical fruit. The vegans came out with baba ganoush.

At first people stood or sat on the nearest stoops. But then a young enterprising dad brought down a shrink-wrapped pack of wood he'd bought for the weekend house and built a fire right in the street.

"Won't the cobblestones melt?" asked the kids who'd gathered round. "Won't the fire spread?" No one knew; this had never happened before.

Becca smelled wood smoke from the fifth floor, looked out her window, grabbed her father's old army blanket, and ran down. Mindy, the super's wife, and Ed from next door scooted aside to make room. And for a little while at least, the old-timers almost forgot to resent the newcomers and the newcomers decided that maybe the old-timers weren't quite so moth-bitten and pleased with themselves.

"We're like a page out of Jane Jacobs," said one of the hipsters.

Food appeared like magic. Ears of Jersey corn from someone's freezer. Chicken kebabs. A braided challah. In the middle was a stick of softening butter, and people were tearing off hunks of sweet bread and using the butter like dip.

Becca placed her hands behind her on the cobblestones. She felt the sturdy surface of the granite that was said to have been brought from Europe as ship ballast, and in the spaces in between she felt what might have been actual earth, and she had a strong sensation of sitting on her slowly spinning planet.

The Jamaican babysitters who'd been invited to spend the night stood on the sidelines in their sensible heels and their tucked-in blouses.

"Sing us a Jamaican song," said the young dads. "We've heard you sing lullabies. We know you sing like angels."

But the good Christian nannies demurred, smiling at the very idea.

The Maltese supers with their tinkling accents brought out a bocce set and gathered around with the Ecuadorans and the Mexicans.

And then, when no one was watching, the Jamaican nannies conferred. They spread out in a line across the street, softly swung their hips in unison and sang a song with a refrain like small waves lapping Caribbean sand: "Comin' down with a bunch of roses, comin' down." Everyone joined in.

"All that's missing is a steel drum," said one of the young moms. And a few minutes later there was a steel drum and Dixie cups, a bottle of Bacardi and a sweating carton of pineapple juice, and they all drank through the dinner hour until the past and the future grew soft and remote.

Becca poked the fire with foil, and sparks rose into the sky. Another dad brought out a stack of downtown Yellow Pages and threw them on the fire. The adopted Chinese daughters of the *New York Times* reporters next door grew mesmerized.

"Fire lettuce," said Sophie, "and fire potato chips."

"Fire lasagna noodles," added Hannah.

Sparks rose and joined against the sky, now a deep shade of teal.

Community Board Chair Emerita Frieda Glaberson and her husband, Sheldon, out for their regular evening stroll, stopped by. Frieda rubbed Becca's shoulders, and Becca reached up and gave Frieda's hand a squeeze. Someone shone a flashlight and for a second Becca saw Camille's ancient, lined face at her window, winking her approval.

Someone produced a box of sparklers, and the kids ran down the street with crackling gold in their hands. Even the teenagers who ordinarily vanished at this hour into cyberspace or mysterious outings with unnamed peers stayed in view and helped.

Tomorrow their machines would whir back into action, and all the little LEDs would glow. The culprit would be found and repairs would begin (after all, if New York City's workers could clean up Ground Zero, they could certainly fix little old Washington Square). But right now nothing was pressing. Tonight was a block party free from pad thai vendors and tube socks. Tonight was a pre-cash society.

Jamie, Mindy and Carlos's youngest, crawled into Becca's lap, and she wrapped her arms around his soft belly and stroked his fine black hair. She'd forgotten how warm bodies are. She could feel Ed's bony knees on her right and Mindy's sturdy thigh on her left, and she looked at all the faces lit a soft orange from the fire; she couldn't remember ever being so happy. The air smelled of roasting meat. Her face and chest were flushed and her rear end was cold, and for a moment of grace the two balanced each other perfectly. This is the way humans are meant to live, she thought. Close to the Earth and the elements and each other. A log settled and sent off sparks, and everyone watched the sparks form lines of text in some gorgeous unknown language.

The sky was having a sample sale of stars, beautiful white stars of all sizes twinkling the way they did in the kids' song, the way they did in the ceiling of Grand Central.

Then an ordinary fluorescent flickered in the distance, and everyone went still. "It's just a generator over at St. Vincent's, folks," said the know-it-all chair of the community board land-use committee. "Don't get your hopes up."

But Becca wished the lights would never come on.

They wrapped up the food and someone dragged over a trash can and a garden hose and put out the fire. The street hissed and a rush of smoky butter-scented steam rose. The black air turned moist and white. And then the sound died down.

The young families gathered up their belongings and went home first.

Eventually there was a caravan back to Becca's building.

Carlos had disappeared as he so often did, so Mindy herded the kids by herself. A few older gay couples, old Mrs. Goldman, the single mom and her daughter. Is there any dark as absolute as a tenement hallway in a blackout?

One by one the neighbors exited the stairwell and groped their way down the hall to their own doorknobs. "'Night," they called, each like a lighthouse keeper climbing the rocks for the night shift.

WEDNESDAY

FROM JAY SUPAK'S SECOND DISPATCH FOR
VILLAGEWEEK ONLINE

A new vocabulary has developed in the Village. With Ground Zero already taken, the area including and surrounding the Arch is now being called Zone A and remains cordoned off with caution tape and sawhorses and cops. Zone B refers to the ring just beyond, where there is no mandatory evacuation but there is also no power. The city has preemptively turned off the electricity temporarily to prevent secondary fires and explosions.

Shrines have appeared. So have slogans on T-shirts and buttons: Peace & love, once and forever. We shall overcome. When will they ever learn? Long Live the Arch, October 2006.

A sister-city program with Greenville, South Carolina, and its suburbs is being organized. On Sunday, the mayor is scheduled to fly down and meet with the families. Delta provided, at no charge, first-class flights home for the widowers.

The recovery of bodies is proceeding slowly.

BAD TOUR

Becca reluctantly met them on Seventh Avenue South near Bleecker, well outside Zone A.

She had tried to call off all her tours for the week. She spent the hold time going through the "vessel": some barely used birthday candles, twisty ties, refrigerator magnets, and down at the bottom, lots of change that looked promisingly silver. Just as she'd done when she was a girl, she sorted it into piles on the red Formica table. She always got the nickels out of the way first—so much bulk for so little worth. When she tallied the piles, she had enough for a scant week's worth of staples.

When she got through to the adult school in Westchester, the woman who'd coordinated it wouldn't hear of canceling. She said a lot of things to keep Becca on the phone—talked of her students' dedication, their class on the history of conflict and oppression, busy schedules, the van that was already hired, a strong pull to be in the Village as an act of solidarity.

Becca said, no, she didn't think it was a good idea. She said the whole area was on lockdown. She said everything was canceled. Her hand holding the rotary phone was shaking from exhaustion, from shock. She was in no shape to give a tour. She didn't even know what she could show them. She tried to brush some crumbs off the sleeve of her sweatshirt and realized they were tiny holes from the bonfire.

And then the woman said, "We understand this will require some extra time and effort on your part and we will certainly compensate you accordingly."

Heaven help us all, Becca said to herself, before she stipulated "cash."

The women were sharper and noisier and New Yorkier than her usual tourists, with what her cousin Joycie called Pilates bodies. This time there were men too. She generally liked men on a tour. She could meet them where they lived, in the world of facts and politics and public policy. They brought a different energy, slightly flirtatious. These men wore shades of tan. Corduroy and leather, hair plugs. Clothing chosen by the wives. Sports jackets, firm handshakes. They looked like actors in a commercial for financial planning or a high-end resort.

Often on a tour she broke into a folk song. Or recited "Annabel Lee" or "The Raven" or some lines from *Leaves of Grass*. She also knew her local birds and her botany and kept an eye out for corn growing in a tree pit, an unusual bird beak poking from a soffit to delight them. But she couldn't find her way to pleasure today. And besides, the group wouldn't shut up behind her.

"There's supposed to be a fabulous pizza place on Bleecker, one of those ones with the official blessing from the pizza gods in Naples."

"Yes, we went a couple of weeks ago with the Fodermans. You have to get the fried pizza dough with the Nutella for dessert. To die for."

"This is going to sound more crass than I mean it to, but do you think prices in the Village will come down now?"

"No way. Hey—remember how everyone predicted a crash after 9/11?"

"We just looked at a conversion down on Wall Street, just for the fun of it. Shoshana's been talking about NYU and we figured we should do due diligence. It's a former bank building, one of those ones with the fantastic steel elevator doors with scenes of work-ethic virtues. Get this. One of the apartments still had an actual vault in the living room. Of course, there's no place to buy a quart of milk for miles around. Crazy."

They talked of their children's MCATs and their kitchen renovations. A woman with perfect corkscrew curls said, "I'm doing a cleanse thing. It's actually great. I recommend it. I feel lighter than air and weirdly focused."

Becca almost turned around and said, *I'm doing a cleanse thing, too. It's called rice and beans.*

"I know what you're thinking, *ketzelah*," said her father. "Be nice."

Usually she gave no more thought to navigating these streets than she did to the blood making its rounds through her body. But with no Arch as home base, the Village felt lopsided and she felt dizzy. She actually got confused for a minute and mistook West Third for West Fourth.

The organizer asked her if she was okay, and she reassured them all. "I'm breathing. It's good to work."

She didn't go down any of the blocks she had taken her South Carolina women to. Every time she stopped to show this group something, they went back to their serious student faces, shaking their heads sadly. "Terrible, the things humans do to each other," said one of the men.

She got stuck for a long time on Eleventh Street just outside Zone A, in front of the rebuilt building the Weathermen had blown up in 1970, the one with the jutting window where a stuffed Paddington lived. It was October, so he was in his Yankees uniform.

But she didn't want to talk about Paddington. She talked about that day, down to the nails in the tubes of the pipe bombs the anti-war radicals were making in the basement of the old house before they accidentally blew it up. She told the story of Cathy and Kathy, the Weathermen women. Then she digressed. She told them about Etan Patz, who had once been babysat by one of her classmates. Lisa Steinberg's gruesome death by her stepfather in 1987. In the middle of the lecture she heard her father's voice say "ixnay, already" so loudly that she whipped around, expecting to see his head leaning out of a car window. And for a split second, she did see it, his round balding head. She shook her own head to clear it away.

She tried to sneak a furtive glance at her watch, something she never did, wishing it was time to march them back to their van, so she could go home and crawl into bed. If only someone might greet her at the door with a glass of wine and ask about her day.

She decided to give them what they really wanted all along, and walked them all the way to the western end of Bleecker Street, which still had power. They came to Magnolia Bakery. They peered in and saw cakes under glass domes, a woman icing a red-velvet cake by turning it on a lazy Susan. The cupcakes had the same palette as the spring line of Coach pocketbooks: pistachio, mocha, raspberry.

The lack of a line in front was the only sign that something was amiss in the Village. They filed on in while she waited on the sidewalk. Her father's voice whooshed in her ear.

Ketzelah, don't phone it in. You're better than that. These are people with clout and deep pockets.

He was right about this gang. Probably they did more to help the poor than she ever had. Wrote year-end checks to Planned Parenthood, the Henry Street Settlement, Habitat for Humanity.

She took a breath so deep she felt a pull in her ribs. Calm down, she told herself. They will post reviews online. Hold yourself together. You're a professional. A phrase from high school theater flitted into her mind, what they all used to say when they flubbed a line: "It's not brain surgery and no one died."

But people did die, on a regular basis. Everywhere she turned today, the blocks were rife with stories of lives gone wrong. All her Village stories seemed like fairy tales with gruesome endings and bad morals. The hypocrisy of Mae West being hauled off to the Jefferson Market women's jail. The waste of Jimi Hendrix, just another brilliant young Black man who died a tragic, preventable death. John Lennon? Murdered by a petty maniac. What about the thousands kicked out of their homes when traffic engineers rammed Seventh Avenue through a hundred buildings to meet up with Varick Street? As she shifted her weight, her hip bone ground in its socket like a pestle in a mortar.

Fashionistas walked down the street in low black boots and pre-torn skin-tight jeans, their hair as flat as sheets of paper.

Inside the women were ordering cupcakes, and Becca started to cry. She hated today but the past wasn't feeling like a very good refuge either. There used to be so many perverts roaming the neighborhood that everyone called them pervs for short. She had been felt up right across the street. One of the many Marc Jacobs boutiques had been a dank, used bookstore run by a known perv. It was understood in those days that you entered at your own risk; you protected yourself. You ran home past the longshoremen with your loose-leaf notebook covering your bouncing breasts. Even her father—peacenik, lover-boy Lew—took her to the schoolyard behind PS41 one evening after supper to show her how to punch a boy. It was considered a life skill.

The first one out was the Indian-looking woman with a bobbing black pageboy, carrying a chocolate cupcake with white icing.

"Can't we buy you one, Becca? They're pretty great. I'd have to run all the way back to Larchmont to work this off, but it's just so darned good."

Becca turned away, pretending to watch the kids on the playground down the street, but the woman could see she was crying.

"Oh dear," she said. She didn't sound anything like the others. She had a lovely accent that turned up at the ends of the words. "I feared this was a bad idea. So soon after. I'm going to get you a Kleenex. Here, you hold this while I find one in my purse."

That was how Becca came to hold a Magnolia cupcake for the first time.

"Let's get you calmed down before the others appear." The woman held out a Kleenex and they traded. "They can be a little...how shall I put it?...hard-edged, this crowd."

Becca hadn't bought Kleenex in years. "This is really soft," she said.

"Oh yes. They embed lanolin in them. I have allergies. They're great. They keep my nose from getting all raw."

The woman offered up her cupcake. Becca refused it; she didn't want anything that was on offer on this street. The woman insisted.

"You're sad. You just lived through a major trauma. Take a bite. I'm telling you it will ease the pain. You need to stimulate your pleasure centers."

So Becca took back the cupcake, top-heavy with icing. She took a tiny bit of buttercream on her finger and licked it. Her mouth watered for more. She peeled off the paper. The cake was so very soft.

White beans, kidney beans, black beans, lentils. Pasta, kasha, rice. That's what she had been living on. And pretzels, lots of pretzels. She didn't even like them but they were cheap and filling. And Baldwin apples from the Greenmarket. The bin with the hand-lettered sign read "tart like lemons, hard like rocks."

Her teeth sank into the cupcake from above and below and met in the middle and her mouth filled with sweetness so intense it almost crossed over into astringency. She had to cough and clear her throat before her system adjusted. Fresh tears came to her eyes. Her teeth, tongue, palate, gums were coated in butter and chocolate. Her mouth said: more please.

The buttercream acted like a hallucinogen, or maybe it was just shock wearing off or the lack of sleep catching up. She looked at the little buildings across the street and imagined time running backward. Decades unlived themselves, the fashionistas went back to whatever suburbs they had sprung from. The boutiques turned back into secondhand shops that called themselves antique stores, then pushcarts sprouted in the street. She saw the mortar of the row houses softening, bricklayers pulling off each brick and returning it to the stack, the stack being loaded onto barges that chugged up the Hudson to Haverstraw or Kingston where they were unbaked in kilns until they turned to loose clay and were scooped onto the bluff on the riverbank, and meanwhile here on Bleecker, the blacktop heated up and flew back into the truck and the cobblestones below it were unlaid and shipped back as ballast on a long, slow trip to Europe.

And not far away the Arch re-erected itself until it stood proud and white and in a flash was taken apart and shipped to Carrara and all the slaves who were buried under Washington Square's lawn grew black flesh over their bones and went back to work and then shrank until they were infants tossed back into their mothers' wombs and then their mothers shrank back into *their* mothers' wombs and all the Africans and islanders were shipped back to their warm lands.

And she grew younger and smaller and her parents appeared on either side to lift her up over every puddle, and then she shrank and disappeared into the womb of Doris Michaelman Cammeyer Steinglass.

Becca forced herself back to the present. She asked the woman where she was from.

"Sri Lanka, by way of Singapore and Brussels," she said. Her husband had been in the diplomatic corps. Now they had settled in Larchmont where she taught middle school. She had come on the tour because she was planning her unit on New York history.

The rest of the group trickled out, sugared up, cupcake papers crumpled in the paper bag, fingertips licked daintily, smiles on their faces as if they'd just had sex.

"Nirvana in a cupcake," said one of the women.

Becca thought, *Just let this tour end.* She bunted for a while. Showed them the old synagogue tucked into Charles Street, and then basically let them drool over the Italianate row houses with their grand stoops. She passed out postcards pre-addressed to the Landmarks Commission but skipped her usual plea for the South Village.

And then she pulled herself together. "Let's talk about a couple of the creative artists who lived around here. It wasn't until Willa Cather came to Bank Street that she felt free to write about the prairie. Ginsburg from Newark and Kerouac from Lowell. It happened to all of them, all drawn here from everyplace else. Twain, Cummings."

"What about you, Becca? Where did you come from?"

"Me? I couldn't come here to make it big. I was already here, born and bred. About five blocks away. A lifelong renter."

She was about to tell them how she'd spent her entire life throwing buckets of money out the window and had no equity. But now, of all things, her mother's voice piped up. "Don't bite the hand that feeds you, Rebecca."

Becca did what she always did when her mother offered advice: ignored it. "Remember when people in the Village used to wear smocks? I can't remember the last time I saw a smock go by on a Village street. Or the last time I smelled oil paint or clay."

The woman who'd asked the question stepped in deftly. "Becca. I guess I hit a raw nerve. I guess the whole city feels like a raw nerve. I bet lots of the greats lived near here. Maybe you could show us one of their houses?"

"Forgive me," said Becca. She did a quick roll call of the block's former denizens (Thomas Wolfe, William Styron, Sinclair Lewis, Hart Crane) and decided to show them the bar on Tenth Street where Edward Albee was said to have seen, scrawled in soap on a mirror, the words *Who's Afraid of Virginia Woolf?* And then it was finally time to lead them back to their parking lot. She got them ready first.

"You're about to see one of the more bizarre, jarring stretches of avenue in Manhattan. Seventh Avenue used to stop at Eleventh Street. The same year World War I began, the city rammed a connector right through dozens of buildings to meet up with Varick Street to the south, where the IRT subway line was cut through. Just like Baron Haussmann in Paris a little earlier. If you look closely you'll see the scars everywhere."

They waited for the light at the enormous intersection where Bleecker and Seventh Avenue and Commerce all crossed at odd angles. Right behind them was the old psychic tucked into the tight triangle of a building, where she and her high school friend Mundo had once had their palms read for kicks after school. The psychic had run her fingers across Becca's palm and declared that she was an *artiste* who would be wise to marry well. The psychic told Mundo he would need to summon all his strength for trials to come. They walked out wishing they had never gone in and decided to console themselves at Marie's Crisis Cafe.

"*Artistes* before weaklings," Mundo had said as he held open the door to the piano bar.

He died in 1983 when they were just starting to call it AIDS.

It was hard to keep a group well herded on Seventh Avenue South, the road out of the Village, with cars trying to jump the lights on the rush to the Holland Tunnel.

Her own voice started to clamor for attention in her noisy head. *Help me*, it said. *I'm afraid I'm not going to be okay.* She felt like the shaved-off buildings of Seventh Avenue South. The aftertaste of sugar sat rank on her tongue.

She sidled up to the woman who had organized the tour. She offered to pay her back while praying, *Please don't let her take my money.*

"Don't be ridiculous," the woman said. "I'm the one who strong-armed you into this. I thought it might be a bad idea, but I deferred to my boss as usual. You'd think I would learn to trust my own instincts."

A new feeling bubbled up: why did people always have to make everything about themselves, and why did they always think they were right? Maybe she loathed New Yorkers, including those who just liked to think they were New Yorkers. She wanted to go somewhere where politeness trumped showing off. Maybe her whole life had been lived in error.

A black car—that is, a New York black car, the kind rich, busy people could order up at work at will—sped to the intersection and stopped in the crosswalk. She could just make out the driver through the tinted windshield. He wore tinted aviator glasses like a movie chauffeur.

She took the flat of her hand, the tender underside, and smacked it on the black hood, hoping to feel the sheet metal give under her. All she felt was fresh pain in a new place.

She made an efficient gesture that said, *What the fuck's the matter with you, you entitled prick?* He pressed the horn as if he would never stop, then gave her the finger as his light turned green.

When she finally trudged up the steps, Carny slowly roused himself to greet her and hawked up a puddle of pale froth at her feet. Her oak floor was dotted with clean patches from where his stomach acid ate the varnish. The cash she'd earned would barely cover a visit to the vet.

She laid out a fresh Duane Reade bag for him to pee on and collapsed on the sofa. Half-read books lay open on the coffee table like an encampment, spread on a ground cover of unread *New Yorkers* that Ed had left in the recycling bin for her.

She hadn't yet dreamed about the women; they seemed to be trapped in a limbo between her short- and long-term memory; her unconscious hadn't had time to know them yet. What she did dream was that she was being sold as a tear-down. She was also being marked up for cuts like a beef cow. Instead of flank and standing rib, her parts were zoning designations: M3 and C1-9.

That dream bled into another, this one cut-rate, made up entirely of memory. She needed a copy of *Hedda Gabler* for school and the library was closed. She went to the store on Bleecker Street where her mother always told her not to go. The man cornered her in Used Drama. He told her she was beautiful. His hair was slicked back with Brylcreem. She kicked him in the balls, not hard; he was old.

The gas is back on in the A Zone. All but four streets around the periphery of the Square have been opened back up. All news outlets have, of course, interviewed the mayor, but former mayor Ed Koch, who happens to live right across the street from the site, is again the man of the hour.

"Oh yes, saw the whole thing from my window," he said. "Felt it deep in my bones, almost like a stomachache. No—more like a heart attack, and that's not just a figure of speech in my case. Our beautiful white arch, our wonderful, wild democratic park where people come to sing and to feel comfortable being themselves. Whoever wanted to destroy that? One sick cookie is all I can say."

ORIGIN STORY

Becca hated the basement steps, so shallow they forced her to turn sideways to fit her wide feet on the sloping treads while bending so as not to clunk her head on the door frame. The walls were made of some kind of red-black igneous rock that looked as if it had been hacked by hand, with mortar that appeared to have been slapped on by the world's laziest builder. It was an entrance that cried: *Give up, you don't want to go down here. Leave us skeletons be.*

She made it her business to have as little to do with this place as possible. But when she checked again on Camille, Camille said she was trying to organize her Ironed Curtain papers and asked Becca to bring some things up to her. Camille was one of the few people in this world Becca couldn't say no to, and besides, she had nothing else to do. It smelled of mildew and felt clammy. Plastic pumpkins, Christmas tree stands, sacks of kitty litter, glue traps. The plastic of a garment bag with dust as thick as velour. The floor had once been concrete, but it was returning to dirt.

The front of the basement wasn't so bad because a little light came through from the street. But the back, where the boxes were, was medieval. A bulb with a pull cord that you had to grope blindly to find, provided the power was on. Rime on the stones. Hoses and dials, ductwork. The furnace was a big red tank with fire whooshing inside, no electricity needed. The low ceilings were made lower by pipes, no knowing which ones would burn your skin off. Becca thought she saw something scurry and then everything seemed to scurry, even the rock salt. All the stuff that people without means judged too good to throw out but not good enough to live with. All the stuff that either would be useful one day or would eventually be tossed by the next of kin on the curb for Sanitation. She started shining her flashlight on boxes. For Camille, only for Camille.

The box that stopped her and made her forget all about Camille was simply marked in black, 5F, her apartment. There wasn't enough writing for Becca to know who had held the magic marker or when or why. It was covered in packing tape, but she could read where it said Burry's Fudgetown, a kind of cookie as long gone as her family. The tape had yellowed, but it lay flat and straight and wound all the way around. She ran her fingers over it. She decided it was the work of her mother; nobody could seal things up like Doris. This was a box ready for the second flood. But her mother had decamped from here after the divorce as fast as she could say "Mamaroneck" and "remarriage." Becca couldn't imagine what she had deigned important enough for this kind of care.

She picked up the carton, medium heavy, and made her way up the steps, somehow getting all the doors opened and closed until she was in the concrete backyard. Everyone called it the bunker, but the light was good for reading, and Becca hoped there might be something worth reading inside. She set the box on the broken Ping-Pong table and pulled up a white plastic chair. She blew dust off the carton. Using the screwdriver on her keychain, she carefully sliced through the tape and pulled up the flaps. She buried her nose inside, hoping she might catch a whiff of her father—Barbasol, cigars—but all she smelled was basement.

What she was really hoping for were clues of her own existence—some proof that she'd been brought into the world for any kind of reason, with any kind of love.

What she found instead was a couple of yards of cotton fabric, folded into a neat square, a perfectly pleasant green and blue stripe. It sucked her straight back to a part of the past she least wanted to revisit.

The fabric was supposed to have been made into curtains. It was her father's thrifty plan, and her mother had gone along with it just long enough to make the trip to the yard-goods store. Much later, after the fabric had sat in its bag on the side table for a good long while, her father had torn the bag open and held the fabric up to the window. "Four seams and a rod!" she remembered him crying, almost in tears. "Four seams and a rod was all I asked." And she remembered wanting to get up from the sofa and stand by his side with the same rallying cry.

Under the fabric she found some random household stuff, maddeningly uninteresting—a pair of fussy silver candlesticks, badly tarnished, that she had never much liked, and the same kind of Elgin folding alarm clock every household used to have. The next layer was a batch of newsletters from the year her father was secretary of the local Democratic club, which Becca was grateful for; she set them aside to go through later. She had to smile at the next document, which offered proof of her own existence all right, but of the most anodyne sort: her vaccination records. The bottom half of the box was stiff white layers that she assumed was padding. It turned out to be a satin wedding dress and a veil. Becca gasped.

She pulled it out and held it out to inspect. It was short sleeved with a sweetheart neckline and little satin flowers sewn on at wide intervals. In fact, Becca decided there was something grudging in every part of the dress: the plain short sleeves, the uncreamy bluish white of the satin, the narrow little bodice, the row of satin buttons that had no buttonholes to meet them on the other side, just a metal zipper tucked into the seam. Becca checked the label. It had no designer's cursive name, not even Bergdorf or Bonwit or Saks. It was an off-the-rack dress from Gimbels, the kind you bought in a hurry and on the cheap, not at all her mother's style. No wonder there had been no wedding photos on display.

She folded the dress back up and set it on her lap. When she lifted the box to the sun to be sure there was nothing else in there, a small packet slid to one side.

It was a bundle of letters tied with a piece of string, red and white like the kind on bakery boxes. The envelopes were worn flat, as if they had been either neglected or treasured, it was hard to tell which. And when Becca leafed through them quickly, trying to keep the oils from her fingers from penetrating the soft paper, hardly believing what she had in her hand, what she had almost missed finding, she saw that most of them appeared to be from Lewis Cammeyer of Stanton Street to Doris Michaelman of the Grand Concourse. Some were handwritten and some typed, the ink faded. She pulled out one of the hand-written ones at random. There was his odd, improbable cursive, large and decisive-looking and yet hard to read, so unlike the rest of him.

She read.

> They put me off at the employment office, but tomorrow is Monday, day of serious business, and I shall prevail (as soon as I get this mailing out and the union hall reserved). Ralph knows a fellow who knows a fellow who knows Leadbelly, so keep your fingers crossed. This could be big, big, big. Kiss the envelope three times for good luck when you read this.

> p.s.: Big, I tell you. Your completely devoted slave, Lew.

Becca had a strong yearning to run and show someone the secret she'd stumbled on: the actual written voice of her father, charming and young and alive, if unemployed. If her cousin Joycie were still in Forest Hills and not Arizona she would hop on the subway right now to share them with her. But all she saw here were the fire escapes, slivers of other buildings beyond, the violets growing out of the cracks in the concrete. She would have to make do, as usual, with what was at hand: her own memory. Her history-major mind got right to work reaching, reaching to make sense of his words on the paper. She couldn't remember her father being out of work. And while he had passed his love of Leadbelly on to her, she couldn't remember any stories about snagging Leadbelly for a union rally or a concert. Ralph, Ralph, Ralph, she said to herself, but try as she might to call one up from the past, no Ralph appeared. Nor could she imagine her father excitedly sharing his news with her mother or expecting her to kiss an envelope full of germs from the mailman. But being Doris's slave—that was no stretch; that was prescient.

Next she pulled out one of the typed ones that turned out to be the first typed one. It was a single sheet of onion skin folded in half and then in thirds to fit inside the plain envelope. Becca carefully unfolded the folds her father had made, the same folds her mother had unfolded and refolded, maybe more than once.

> Okay, no more complaiming about my penmamship. I am the proud owner of a secondhamd Underwood. It has lovely round keys rimmed in fold I mean gold and some day soom I will learn quich ones are where. Just call me Archy. Or Mehitabel. Which one is the typing cockroach? Wait…don't call me a cockroach!

Becca laughed out loud at her goofy father, at the possibility that he and her mother had once been in love. The concrete of the bunker bounced the sound of her laughter back at her.

The next one had no envelope. It was fatter and had been written a little later, judging by the slightly improved accuracy of his typing.

> You know what I keep rememberering? That day when we all went to the Rockaways. Actually, we only went to one Rockaway as far as I can figger. We thought we were so suave, but me and Bill and Ralph didn't even have the chutzpah to sit with you goils. I watched the way you and the other two braced yourselves in your little sunsuits—is that what you call those outfits?—every time the train lurched. The sun was in your eyes and you were the omly one with enough brains to put on sunglasses. And I thought: yep, that's the one for me. The still one in the middle looking out at the world, not back at herself. She's not a goody two shoes like Aggie over there admiring her own ankles and fingernails. And what's her name on the other side who giggled every time you looked at her. You

also had a first-rate pair of legs if you don't mind my saying, even in those funny sandals all the girls were wearing
with the nooses around your lovely ankles.

The boys and I had already done the divvying, but
of course we hadn't consulted any of you. Were you
impressed with what mensches we were when those old
ladies got on and we all leapt up?

Not many cities have ocean beaches within the city
limits, I don't imagine. LA, Rio, Miami, Tel Aviv, Sydney.
OK—I take it back. Apparently a lot of cities do. But the
thing that kills me about New York is that you can hardly
believe it's possible. You stand anywhere on the island of
Manhattan, take for instance here on the dirty old East
Side and you can hardly believe that a nickel away there's
sand and waves and boardwalks. There's primeval forest
right here in Manhattan. And a huge harbor. And maybe
one day soon there will be Doris Lilian Michaelman of the
Bronx, who, I will say once again, I would very much like
to make Doris Lilian Cammeyer. Am I being presumptu-
ous? Hell, yes! But I know how to bide my time. I know
how to play the odds, and I like my chances. I like them
very much. Yours, Lewis.

Another began:

You are not the sweet nothing sort, so I will whisper tart,
tangy nithings I mean nothings. Wish me well. Tonight
I have to run a meeting that's going to be LOUD and
maybe UGLY. I have a secret weapon. I pretend I'm you.
The noisier they get, the quieter I'll get. I'll fix 'em with a
gimlet eye. I'm not sure what a gimlet eye is, but I know
it's sharp. Say yes, my love. I live for the word yes slipping
from those ruby lips.

When did it go wrong, or was it wrong from the start and Lew
was too sweet to see it? She hadn't dared to look at the rest of
the pile or at her watch; she wanted this moment to stretch out
as long as possible. The sun had moved and new tree leavings

had fallen on the Ping-Pong table. Becca got up to reposition the chair out of the shade so the light could shine on his words. So when she flipped to the next one, she was startled, even embarrassed, to see her mother's narrow Palmer script on the envelope. She tried to think it through—they had all lived in the same apartment for years; maybe it wasn't that odd for the letters that crossed each other in the mail to end up in one place and get shoved into the bottom of a box.

> Dear Lew, You are very sweet but very poor, and one of those things will not fly here on the Grand Concourse, where certain people take the word Grand very much to heart. Please tell me you got the foreman job. Rents are cheap and all, but not free if you want something halfway civilized. Yes, I know you'd like nothing better than to see me naked in the tub in the kitchen. But let me tell you, mister, a lady needs a tub with a door that shuts. I will cook on a two-burner stove, I will live with a half-size ice-box, but I draw the line at bathing in the kitchen.

How quickly, Becca thought, teenagers leapt into adulthood back then, and how ridiculously ill-prepared they were. No wonder her own generation refused to grow up.

> There's an ancient brass clock on the mantelpiece, *Doris continued.* It's rattling and driving me insane, and I keep going over and adjusting it, but it keeps right on rattling.

It seemed irrelevant, and Becca could almost feel the cold feet and hear the awkward pause as her mother tried to back-track to safer ground. Next paragraph:

> My friend Shirl and I went to see "Saint Joan" on Broadway. Very thought provoking. The clock stopped rattling. Will wonders never cease. Yours, Doris.

There was one letter left.

> I have a clock that rattles and makes me nuts too! Let's put them side by side and maybe they'll make rattling babies. Doris o Doris, how I adore-us. Shining likes a star-iss,

please don't go far-iss into the foress. I'll send my uncle Morris with a search part-iss. You see my poetry is rich like the rest of me. I can't afford a carriage ride in Central Park but come to the Village with me. We'll listen to jazz. My treat.

It wasn't much of a stretch for Becca to imagine the final missing letter. It would be from Doris, and it would be very short. It went something like this:

Dear Lewis, I would call except that little pitchers have big ears and so do certain big ones. There is something important I have to tell you. Meet me you-know-where on Thursday after work.

The postmark of this one, unlike the others, which had faded, would be clearly visible, and it would be a date approximately a week before Doris got on the IRT, maybe corralling her friend Shirl, for a quick trip to Gimbels. It would also be a date approximately eight and a half months before Becca's birth.

It was getting chilly. There was a crack in the chair that was pinching her in the back of the thigh. She put all the letters carefully back and she sat there staring at the envelopes in her lap. It was the days before zip codes. An individual seemed more unique then; it seemed possible that from where he was writing on Stanton Street, there really was no other Doris on the Grand Concourse.

It was almost four already. She needed to go back to the basement for Camille. She needed time to get upstairs before the daylight faded. But she sat in the plastic chair and finally said it out loud to a pair of sparrows hopping around the concrete wall: "I should never have been born."

This was what Becca knew, although it was hard to say anymore how much of it she'd been told and how much she had made up: Her parents had met at a rent party in a tenement in the Village called The Rebecca.

The entrance fee was a few coins dropped in a pipe tobacco can. In those days there would have been a curtain of brown wooden beads in the kitchenette doorway. There would have been clamshells full of cigarette ash on the coffee table and the windowsills, and maybe a brooding photographer with a Brownie, a cousin of the hostess wanting to show in galleries. Someone would have made gin punch and poured Wise potato chips into a bowl. A record player on the countertop played obscure blues songs and new jazz. Everyone claimed to be an artist or a longshoreman or better yet both, but many were actually receptionists and salesmen or students on the GI bill.

Lew was buddies with the hosts. Doris didn't know anyone, but her friend Shirl did, and the party had been sanctioned in the Michaelman household because the Michaelmans and Shirl's parents knew each other from shul. Lew had developed some muscles working on the docks over the summer and walked in his high-waist pants with a new swagger; Doris, slender and sinewy, wore a fully fashioned black turtleneck and slacks from the kind of place she usually shopped, maybe Rogers Peet. In the dim light he mistook her for a free spirit, and she mistook him for a man about town. They talked all evening. They both loved plays. They both were looking to escape their families.

The party reached a pitch. There was suddenly slow dancing in the living room hardly wider than a car on the A train, and just as swoony now that the punch was coursing through every body. The dancing turned to groping, the crowd broke down into smaller units (in one corner an uneasy threesome kept forming and breaking apart). Lew was rarely first at anything, but he managed to claim Doris and lead her into the small bedroom where together they claimed the mount atop the bed. In the living room the needle at the end of the Bakelite arm skipped over and over until someone leaned over and pulled it off the Charlie Parker.

"You're like a model in a *Vogue* magazine," Lew said, groping at fabric and zippers and hooks. "You have elegance AND you have brains." That, it turned out, was the ticket to the warm body of Doris. She lifted the turtleneck over her slender head and tossed her hair back into place.

Young Doris did it with young Lew, on a pile of strangers' scratchy coats. It was an old story. She did it forgetting all about Shirl, who was waiting to ride the IRT back to the Bronx with her. She did it to stick it to her overprotective German Jewish mother. She did it because Lew was cute and wanted her so badly and she did it hard and fast and rash and loud. It might have been her first and last rash act.

Not in My Backyard

The sparrows scattered at some movement, and Becca thought she heard a woman's voice calling her name. She wasn't sure the voice was real; she wasn't sure anything was real. She looked up from the letters, shaking herself back to the bunker, circa the terrible autumn of 2006. She had spent more than half a century right here at The Rebecca, where she was pretty sure she'd been conceived.

And there was Melora Ross's white-blond head sticking up from the other side of the wall, a wall that had once been a conduit between them but over the years had become a rampart. They exchanged wary hellos.

"I saw you from upstairs," said Melora. "I don't mean to interrupt. It's kind of the last thing I want to do. I'm sure you have a lot going on, but I'm having kind of a…" She and Becca hadn't said a word in years. Melora's voice came rushing back into her ears, its odd harmony of seasoned woman and little girl, the homey hint of Nassau County that always snuck through.

"Look—I come in peace. I'd put my hands up except that I would fall off the wall. Listen, I don't know what to say about the Arch. I'm really sorry. I can't imagine what you're going through…"

Becca could see that Melora was trying, but also that she wanted something. "Is that why you climbed up the wall? To tell me that?" Becca asked.

"Actually, I need to ask a favor," Melora said, screwing up her face disarmingly.

Becca did not want to be disarmed. There was too much history, history every which way she turned. She slowly put the dress and everything else back in the box, cushioned it with the curtain fabric, and tried to close it, but the contents took up more room now.

"You're not saying anything. This is hard enough already. At least say something."

"I was kind of in the middle of something," said Becca, wondering what she could possibly have that Melora Ross might need.

Melora's hair was still tousled in just the right way. She wore a taupe sweater. She had the tiniest wrinkles all over her face; they suited her.

"Listen. There's a ruptured pipe or a backup or something. In my basement or maybe the backyard. What do I know?—I just sell houses, I don't dig inside their guts. Maybe it's something from the Arch. And don't tell me to call a plumber. *You* try calling a plumber two days after a bomb goes off in a neighborhood full of crappy nineteenth-century plumbing. And while you're at it why don't you ask how much they charge just to make the house call before they do anything. I'm all alone over here and there's a flood and I don't know where it's coming from and my hose rotted out and please, pretty please, can you just throw me a hose and turn on the water?" Melora's eyes filled with tears.

Becca looked around. She saw trash cans, rusty trikes, a Super Soaker, and a lot of unspecified odds and ends, as if the basement had burst its bounds and shot tendrils up here. Finally she found the hose in a corner and handed it up to Melora. Then she went to the spigot, which squeaked and squeaked and then sent water shooting up her pants legs before it filled the hose.

"You're lucky the water's on," Becca said. "If the super were actually doing his job, he would've turned it off for the season already."

Becca didn't even walk down Melora's block if she could help it. It was just habit by this point: her feet would turn elsewhere like a streetcar. Even on tours. It was easier that way. Becca blurted it out despite herself: "Do you need help?"

"No, that's okay. It's really nice of you, but I'll manage." They passed offers and refusals back and forth a couple of times until Becca carefully tucked a tarp around the box for safekeeping and put the box inside the back door, dragged over the chair, and after a few tries and after making the crack in the seat bigger, got herself up on the wall, which she used to be able to do without a second thought, and lowered herself down into New York real estate Oz.

Melora's backyard was twice as deep as hers and a hundred times more green. The maple that Aaron and Cole used to climb was starting to turn red. The teak chairs and flagstone path were new since she'd been here last. The path circled around the back and split to make way for a koi pond ringed with a wall of flat rocks. The weird thing was, it didn't look so hot up close. Lichen was growing on the paths and the chairs. The violets were starting to take over.

"Since you're here, and let it go on the record that I did not beg or even ask, would you help me save the koi? I'm afraid they're going to die; the pump's not working. I put them in the bathtub downstairs, but there's sewage backing up."

Lots of Villagers talked with their hands, but Melora talked with her arms. Becca had forgotten this, one of the many things that irked her about Melora—the way her arms acted out her tales, the way they often got ahead of the story her mouth was trying to tell. Becca couldn't help herself. She started to snicker. She turned away so Melora wouldn't see. She wasn't even sure what was funny: Melora and her rich people's problems, or the relief of escaping from her own world for a few minutes.

"Shut up. They're the best pets I've ever had. I'm responsible for their lives, and I'm failing them."

"Where's Niko?"

"Not here, that's for damn sure. It's a long story."

"What about Fabienne? Doesn't she still work for you? Seems to me I see her around sometimes."

"That's a good question. Does it count if you have a cleaning lady but she appears to have moved to Haiti? Niko seems to have stopped paying her. Leave it to me to have a housekeeper who reverse immigrates." Melora suddenly stopped to give

Becca a strange once-over and Becca thought maybe she was going to make a crack about her sweatpants. "I'd forgotten that about you—how the fuck do you remember Fabienne's name? I can barely hold on to it and she's been working here for fifteen years."

"Isn't there *someone* you can call who knows what they're doing?" It occurred to Becca, maybe for the first time, that people who lived in townhouses had money but not supers.

"Well, duh." Another Melora habit. She launched into another long explanation about an AWOL handyman.

"Well, okay," said Becca, "let's get to work."

It wasn't a finished basement as much as a whole extra loft-style apartment, with separate areas for a futon, a desk and bookcases, dumbbells and a yoga mat, and a bunch of old toys that no doubt still bore Aaron's fingerprints. Melora led her to the guest bath, where the fish were madly flailing in the tub. There was a giant net lying across the counter. Before Melora had a chance to warn her, Becca scooped up all five fish in the net on the first try. She wouldn't have admitted it, but she was delirious with busyness, with the competence of her own hands, with showing up Melora as the calm, sensible, action-taking one.

Then the fish started flailing madly, as if trying to turn themselves inside out. "Where to?" she asked.

"Laundry room," said Melora. "Hang on, let me try the water in there. I think it runs on a different line." She disappeared. Becca heard water pouring full force.

The koi were flipping and flopping in the net and spilling water in all directions, such a violent action it seemed like there was malice and not just self-preservation involved.

"Okay, seems clear enough," Melora called.

They stood watching the fish flail in the net while the sink filled. They had gorgeous skin—orange, yellow, white, black, stripes, spots—but unfortunate faces with their underbites and blank little eyes. When they sucked the air in search of nourishment, their lips became perfectly round like the top of a small condom. She wanted to tell them to conserve their strength, but they kept flinging themselves against each other. Maybe this was the life force. Maybe it was death throes. It was hard to tell the difference.

When the sink was filled a few inches, Becca gently released the fish, taking care not to knock anything over with the other end of the net. They flailed some more and then calmed down.

"Thank you," Melora said quietly.

"You're welcome. Do they have names?"

Melora nodded. "The parents are Mick and Carly. The babies are Monica, Angelica, and Al, for Al Jolson." She shrugged. "It seemed funny at the time."

Becca winced, but let it go with a simple "very PC of you." Then she asked, "What if the power doesn't come on?"

"You mean existentially or for the fish? For the fish, there's a koi guy, or there used to be, but I don't have his contact info. Where do you even look up a koi guy? I'm afraid about the chlorine," said Melora. "I might be making this up, but I think maybe the pond is supposed to filter it out."

And now Becca lost all patience. Five minutes with Melora and she felt like swearing like a sailor. "If you're going to have a koi pond, presumably you learn to take care of the fucking koi."

"That's the problem. The koi were fucking. They made koi babies. There used to be two of them, and they fit just fine in the sink. And besides, this household is kind of a lot for one person to keep a handle on. You're the expert—presumably when this house was built, people had servants."

She was right. A family would have had at least an Irish "girl." In the earlier, statelier houses, the ones from the 1820s, they might have had a slave or two. They had someone to tend to the horses and livery. They had a cook and a nursemaid. But Becca didn't want to grant Melora the satisfaction.

"Can't you rent out a couple of floors?"

"Duh, why didn't I think of that." Melora clunked herself on the forehead and pretended to lose her balance from the impact. "To rent an apartment in a one-family house, for your information, requires little details like kitchen facilities, and separate entrances and a husband who lets you know for sure that he's not just taking another little hiatus from his twenty-year marriage."

And here they were, right back in their old stances. She used to love showing Melora all the ways she was behaving like a spoiled brat, and Melora reciprocated by calling out Becca for self-righteousness and reverse snobbery. Funny that it's called a dynamic when it's such a static thing.

WANTING OUT

If depression were a garment, it would be gray sweatpants, stretched in the knees, pilled inside the thighs, smelling of stale human. It came on hard and sudden, and by evening it seemed the only world Becca had ever known. She tried reading by a flashlight but the night kept blooming blacker and blacker all around the beam.

All the sounds that ordinarily drove her crazy ceased: Ed's weird taste for house music, old Mrs. Goldman's TV turned up for the local news, the humming fluorescent tubes in the kitchen. Now she heard sounds that must have been there all along—flies banging the window, mice in the walls. Meanwhile, the locust tree outside her window dropped its leaves but seemed to be budding all over again.

Becca wanted out. What a disappointing planet this turned out to be, and if she could only find the energy she would get up and find another less laden with gravity and guilt and rank unfairness. She lay on the sofa until her body announced one of its tiresome needs.

She had always been a good sleeper. She slept at night because nobody but the most benign of ghosts could penetrate this tenement fortress, not through these mighty sash windows, not five flights up in her airshaft aerie, not with neighbors all around. She slept because so many of her worst fears had already come to pass. She slept because Aaron was fine. Even half destitute, she slept knowing she had work she loved.

But now it was ridiculous, the state she found herself in. She had read about it but never understood it: she was depressed because she had survived. What sense did that make? She should be up and out, behaving like a grateful survivor, cherishing every bite of each sandwich. Survivors started foundations and somehow suddenly knew how to hire people to do the paperwork. They did speaking engagements. They knew the Soroses.

Becca couldn't seem to move except to shift the weight now and again from her bad hip to her good one. The springs in the sofa were going. She was going, but nowhere fast, with no one to rescue her. It always came to that—where was her safety net? She stewed in self-pity, desperately missing her Forest Hills cousin Joycie, who was with her husband, Richard, in Flagstaff. They were staying with his aged mother while she recuperated from knee replacement surgery, but Becca feared they were actually doing a test run for a permanent move to Arizona.

The A-frame village of started novels grew on the coffee table. There were also unpaid bills and an unused Metro-North ticket Ed had handed to her, part of his failed mission to get her to visit her mother in Mamaroneck.

She grew hot, she grew cold. Blanket on, blanket off. Blanket on the floor with Carny on top. Cheek buried in Carny's flank listening to the sound of his heart. Carny. If not for Carny. She had made him a potty of newspaper on top of a sheet of PVC. She had put out dry food. He didn't like any of this, but he was a better man than she. He accepted the planet he'd been handed, the shitty planet Earth. Occasionally he looked up at her with his long ears lying flat, looking like a mourner in the crowd in a Giotto painting.

Something would have to give soon, and somewhere inside Becca's despair she understood this, but all she could do right now was wait, sending out an occasional sigh, the faintest of SOSs. She worried the dead women's names like a rosary: Jackie, Connie, Mary Anne, Laura, Wynnette, and Sheryl.

For practically the first time in her life, she lost track of when she had last eaten, but she could remember what because she felt the film on her tongue: the last of the chili she had made the last day, because now the calendar had split into a BC and an AD. That had happened on 9/11 too, but back then, as she recalled, it hadn't felt anything like this. There had been no paralysis then, just a surfeit of action and crystalline days. That had happened far away in nobody's neighborhood.

After a while her body made a new request: air, it said. She opened the window and stuck in the dowel to hold it up. She breathed, but it didn't feel like nearly enough of the cool night air. She moved the horsehair chair so she could put her arms on the sill and stick her head all the way out. She gulped air. Outside there was nothing but air. She wanted to fly like a bat in a sloppy, flitting pattern and never worry about crashing. The sky was as close as blue comes to black, so much sky, really, and so few interruptions—a few humans crisscrossing, buildings poking up.

A slight breeze blew into the room and suddenly Becca thought she might die if she didn't get some fresh air. She swiveled her feet to the floor and shook her head to clear it. For a few minutes, despite herself, she would wriggle out of the depression like a loaded backpack.

"Carny," she said, "we're going out."

She felt for her fleece and his leash on the coatrack, grabbed her flashlight, tucked her thermos of decaf under her arm, and headed to the stairwell.

This time the steps felt as familiar as her own thoughts. She knew the divot in the step that meant they had reached the third floor, the bark of flaking paint on the cool iron railing that announced the second. The only sound was their echoes as they rounded each bend of the tiled hallways and the click of Carny's toenails on the steps' metal treads.

They fumbled their way through the vestibule, which was barely long enough to fit Carny and hard enough to maneuver during the day. When she pulled open the heavy door, the glass wobbling inside its wrought-iron grill, the dark and the cool hit like a slap to each cheek, exactly what she needed. There was still half a moon up high above the tall buildings over on Sheridan Square. Carny peed on the sidewalk and she could actually hear the splash. They sat down on the stoop. They were the only ones on the block.

Her favorite place on earth had blown up and possibly taken her livelihood with it. No one knew yet what would happen to it. Was Washington Square like skin that slowly and imperfectly seals itself anew over a wound? More likely it was like bone that outdoes its original form and grows burls to protect the damaged spot. She could still faintly smell the smoke. In the daylight the sidewalks nearby were chalky with the dust of sheetrock, the pale ginkgo trees burned black, the white Arch in charred crags behind police barricades and caution tape.

The family in the townhouse across the street had set a candle in each window like an old New England house at Christmastime. The light was austere and beautiful. In the third-floor window, she saw a little girl getting ready for bed. The girl raised her arms above her head while the mom lifted off her shirt and lowered a pajama top. Her head popped out and her straight dark hair resettled itself around her face. The girl twirled like a ballerina. Now the girl begged her mom for something and the mom shook a finger no. The girl hopped up and down, clearly trying to wear down the mom's resistance. She won.

Now they stood side by side facing the window. The daughter pulled at the mom to get her to bend down, and she disappeared from view for a minute. She came back with two bowler hats, which she placed on each head. They stood still and then, at some signal Becca couldn't hear or see, they brought their hands up toward their shoulders and clicked their fingers in unison. They were both very thin and long-legged, one a miniature of the other. Then they did a perfect little Fosse routine, hands swiveling and flipping behind them, legs step-kicking sinuously and then crossing over each other. Both of them smiled a secret smile, having no idea they had a witness.

The mom looked out the window, sighed, and blew out the candle. Becca poured herself a cup of decaf, which was still nice and hot.

"Carny, babe," she said as she had said a thousand nights before. "Bedtime for Bassets." And they went upstairs to bed.

She awoke in the middle of the night. Her tourists were dead, no one was claiming responsibility, and insomnia was a gray Communist country. She got out of bed, put on her pilled terry slippers, and stood by the window. Carny roused himself when he noticed the bed had gone cold, jumped down, and waddled over. She reached down and patted his fat flank, solid as a millstone.

The windowsill was dusty, the child guard rusted away. She braced herself to open the window, hearing the mysterious sliding of sashes and disturbing of springs inside. The wind had died down and the moon was lighting up the super's junk, and beyond, she could see the placid surface of Melora's koi pond.

A cat fight was in progress beside the pond between a huge marmalade cat and a scrappy little white one with random patches of stripes. They circled each other with that silence only cats can manage. Tails swishing. Each time they turned, their eyes caught in the moonlight and glowed green like cyborgs. She assumed they were fighting over real estate—in the end, wasn't that what all New York fights boiled down to?

The cats took forever to make their moves. They placed their paws gingerly on the ground, stepping around Melora's yews and Melora's oakleaf hydrangeas.

She grabbed her clock and turned it until the moonlight lit the hands: 3:23. She tried to clear thoughts of tomorrow and yesterday, but they always crowded the present moment like obese subway passengers on either side of her, wheezing sour breath onto the present. *Look at the mess you've made, you fuck-up*, said the past; it spoke this way at 3:23.

THURSDAY

FROM JAY SUPAK'S UNPUBLISHED REPORTER'S
NOTEBOOK

Who knew the city has this power with the power? It can turn off the juice building by building, declaring: you, safe; you, not.

The tabloids have gone to town with photos and profiles of the six women. *The Times* has created a special section tucked inside the Arts, with a special Arch logo designed by R. Blechman, master of the poignantly wiggly line. The local cable news network has all its reporters covering the aftermath from its headquarters in Chelsea Market, giddy with purpose. CNN opportunist Anderson Cooper, who lives two blocks below the Square, has set up a camp to report live all day and all night. A media circus, say the old Villagers, who are finally getting some respect again.

The mayor is going with an entourage to South Carolina, with all the media outlets following, and for two or three days the story will be a grim tragedy and a feel-good human-interest tale, and then it will fade into the background like all novelty stories—the aspiring actress knocked onto the third rail by the crazed homeless person, the burning Bronx nightclub full of immigrants, the world's most famous kidnappee—Etan Patz.

A collective mood develops, or at least is reported by the people at the city desk, and the myth-making begins. If 9/11 was all about horror and the resulting solidarity, the bombing of Washington Square is all about the other shoe dropping, about getting the hell out, about the ground opening up, about uncertainty. This time there is little cathartic or unifying about the experience. A sense that the previous five years have collapsed—a half-a-decade-long twiddle of the thumbs.

First Order of Business

Renee the employment agent, whose card had been sitting on Becca's bureau for months, was overweight too, but in a hard-packed, sexy way, with carefully applied makeup, lots of it. Cleavage poked out of her red jersey top with elaborate criss-crossing swags across the chest. *Go ahead*, she seemed to be saying: *I dare you to call me fat.*

Becca was wearing her one good suit. She had splurged on it years before when she started teaching at the New School. She had loved that good maroon wool suit and kept it zipped up in a garment bag at the far right side of her closet. But when she pulled it out, terrible things had happened. The skirt had always been a kind, forgiving skirt, but now it looked ridiculous with its little pleats and long hem, and the two eyes in the waistband wouldn't begin to meet the two hooks. She spent the whole morning in a frenzy with the jacket's armholes and her seam ripper, ripping one stitch at a time, excavating through seams and lining and interfacing and more seams until finally she freed the mammoth shoulder pads and could ease them out and stitch everything back up. Even her good brown work shoes and pocketbook, shoved on a shelf, had turned on her. She put on Camille's beautiful locket, figuring it would bless the rest of the dowdy mess like a priest swinging a pot of incense on a chain.

Renee reached out a hand for shaking. "First order of business," she said, picking up Becca's resume with the other hand. Her lips pushed to the side of her mouth in some kind of contemplation that Becca couldn't read. For a second she made an impressed face. Then she looked Becca straight in the eyes.

"First of all, don't worry. I'm not horrified. I get lots of women who don't have traditional career paths. Tech skills? PowerPoint, Photoshop?"

Becca gave one continuous shake of the head.

Renee flicked her hair with her red fingernails. She came down a notch and asked about the Microsoft Office Suite.

Becca had a computer. She wasn't a complete Luddite. It was even an Apple, a laptop. It had been Ed's. Ed had expensive taste that he could indulge because of the cheap rent. It still had his password: KandyKorn37. "I took good care of it, and I deleted my most intimate files," he had told her. "It's as good as buying a reconditioned one at Tekserve. Use it in good health, sweetie." She made him a big batch of chili to repay him and put it in plastic containers for freezing. And when she still felt beholden, she baked him a Russian coffee cake, a yeast one.

"I'm a Mac user," said Becca, having no real idea what Microsoft Office Suite was, knowing only that "Mac user" acted like magic on certain people.

Renee suppressed a sigh. "Listen, Becca, it's pretty brutal out there. You have no idea how competitive this workplace is. I can see you're not going to make this easy for yourself. Here's what I'd like to do: run a battery of diagnostics, all aimed at figuring out where you'll fit in best."

Renee wasn't stupid. She just lived in a stupid universe and played by stupid rules.

"I know by now what I'm good at," said Becca. "There must be some companies that still need research and organizational skills. Or put me in an art gallery. I'm good with the public."

She was rubbing Renee the wrong way, she could see. She couldn't do this anymore. She couldn't ever do this. But she needed the money; she would have to try.

"I'll be straight with you," said Renee. "Unless you have a degree in art history, they want someone just out of college sitting at the desk who's willing to stay late and pour white wine at openings, and look good doing it."

Her pantyhose were too tight. She felt itchy all over, as if she'd developed an actual allergy to offices.

"Listen," said Renee. "I don't like to promise anything I can't deliver. But I'm going to make some calls. I need to know that you'll go out on any interviews I set up and that you'll put your best foot forward." She took out a red Flair and put lines through the resume with arrows and new headings in capital letters.

"Go fix this and email it back to me later today. I don't care if the power's out. Here's what could happen. Some big company could be looking for a creative mind. Or someone will be looking for someone to do something boring but that requires half a brain to get it right.

"There are a gazillion online tutorials. BMCC has cheap classes. Go teach yourself Dreamweaver or PowerPoint and how to use an Excel spreadsheet and then we'll have something to talk about."

I can learn, she told herself. I can change. People change.

"And one more thing," said Renee. "There's a store around the corner, what my mother would have called a 'schlock house.' It has a thousand cardigans, nice roomy bias-cut ones. Dirt cheap. Insanely flattering. The poor woman's Eileen Fisher. Go splurge. For twelve ninety-five you'll look nice and you'll be a hell of a lot more comfortable than you are in that power suit, and a comfortable woman is a woman I'd rather send out to my clients."

Becca passed the schlock house on the way to the subway. She went in; she would at least pretend. She picked out a dark green cardigan with no buttons and went into the small communal dressing room with indoor-outdoor carpeting and a thin curtain. There was one other woman in the room, about the same age and build.

The sweater hung down almost to her knees in the front. "It feels like cheating somehow," she said to the woman.

"I know—isn't it great? It's no one's business what's going on under all this fabric. Don't look so panicky. It's just a sweater."

"It's the job interviews that go with the sweater that are making me sick to my stomach."

"Hey—I needed to go back to work after my kids left the

nest, and I couldn't imagine who would want to hire me. So get this—I'm telling my chiropractor's administrator this, and she says, 'I'm moving to Florida. Want my job?'"

"Had you ever been an administrator before?"

"Listen. If you're a mom, you've got your master's in administration. Don't let the software freak you out. If you've got half a brain you can learn it. Here's the secret. The twenty-somethings know the software and they'll make you feel like Methuselah, but that's to cover up the fact that they don't know squat about most other things. Have no idea what a verb is. No one's ever taught them to write a decent English sentence. Their cultural frame of reference is about this wide," she said, pointing to the leg of a pair of skinny jeans someone had left on a hanger. "I mentioned Charlie Chaplin the other day and got a blank look. Not to mention they're so self-absorbed and worried about out-PCing each other that they kind of lose sight of why. And it makes them weirdly cautious, I find."

She asked Becca for her card. Becca shook her head.

"Get some. They're cheap. Not even because they're that essential. More because they make you feel like a professional working person with something to offer. Mind if I ask what kind of work you do, or want to do?"

"Not exactly the kind of job they advertise on Monster. com," said Becca.

Our Lady

In the afternoon, clouds came from nowhere and settled like a lid on a pot of soup. Soon it was pouring. Villagers agreed: This we do not need.

The doors of Our Lady of Pompeii were still locked when Becca and a crowd of others began arriving for the hastily called meeting. People piled up on the sidewalk, going over what they knew, checking their watches. The flyers said 4:30; it was 4:30. It was definitely Thursday, though some of them had to review to be sure: Monday was the bomb, Tuesday was all the shock and irrational exuberance, and Wednesday was when the power was supposed to come back on but didn't and the mayor finally gave his big press conference, which of course they couldn't watch because they had no power. So, yes, it was definitely Thursday.

Someone finally opened the doors and Becca descended with the hordes to the cafeteria, which was warm and damp and smelled of cheese and disinfectant. The cafeteria had its own generator, and wan emergency light added five years of worry to every face. The newcomers tried to be polite as they stepped around the stooped, gray-haired, palsied renegades and claimed tables for themselves; the instincts of high school were apparently still in force. If you didn't know better, you might think it was years of meetings like this that had aged the old fighters. Maybe it was. Some of them used to be beautiful. Most were still sharp as ever, some were nuts, sometimes the sharp ones were the craziest. People unzipped boots, shook out raincoats. Jay Supak appeared from nowhere, hovering in his creepy, silent way, down on his knees, up on his feet. He came up to her and haltingly asked if he could stop by her apartment to take her picture after the meeting, and because the editor was an old friend of hers she reluctantly agreed, and tried to put the thought out of her mind.

She took a seat near the front. Her mind was racing from her attempts to rewrite her resume and her hip was aching from the damp, so she put her leg up on a chair. Her pants were wet up to the calves. She surveyed the room. New faces. Prettier and better dressed and taller than the regulars. Blackberry and Burberry people. The seats were the great equalizer: they all sat in hard fiberglass chairs the color of bandages with an opening in the rear end that looked vaguely surgical. Umbrellas kept sliding and falling with a clunk.

"There's a sign-in sheet circulating, people. Keep it moving, please," cried the community board chair. The newcomers hadn't brought pens and had to share; maybe they didn't use pens.

The chairman had poor posture and stringy silver hair that he used to wear in a ponytail until it grew so thin he would have needed an orthodontic rubber band and steadier hands. He stood up and put his hands out face down and called, "People, people," but they wouldn't subside, so he put his fingers in his mouth and let out a huge whistle, while a Con Ed guy stood by not giving a thing away as if he'd been through all kinds of seminars on handling hostile crowds.

The whistle did the trick. Even Mrs. Goldman, who was sitting four tables away and could be heard clearly complaining about the battery in her hearing aid, finally hushed up.

"A little trick I learned in the schoolyard of PS 177, Coney Island Avenue," said the chair, overestimating his ability to charm. No one laughed.

"No speakers' cards tonight," he said. "This is not an official CB meeting, though we did manage to get a couple reps from the electeds to come speak. We have reports from Con Ed, the Sixth Precinct, and three of the standing committees."

Then he very quickly recited by heart, as he did at every meeting: "Let me remind the regulars and warn all those who are new to our little world, community boards have no legislative authority, only consultative, investigatory, and advisory powers."

The vice chair leaned over and said into the mike, "Don't you love the way he says that?" A chuckle or two.

People were still trickling in. The din began to build again. Nothing like a bomb to bring out the hordes, someone said. Three days in; apparently it was okay to joke now. People compared notes about cold meals, dark nights, the slowness of the investigation. Everyone was torn between keeping the freezer closed and using up what was in it.

And then when the room was full and everyone finally shushed up, in walked Melora Ross, her hair wet like the others but in its wetness resembling white tulip petals. She wore a short belted raincoat and short black boots, her legs long in between. She sucked in her breath as if to say, I'm sorry to interrupt, don't mind me, I'll just tiptoe in. She looked helplessly across the sea of linoleum tile and tables.

Becca looked at Melora and then at her own foot. Her walking shoe, which had seemed neutral a moment before, was now squat and old-ladyish and sad. She lifted it off the chair, placed it on the floor, and gestured to Melora as if Melora were some neutral person and she an ordinary Samaritan. Melora walked quickly across the room, pulling in her elbows and her big leather pocketbook to make herself smaller, and sat down, mouthing a thank-you. Becca mouthed back a you're welcome.

"Okay," said the chair. "This is how it's going to work. We're flipping the usual order. Because I know everyone is feeling anxious after this tragedy, first we're going to let you speak. We'll take questions from the floor for fifteen minutes and not a minute longer. And then we're going to sit quietly like good girls and boys and listen to the experts."

Hands shot up—veined, bony, swollen at the knuckles, shaking, more than one wearing a drugstore splint. The floating hands of old dancers and the earthen ones of old sculptors. Not a lot of wedding bands. Sprinkled around were a few more beautiful but less well-used hands, tanned.

Without being called on, an old man on the side rose up as mighty as a volcano and shook the walking stick that appeared to have been carved by a grandchild in shop class. "Can you please explain," he boomed, "why we've been without power for three days when after 9/11, an event on a magnitude at least a hundred times bigger, no one lost power? The mayor doesn't see fit to give straight answers."

"I have to ask you to wait to be called on," said the chair. "Obviously that question is forefront on everyone's mind, and we will hear from Con Ed in a little while. Folks, we've got this tiny little mike with a teeny little clip. I'm going to ask everyone to use it, not that I think you lack vocal power, but I know the acoustics down here leave something to be desired."

Hands shot back up; some had never gone down. The chair scanned the room slowly and then called on Melora. She looked panicked. She stood up. The room went quiet. Her shiny coat crinkled. She started to give her name and address, but the chair stopped her and motioned for her to come to the front. "Oh, right," she said, and turned red. There was trouble with the microphone.

Melora loosened her raincoat belt. Under it she wore one of those shirts so fashionable it was the color of cement and had a raw edge. The chair fiddled with the mike clip until he got it to stay put. Melora gave her name again. He made a slow spinning motion with his forefinger until she figured out that he was telling her to turn around so the audience could see her. She gave her name and address a third time.

"Can you tell us your affiliation, please?"

"I work in the neighborhood, for a local business."

"Can you please be more specific?"

Melora took a breath, clearly aware she was going to say something people would not want to hear, or something they would love to hear so they could make snap judgments about her. The room was filled with people who, like Becca, had railed against the elevated highway called Westway, against jail barges parked on the banks of the Hudson, against luxury apartments on the piers. They could tell you the difference between SECR and SEQUA. They knew what ULURP stood for and sometimes in quiet moments would say the words to themselves: Uniform Land Use Review Procedure. Some of them had been part of Save the Village itself, Jane Jacobs's path-breaking organization, a group of mothers that fended off power-mad Robert Moses's nefarious schemes in the 1950s. In other words, they had railed against every real and perceived threat to their neighborhood and way of life, and even given the week's events, many still believed the worst threat to date was from people exactly like Melora.

"I'm a realtor, at Downtown Domiciles."

No one said a word, but Becca felt it building, the room turning from two hundred separate humans into one big one with a single giant agenda. Becca understood that this is what history was made of. Especially when there was no obvious enemy, the need to forge one from whomever was available was great.

Melora was shaking. "I have kind of a subspecialty in townhouses," she said. Becca winced at the way her voice rose at the end of the sentence. "I happen to know a little bit about nineteenth-century row houses. Many of you, I'm sure, know that they were built quickly, as middle-class housing.

"I know everyone's having a really hard time, and I know the city is trying to fix it," she said. Mrs. Goldman let out snort. "But I have a problem from the—" no one liked to say the word bomb— "the Arch and I don't know quite who to turn to and I thought maybe I'm not the only one. I know people died, but that's why I came."

"Ms. Ross," said the chair. "Take a deep yoga breath and state the problem as succinctly as possible."

"I live in a house that was built in 1848," said Melora, much steadier now. "I had some damage to the feeder line to my plumbing. I thought I was lucky, that that was all. But now I think the foundation has been damaged. And since my house is up against all the other houses on the block, I think it's very likely mine isn't the only one. And I'm not sure what to do."

"I am very sorry to hear, but wouldn't this be a matter

between you and Buildings and your insurance company?" Becca was afraid Melora would say, *Well, duh.*

"Yes, of course I called my homeowners," she replied, seizing a tiny bit of power. "That's not why I came. I came because I wanted to let people know there might be other dangers, ones that aren't so obvious. The majority of the housing stock is old, as you know."

Becca watched her shift her weight and move her long arms around to try to find someplace where they might seem to belong. Melora had told her years ago that she'd never acted in a play; she had horrible stage fright. This was not easy for her.

"A crack in the foundation can be a really dangerous thing, and I just thought maybe other people who live in houses like mine ought to be told what to look for.

"And one more thing: this is smack in the middle of the historic district, and Landmarks is really strict. You can get a violation if your newel post doesn't have the right kind of acorn or isn't screwed into the right part of the railing. So, what I'm asking is whether you...I know there's a Landmarks committee that reports to LPC...whether some of the usual paperwork can get waived if people need to replace a standpipe or the like." She moved her hand, because it was so hard not to confuse one kind of waiving with the other.

To Becca's amazement, the chairman stuck his lower lip out and moved his head back and forth in serious consideration.

He turned to the woman beside him. "Lottie? What say you?" Lottie, the chair of the Landmarks committee, Becca knew, was a fussbudget.

"I think it's a perfectly sensible request," decreed Lottie. "I will see what I can do." Melora looked shell-shocked with success.

Someone in the back near the soda machine yelled, "I feel for the woman with the white hair, I do. But we have more pressing concerns here than hairline cracks in townhouse foundations. Like we have businesses, including mine, that are going to be bankrupt by Saturday if we don't get power. We have senior citizens who aren't getting enough to eat. If it gets cold like they're saying it's supposed to tomorrow, we're going to have some real health and safety issues. Let's move on."

"We've set up a network for our housebound seniors," said the chair. "Each building has a captain, or several in the large buildings. Westbeth—yeah, well, that's a nation unto itself, not to mention the largest voting bloc in the West Village, so I'm not too worried about the folks there."

There was a smattering of here here's, one stray boo.

The officer from the precinct with the huge muscles, the sort with arms too big to lie flat at his sides, had to keep airing out his armpits.

"Where's the sign-in sheet, folks?" cried the vice chair. "Let's keep it circulating."

"By the way, let's give a hand to the generous donors of all those goodies in the hall, Donna Karan, Florent Morillet, the Rudin family," added the chair. "We've got some peanut butter and some bread. Over at the office in Washington Square Village we've got some sleeping bags someone donated (still sealed in plastic, so no worries about bedbugs.) Coat donations too. I'm told the power should be on well before the weekend, but we've got plenty of reserves just in case."

At this hint that relief might not be coming, a protest gathered strength. They were tired of living on hope. Hope was like chicken breasts in a warm freezer.

"Listen, people. May I remind you that I lack omnipotence. I cannot wave my magic community board wand and get the power back on."

He called on more people, who came up and asked their questions, told their stories. The fifteen minutes went by quickly.

Before the chair had even finished introducing the Con Ed guy, a hiss broke out. They'd gone remarkably easy on Melora; Melora had managed to win them over, damn her. But now they turned. The hiss sprang spontaneously from all corners of the room. It was the "om" of the old Village, and Becca's tongue automatically placed itself close to the roof of her mouth for maximum sibilance and she looked up, half expecting smoke to engulf the table up front. The beautiful thing was that the newcomers, the nouveau Villagers, participated in the hiss, the great hiss of 2006, and she could feel the angry joy, because a group hiss was always so much greater than the sum of each individual hiss.

The Con Ed guy introduced himself and put out his giant hands until they calmed down. "The problem is, there are multiple overlapping problems," he said. He dovetailed his fingers. "This guy or this organization, whoever the perpetrator was, either they were very clever or very lucky, because they hit not just one but four sensitive juncture points. Think about the street in cross section, okay. It has these levels, layers." He got a smarmy smile on his face the way Ronald Reagan used to when he was about to introduce levity. "Since we're here at Our Lady of Pompeii, like a lasagna if you will. There are different utilities taking up different ones, stratums. We have the best guys in the world, I mean on the whole planet, working as fast as they can to restore your services."

Becca, meanwhile, kept the corner of her eye on Melora, who had stood her ground and now was taking it all in wide-eyed. At one point Becca snuck a glance and found Melora looking right back. They both quickly looked away.

They'd met almost twenty-three years before, a few blocks away in the maternity ward at St. Vincent's. The nurses had decorated their station with pumpkins and skeletons, and outside the window at the end of the hall the sumac and the maples were brilliant red. They met in the hall, where the nurse shooed them from their respective rooms to get some exercise while their infant sons slept. They got to talking as they shuffled down the slippery hall like old ladies. Melora was much younger and a head taller than Becca, but they seemed so alike then, wearing the same blue Dacron hospital gowns and aching in the same places. It turned out they had both had C-sections on the same day, performed by the same midwife, and their sons had adjacent bassinets in the nursery. The boys took after their respective fathers. Aaron was pale and bald; Cole could have been Kohl or Coal—a head of oiled black hair, like a baby crow. Melora's room was overrun with Niko's noisy relatives from Astoria. One day Becca's mother came in from Mamaroneck with her husband, Ben. She sat on the edge of the vinyl chair with her legs tightly crossed, as if she were afraid another one like Becca might slip out. The minute Doris and Ben left, Becca, weak and leaky, somehow got out of the bed all by herself, desperate to find her tall new friend to wipe the taste of the visit away. Melora was already on her way to find Becca and they almost fell into each other's arms in the hall.

Aaron and Cole never walked. They hopped on one foot, they balanced on ledges, they ran flat out in their sneakers. She and Melora took them everywhere. They went to the Thompson Street pool and caught the leaping boys in their hands, all that puppy skin sliding up and down their ribs, their toddler bellies shiny with sunscreen, their eyelashes many-pointed stars. They went to the Marionette Theater, the Hall of Science; they took the D train to the aquarium at the end of the continent in Coney Island, where they grew so enchanted by the beluga whales that their PB&Js were all hot and floppy by the time they sat down to eat. They got falafel from the falafel man on MacDougal who greeted them like friends from the old country. Or they went to Two Boots and all ate their pizza in little squares, and if they'd had a good work week they'd get Italian ices and suck all the flavor out of the paper cups until their mouths were dyed blue or orange, the official colors of New York.

And when they were too tired to travel, Washington Square always welcomed them in. One endless August afternoon early on in that era, not enough sleep or iron in their systems, they swung the boys in the bucket swings of the baby playground and they miraculously both fell asleep. They lifted them to their strollers, just experienced enough by this point to get their fat legs out of the openings without snagging their ankles and waking them up. They took off their own sneakers (having given up sandals for the duration of the sandbox years), used their pocketbooks as pillows under the hard green Parks Department benches, put their baseball caps over their faces, watching the starbursts of sunlight through the air holes and, with a lullaby improvised out of the M8 bus, the swings' squeak and the pounding of a far-off jackhammer, they too fell fast asleep for a blissful hour, only to be woken by a scolding mom who said that anyone could have absconded with the boys. For years after, neither of them could hear the word *abscond* without cracking up.

Threshold

Later, when Becca opened her apartment door, Jay stood in the dark hallway with a flashlight and a sack, like a peddler, and nodded the way he always did when they passed on the street, as if a hello were far too precious to spend on her. Carny gave a quick sniff and walked away.

"No vest with all the pockets," she said. "I almost didn't recognize you."

"No tour-guide cape. Almost didn't recognize you either," he replied. One side of his mouth turned up, as if he had never attempted a smile before and wasn't sure how to work one. She watched him pull a data stick out of his pocket and then hitch up his jeans (being one of those men whose rear end was the same width as his middle). "Everything I need's in here. It's liberated my torso. Of course, electricity would be handy too, which is why—" he opened the sack and showed her the portable lights inside. "This is insane to try this late in the day, but you're the woman of the hour. They decided they need you on page one." His voice trailed off into nervous half-sentences about the bomb and the power and his editor.

All these years sitting in the same hearings, walking the same streets, and Becca was not sure she had ever heard him speak more than a sentence. How strange, she thought, in a week already filled to the brim with strangeness, to watch a still face animate with speech, to see the jaw work and the lips form words (possibly humorous ones) and hear the timbre of the voice (baritone, with a mild borough or Jersey accent). Standing there in his anonymous navy-blue guy clothes, Photojay, it turned out, might not be quite a total pill.

It had been a while since a man who wasn't Carlos the super had crossed her threshold. She wished one of the thousand wishes of the tenement-dweller: for a foyer—someplace to put him that wasn't out but wasn't in either. "I have to tell you," she said, reluctantly taking the parka, one of those heavy but slippery ones from the world of men, and motioning him in, "this is not the kind of fame I wished for. Just tell me what to do and let's get it done while there's still a little light."

He narrowed one eye as if it were a body double for his camera lens and surveyed her candlelit living room. She suddenly felt protective of her corduroy sofa with the throw pillows she had made years ago, her horsehair chair, the glass-front bookcase she had rescued from the curb. Even her lumpy, overpainted plaster walls looked vulnerable in the flickering light.

He got his voice back. "How about we put you on the sofa with the quilt in the background—Becca Cammeyer in her indoor Boho element. I'll need a little time to set up."

"I had no idea this was going to be such a production," she said.

"Then you've never sat for a portrait."

"I thought you were a photo*journalist*." He had snapped her picture for the paper before, at rallies, always with her mouth wide open in mid-protest, or with her bullhorn, homemade placards all around her.

"Can't a person be more than one thing? You're a tour guide and an activist."

"Okay, okay," she said.

As if to prove his fine-photography bona fides, he began moving deftly around her room. The chains on her table lamps didn't even clink against the bulbs. He brought one of her kitchen chairs over and carefully clamped lights on its back, then opened up a screen of reflective fabric.

He was lighting her like a meat-market model.

She looked down at herself. The temperature had dropped suddenly after the rain. She had put on a decent wool sweater, with Camille's locket. Below: her usual black pants over her old silk long johns and black walking shoes. Her hair was in exile in a bun. But candlelight was forgiving, and what did it matter what Jay Supak saw or thought? She felt for the locket, half out

of nerves, half a reflex left from the chain-snatching eighties.
It was safe and warm, resting in the nook between her breasts.
When she glanced up, he was looking straight at her.

She panicked. She grabbed a candlestick and excused herself
to go into the bathroom. She unwound her hair. She had a sample of fancy hair gel she'd been saving for some other life, and
she squirted out a little bit and ran it through her hair until it fell
in silver and brown waves around her face. Then she pulled out
an old bag that contained a fistful of makeup she'd somehow
accumulated over the years, mostly from the Halloween costumes of Aaron, the perennial zombie. She combed mascara on
the tips of her lashes and put on a little lip gloss, which shimmered in the light, and took a deep breath and opened the door.

"You look nice," he said. The smile was still on one side of
his face, but it was bigger. She smiled back. Instead of cracking
as her lips usually did in the fall, the gloss protected them. She
had a feeling of lightness, as if they'd both flung off weapons
and shields that had been cutting into their muscles for a very
long time.

He stepped aside to let her sit back down. "Ready?" he asked,
and she said, "Yep, I think I am." He kneeled in front of her
and snapped from one angle and then got up and tried another.

"Turn toward the window," he said, and because it was less a
command than a suggestion, she did as he asked.

"Look," she said. "That can't be flurries, can it?"

Snowflakes were not falling so much as taking excursions
through the sky. He came over to the window and watched
with her.

"It's the last thing we need this week, but it sure is pretty," he
said. "Look—you can see the pattern on that flake." A feeling
stirred inside her, so old she barely recognized it at first, as if
the heat had just come on for the first time all year and was
slowly rising from the basement.

The shutter clicked again and again.

She hadn't wanted him in her apartment. She had agreed to
do this at the meeting just so she could get a seat quicker. She

had thought he was a jerk, and a hack. Of course, she thought that about a lot of people; it saved on heartache and Becca was nothing if not a saver.

He put his hand on her chin to change her angle slightly. It was just a gesture a dentist or a hairstylist might make, but a tremor ran straight through her, hot and cold, silver and gold, Scotch on the rocks when it fans out beyond the swallow. He snapped three more times and said he was done, and she almost yelled, "No!"

He detached the lens and lowered the camera gently into its case. She could make him coffee, but the milk was sour. The beer was warm. She could offer pretzels. Or had she finished the pretzels?

In the end she offered up what a Villager always gives freely: a topic for discussion.

"So, you don't think it was one of ours, do you?" This was a fear that had begun to sprout in the vacuum as the Village awaited news from the investigation.

"You mean like that muttering guy in Father Demo Square with the dandruff and the military beret from who knows what army?"

She nodded like mad, because she had thought of him too. Jay had smallish teeth and looked like a little kid when he laughed. How strange, funny-strange, to know all the same people but not each other.

"Or that woman with the pit bull who snaps at your grocery bags outside Gristedes," she said.

"Could definitely be her. But I think it's that weaver with the—" He traced a long, asymmetrical garment.

"And the dramatic brooches."

He nodded at the brooches.

"It's not funny," she said. "We shouldn't laugh. People are dead." But the living room, where she had planned to spend the evening curled in a ball, felt safe for laughter for the first time all week.

In the lull that followed, his eyes came to rest on her

memorabilia on the bookcase: a piece of the old Miller elevated highway, buttons from campaigns no one else remembered, a feather from one of Bella Abzug's hats.

"A shrine. I kind of figured. Where's the statuette of Jane Jacobs with incense all around it?"

"That is not a very good way to endear yourself to your subjects."

"Sorry. Couldn't resist."

He pointed to a black-and-white Polaroid, the old kind with the white border, the kind you had to rip out of the camera and douse with chemicals. "You don't see a lot of these anymore."

The photo was one of the few in her possession that her mother had taken; she couldn't remember why—maybe her mother had won the camera in the divorce. It showed her on a pony, from the days when there were vacant lots up and down the far West Village with truck farms and the man everyone simply called the pony man. For a nickel you could ride one around the dusty lot. She was wearing an oversized white oxford-cloth shirt of her father's—that had been a style then— and a pair of paisley bell-bottoms.

He picked it up and looked more closely. "I'll be damned," he said. "It's the pony man. I have one exactly like this, but with me on the horse."

"No way—you're not from here. I know everyone from here."

"A little proprietary, aren't you? Did you ever consider a person might have grown up in Perth Amboy and have an aunt and uncle on Bank Street that he visited once in a while?"

"Ah, I guessed Jersey." She asked about the aunt and uncle, but the names were unfamiliar and they were long dead anyway.

A conversation could withstand only a couple of lulls before reaching either a ragged end or a portal. He opened his mouth and she willed him to shut it again, because she could imagine a dozen ways he could botch this.

"You know," he said, "I was there at the big meeting the night your father died. I remember the whole thing."

She stared straight at him now. He had gray-green eyes and he had found something perfect to say: "You were sitting way on the side. You were doing homework. You had braids."

"You remember I had braids? I was seventeen. That was decades ago. You are scary, Photojay Supak."

"So they tell me."

She remembered the braids too, the pleasure of working the three kinky strands into a single smooth cord, the way at bedtime she would undo them and her hair would still be damp, and the smell of Wella Balsam would fill the room and moisten her peasant blouse.

She asked if he remembered her father.

He hesitated and smiled slightly to himself.

"I remember he was a major pain in the rear, but that people liked him anyway. I know he once said he was up to his *pupik* in papers, because my grandmother used to use that expression too. I remember he wore big heavy belts that looked like they were weighing him down."

Tears formed because her father was the first of so many people she had lost, and she missed him so badly, and here was Photojay Supak, of all people, bringing him back to life in her living room, piece by piece, just for a minute.

"He made those belt buckles," she said. "He welded in the basement. He was very proud of them. They were the ugliest things I ever saw." She went over to the shelf and pulled out the one she still had. It had his initials, LC, one atop the other like the Yankees logo but lopsided. She handed it to Jay.

"Lewis Cammeyer, right?"

"Now you're really freaking me out."

He shrugged. "You kind of remember a guy who goes into cardiac arrest in the middle of the very first community meeting you've been sent to cover as an intern." He handed back the belt buckle. "You're right," he said, smiling. "It's hideous."

"You know how parents always used to make kids zip their jackets? I wouldn't go out in public with him until he zipped his, just so no one would see the buckles."

She had an idea. "You don't have any pictures from then, do you?" she asked.

He shook his head. "Didn't get my first camera until way later."

"You mean you weren't born with a lens in your *pupik*? Your parents didn't put a Fisher-Price camera in your crib?"

He smiled. "The photography was sort of in self-defense. I liked to work alone; it made me nervous having to travel with a photographer. So I taught myself pretty much. And somewhere down the line I realized I was better with the pictures than the words."

They were sitting down now. She was on the sofa. He was on the horsehair chair, running a finger carefully over the braid trim. Was it just a few minutes ago he had rung the bell and she had wished, of all things, for a foyer?

Now he was on the sofa beside her. The molecules of the apartment seemed to part to make room for him. She looked into his gray-green eyes, and at his lips. Lips for scowling, lips for chewing, lips for chapping in the cold, lips for holding back words or letting them out, words that could be kind or cruel or just sarcastic. She had almost forgotten about lips for kissing.

She had also forgotten how much heat one human up against another could produce; she'd been cold as long as she could remember, but she had a theory: it was better that way, because it was easier to produce warmth in a cold room than to create cool in a warm one. She reeked of camphor and itched from the sheep's wool. He peeled off her sweater and the silk long johns, and they laughed because there was still a T-shirt under that.

"Is there anything left in your drawers?"

He removed his own sweater and shirt and (knowing she was no bargain) she was pleasantly surprised to find his torso wasn't half bad, though there was a bit of a belly. He had some muscles and some hair. They knew all the same people but not each other. Snowflakes wandered in and lit on surfaces. One landed in his hair, and she saw its pattern and its perfectly flat surface. Another lit on his fingernail and one on his sock. She was pleasantly surprised by his socks too—nice clean new rag wool socks the color of oats. Men's white undergarments.

"Would you mind terribly if we took this really slowly?"

"I'd mind somewhat," he said, running his hand through her hair.

She ran a hand over his straight black chest hair, not even touching his skin. She hadn't been to the land of men in a long time. It was like returning to a place where she had spent her vacations long ago—the salty, low-tide smells, the warmth.

The snow was starting to stick to the locust tree out the window, softening its bony branches. It was still dark and silent on the street, but the snow made a glowing light. Becca was amazed that Jay knew how to do this, and do it well, that all humans harbor these abilities and appetites, as if he could play the classical guitar (which actually felt a little like what he was doing to her). You could crawl into your own bed already warmed by another human, and fit yourself up against the whole length of him, and then shimmy even closer and lace yourself to him and then, after a while, when your hand started to go numb, you could both flip to the other side and re-fluff the down pillows in unison.

She had a theory that a dog was better than a man. A dog let you read as long as you wanted and sighed into sleep at the exact minute you turned off the light. A dog burrowed to the foot of the bed and kept you warm. But a man had so many more articulations, and human speech. Jay cupped his warm hand on her bottom and let it rest. And she ventured her own hand onto his. The muscles of his bottom tightened for a second. He was warm and lean, and she was surprised that it felt so simple. You could just flop into bed. You could not be lonesome anymore, or cold or frightened, at least for a little while. She turned to face him. She felt the electricity of the hairs up and down his body as they rose to meet her smooth flesh. The hairs on his legs, his groin, his belly, his chest, the whiskers on his cheek, the fine hair on his head—they cushioned the length and breadth of her. She put her arm around him and put her face in his neck because he was so much taller, and she began to cry softly. She could hear the blood traveling through his veins. There wasn't room for Carny and Jay, so she got up in the dark and brought in Carny's blanket from the living room, and Carny, bless him, consented to lie beside them on the floor and keep them safe.

She dreamed she was lying on a beach in the sun. The warmth felt like a lovely weight resting on her skin. She had nowhere else she had to be. She rolled onto her back but the sun became too bright. The light snuck in through her tear ducts; it leaked through her eyelids, making patterns of pulsating yellow and white dots and paisleys. She tried to shield it with her hand, but it slipped in through the spaces between her fingers.

She woke up just as the rays were turning to lasers aimed for her eyeballs. She had no idea what time it was. Jay was asleep beside her. It was very hot in the bed and very sunny outside of it. It was somehow too sunny. With a tremendous effort she stuck her hand out and felt for the clock, which said it was only 5:30. Slowly the realization arrived: the power had come back on. The switch on her old bedside lamp felt the same in the on and off positions; she must have left it on when the power went out.

In the light there were so many details. Fear set in. Her knuckles, sitting outside the quilt, were beginning to swell with arthritis. The bones on the back of her hand formed a large letter *W*, like an embossed Wannamaker's envelope. The skin was flaking from her index finger, there were ridges in the fingernails, and her father's old class ring was worn thin in the back—like the enamel of her front teeth, the brass of her mailbox key. She tucked her hand back under the covers, where it was very hot. This is not good, she told herself—going back to a life of vanities, of trying to make herself pleasing to others.

She didn't want to get up and dressed and have to feed him, didn't want to sit at the table in her terrycloth slippers. He would pull his clothes back on. She remembered the textures of men's clothes, the soft, almost dusty feel of their blue jeans, the flimsiness of their worn-out jockey shorts, the pilled terrain of their flannel shirts. His pile of clothes sat on her desk. His man wallet poked out of the back pocket of his Levi's. His hand rested on her hip. She didn't dare move it.

How many auditoriums and meeting rooms had there been between them? How many still to come? How many times had he snapped her picture while her mouth was open and her finger jabbing as if the very air were Donald Trump's chest? Page five of *VillageWeek*, photo by Jay Supak. They'd kept their socks on against the cold. She wore black men's wool dress socks, which had, until now, seemed like a sensible choice because they were warm and yet thin (and she had biggish feet for a smallish woman). Her bathrobe was on the hook on the back of the bathroom door. She would have to pull back the quilt and swing her feet to the cold floor and walk to the robe.

Jay stirred. She stiffened. Complete opposite of last night, when he was the one who had stiffened, and she the one who had stirred, lain wide open on her back, and let him in. Gone the days of diaphragms and spermicidal jelly. It was too easy now, but also too hard. She had closed back up; she was used to being closed; she liked it that way. He had left a sticky residue. She feared he would "honey" or "sweetie" her. She thought she would prefer it if he nodded and walked away without saying a word.

"Power's back," she reported. Everyone else in the Village had been waiting and praying for this moment.

He smiled and said, "You mean we can't just stay here all day?" She felt like saying, Would you stop being a nice guy and just leave?

"Nice quilt," he said.

"All out of old clothes."

"You mean you made it yourself? A woman of hidden talents." He pointed to a bit of hand-block cotton. "Whose was this?"

"An old dress of mine."

"You had a dress?"

"Many."

He pointed to a patch of plaid that still had the shirt pocket, buttoned shut. "This?"

"A guy I used to know."

"You knew a guy?" he said. A guitarist she had hung out with for a summer once. All that remained was his pocket.

"Morning," he said, smiling broadly. "Doesn't this dog need to go out?"

Thank heaven, she thought. Because she felt she would suffocate if he spent one more minute in her space.

She lunged for the robe, grabbed her pile of yesterday's clothes, and ran to the bathroom. She didn't wait for the water to get warm—it was a long trip from the furnace. She scrubbed herself with an icy washcloth that had no power to absorb. She banged her elbows against the walls putting her clothes on.

He dressed and went downstairs with her. Carny's toenails clicked. Jay wanted to get them coffee and bring it back up. She said she had a ton of work to catch up on, what with the lights back on, which was true; she had a resume to revise. He tried to hold her hand. She switched the leash to that side. What had she been thinking? In the daylight, he had dandruff, and a bald spot. She wasn't vain; she wasn't picky. It wasn't that. It was everything else.

The snow had seduced her. It had happened before. One evening in the winter she and the Viking went for a walk and it started to snow. The quiet westernmost blocks of West Fourth Street were perfect for a walking date (though of course neither of them called it a date) because the sidewalk was so narrow that you practically had to walk arm in arm, navigating around the tree pits.

They played a game called Let's Pretend We're Foppish Capitalists.

"I will buy you a house, any house," he said, throwing out his long arm in a gesture of magnanimity. They passed tiny brick houses and an ancient downstairs restaurant called Fedora's. They looked into the living rooms of their fellow Villagers. They came upon a perfect specimen of the Greek Revival, before the austere houses of the 1840s gave way to the tall, showy Italianate style.

"I daresay I choose this one, sir," said Becca. "It shall meet our needs quite well, I do believe," and since they were just playing she slipped her arm into his.

And the Viking said, "I shall call upon my bank in the morning. Your wish is my demand." But he shrugged off her forearm and instead slung his arm around her and let his hand dangle down.

"Now, where shall we dine?" she asked. "I'm in the mood for pheasant under glass."

"Yes! Let us eat the peasants we see in the windows," he exclaimed. "For we are rich capitalists and that is what we do to amuse ourselves, to fill the emptiness inside!"

She was afraid he would get angry when she couldn't help laughing at his faux pas, but he was in a jolly mood and let it pass.

He began humming a tune she didn't recognize. He told her it was his favorite Swedish lullaby. "One day I will sing it to the little ones in the nursery." This was the first time he'd mentioned children, and though he was still pretending to be a foppish capitalist, she blushed. She wanted to throw her arms around him, but, more like a nineteenth-century lady than she cared to admit, she dared not.

"Teach me the song," she begged. "I want to know everything you know, and I'll teach you everything I know."

He just kept humming. The snow was sticking. A deeper hush fell over West Fourth.

"Does this remind you of your town?"

"Hell no," he said, one of the American expressions he had made his own. "And don't call it 'my town.' It was never mine. It was filled with bankers and functionaries. Why do you think I came here?"

"I meant the snow, silly."

They passed the old Spanish restaurant filled with happy patrons and pots of paella and pitchers of sangria with wooden spoons sticking out of them.

She and the Viking went home and ate tuna fish sandwiches with beer. She was working on the quilt then, waiting for his shirts to wear out enough that she could steal some pieces from the parts that were still solid and add them to the bits and pieces she had saved from her and her father's wardrobe. After dinner they listened to jazz and she sewed on the sofa with her feet tucked under his thigh while he read a big dense book of philosophy and politics. And they split a pink grapefruit and let the juice run down their arms and then they made love, twice.

FRIDAY

CITY AND COUNTRY

The Harlem line commuter train whooshed through the tunnel under Park Avenue, sucking Becca and Carny to Doris. Harlem sped past—Schomburg Center, this hospital, that hospital, whole square blocks of tenements newly reborn from seventies blight, courtyarded mini-projects rising from the rubble, as if you could snap your fingers and fix what was broken.

Then barely a lurch of the tracks, the skinny green-brown Harlem River spanned by a row of iron bridges each built by a different engineer, and plop, they were on alien soil—the mainland, the Bronx. Metal clanged other metal and seemed to say, *Bad idea, bad idea.*

She was on the train because Jay had buzzed her in the morning, this time with a paper bag that he held out like a kindergartner.

"You can't possibly turn away a guy who comes bearing crullers from the Donut Pub," he said, standing there with his dandruff and his lovey-dovey face.

"I can't do this, Jay," she said. "I'm sorry. I've lost the knack. I need my space, what little I have." And then as she turned to look at her little space, her eye landed on the Metro-North ticket on the coffee table.

"Besides," she added, as her mother suddenly shifted in status to lesser of two evils. "I'm on my way out of town."

The oil stain spread on the paper bag. He laughed a bitter laugh.

And because Becca had a rule about telling the truth, she walked all the way to Grand Central with Carny and got on the train. Cables overhead rose and fell like EKG readouts. The train sidled alongside the interstate, it roared through tunnels, it rushed past rocky outcroppings. If only she could hurtle toward a different mother, one who might catch her and run a hand through her hair with a "there, there."

She silently cursed Ed. She hadn't called ahead, one of the stupider things she had ever not done. She had tried, a little, but she also kept taking the phone off the hook to avoid reporters' calls. She and Carny came upon a phone booth on Mamaroneck Avenue. Her mother picked up on the first ring. She knew it was Doris by the intake of breath before she spoke. Women of her age who would never sing a note in public performed an aria of "hello" on the phone.

"Hi, Mom. I'm here," she said, her voice going flat in her ears in a way it always did when Doris was on the line. "Mom" may have been the first sound her baby lips produced, but it was a word that didn't come readily now.

"Rebecca?" said Doris. "Thank heaven. I saw you on the news, so at least I knew you were okay. What a terrible, terrible thing. I tried to call, quite a few times." She paused. "What do you mean 'here'?"

"In your town. I took the train. I thought I would come and visit for a little while if that would be okay."

"Oh, for God's sake, Becca. Still allergic to plans, I see. And you expect me to drop what I'm doing and entertain you?"

"I brought Carny. He can entertain us."

Carny zigzagged down Mamaroneck Avenue like a toddler, thrilled by the new smells. She inhaled too, but her sniff was more snobbish. Hair salons, egg rolls—the smells of suburban Jews. In Manhattan you don't need a sense of direction because you're standing on the map, but here the streets meandered in a random way and the earth rose and fell and houses and churches and trees grew straight out of the topography. She got lost looking for her own mother's house.

So much land between habitations. So much wood, so little brick and concrete. The trees had grown huge. The air smelled of soil and fallen leaves. Eventually she found her mother's cul de sac and the mailbox marked *Steinglass*.

Go, get out of town for a day, Ed had said, waving his extra

Metro-North ticket. See your mother. How bad could it be?

She took a breath and rang the doorbell. For a terrible minute, they stared at each other. Doris had shrunk. It was impossible for Becca to imagine she had ever fit inside her. Her hair was recently and drastically coiffed and was an unnatural alloy shade. Her nose still reminded Becca of something you'd buy behind a locked display case at Tiffany's; Becca always feared that if her mother let out one good belly laugh the whole package might break—the skin tear, the noselet pop off and reveal the old honker stuffed inside. Her nails were polished, her midriff spandexed back into a waist. Nothing could camouflage the beginning of a stoop. She wore dark brown slacks and a paisley scarf, knotted over a thin turtleneck sweater, light brown, with fully fashioned sleeves.

She joined her mother on the concrete stoop, different from a city stoop, just a low platform to keep one's feet above the mud. They air kissed. She smelled a smell from childhood. She used to imitate the commercial in the living room to try to make her parents laugh: Dove is one-quarter cleansing cream, she had said, grabbing whatever was at hand—an ashtray, a copy of *The Nation*—and holding it beside her face.

Doris stepped down to pet Carny. Becca could see her vertebrae poking through the sweater. Doris had always liked dogs, or maybe respected them. Maybe more than people. She patted his flank, the same flank that Becca patted every day, and called him a good boy.

"Has he done his business?" she asked.

"He peed out by your mailbox," Becca said, "and he pooped in the city, so we should be good," and she thought, what foolish questions in a way, but really, these are the questions of a mother, no doubt questions Doris had once asked of her. She relaxed a little. There were safe topics.

"Well, no need to stand out here," said Doris, pushing open the door. Even doors were different in towns. Her mother's was painted dark green, with no metal plate at the bottom, as if only city dwellers had the urge to kick.

All three of them tried to go through at the same time, then she and her mother both deferred.

They stood in the foyer. It was going to be a long day.

"So, tell me," Doris said.

"I guess I'm all right." She held out her arms to show that her parts still worked. "I made it all the way home before it happened." And she told some of the stories, about the widowers, the barbecue the next night, the cold and the dark.

Lew had been the hugger in the family, but now her mother got on her tiptoes and pulled Becca into an awkward embrace. In her mother's presence she had always felt she took up far too much room, and now she felt wide and weighty and far too needy. She started to cry again and feared she would get snot on her mother's sweater. Carny stuck his nose between their shins; he hated to miss out on a hug.

They broke away at the same time.

Doris patted her own pants legs and said, "So—I have bagels in the freezer I can thaw."

And Becca was nearly knocked over by a memory of bagels. They almost never talked about the early years; it was just too fraught. Anything to do with the Village or Lew was tacitly verboten. But Becca decided to try.

"That would be nice, Mom. Do you still buy egg bagels?"

"Egg bagels?" she said, as if she'd never heard of them.

"Don't you remember? Orange breakfast? The Bagel Restaurant, that tiny place on West Fourth Street, when I tried to order everything orangey on the menu? Egg bagel, sunny-side-up egg, orange juice, marmalade. And I cut out the egg white and fed it to Daddy because it didn't match. And then you let me rummage through your pocketbook for more orangey things but all I could find was your lipstick, so we put that next to the spoon."

Doris shrugged. "I'm afraid my memory is not what it once was, Becca. Besides, you were always the historian in the family."

The house had shrunk too, the way things that loom large in your memory do, but it also seemed brighter.

"Funny, I don't remember there being a bay window," said Becca.

"Right you are, as usual. We had it put in a couple of years ago. The windows needed replacing anyway." She reached for the name of the architect but couldn't find it.

"It's not important," said Becca. They looked everywhere but at each other.

"I'm sorry for barging in. I know you like to plan ahead. It's just that everything's a little chaotic right now, and the power's still off, and I really needed to get away someplace more serene, so I thought I would come here."

Doris softened. "A terrible thing, those women. We were very sorry, but we saw you on the news, so we knew you were all right."

She made a "shall we?" gesture toward the living room, a gesture that also belonged to towns and not cities, to home-owners and not renters, and Becca had to admit there was something gracious in it.

Becca remembered the house being ostentatious. She remembered chrome lamps with modernist bulges. Poufy leather sofas stuffed with Polyfil. Huge shiny books about dogwoods and Jerusalem, smelling of photochemicals. But a funny thing had happened. The house was not so terrible. The world had grown more ostentatious around Doris.

"Where's Ben?" asked Becca.

Doris pointed up the stairs with her chin. "Napping."

"Is he okay?" asked Becca.

"A relative term." Her mother arranged herself on the sofa across the coffee table, her feet parallel on the floor and her knees lined up on an angle. She clasped her hands in her lap, her face unsettled, as if she were trying to decide between small and big talk and might end up with no talk at all.

"What's wrong?"

"His heart. I believe the technical term is 'frail.' Whatever you do, don't get old."

Becca said she was sorry to hear it, and she was. Despite her best efforts as a teenager to hate her mother's husband, they had always gotten along.

"I did call, you know," said Doris. "For hours. I got a busy signal. I didn't even know there was still such a thing as a busy signal."

"I was getting hounded by reporters. I left it off the hook."

"I won't even ask if you've ever considered a cell for emergencies. I'm sure it's against some principle or another of yours."

Upstairs, footsteps.

"Oh, he's up," said Becca, hopeful. She and Ben had always been able to talk about manly urban topics.

"No, that would be Melva, who comes Monday, Wednesday, and Friday."

"I can say hello later."

"Yes," said Doris. "He'll be better after a nap."

The mailman came and Carny barked.

"Coffee or decaf or tea?" her mother asked, placing her hands on her pants to get up, giddy with the chance to leave the room.

Becca wasn't sure whether to stay behind like a guest or follow her to the kitchen, daughter-like.

"Stay," she told Carny, already curled on the Oriental rug under the glass-topped coffee table. She went to the hallway where she had a view of all the rooms on the first floor. The redwood deck was covered in brown leaves; a rake had been left out. Inside everything was spread neatly but wantonly across surfaces. The place was spilling over with cubic feet. Huge bouquets of it. She heard the soothing sound of the washer running, what it must feel like to be surrounded by sloshing amniotic fluid. Last time Becca did laundry, she had to peel someone's dried purple thong from the laundromat dryer wall.

The magnets on the fridge came from the homeowners' insurance and the lawn-care people. What was it like to own a piece of property? A huge responsibility, a huge pleasure? No doubt some of each, just as it was a pleasure and an annoyance to rent.

She could have had a different life, an easier life.

Her mother took the bag of coffee out of the huge freezer and filled the carafe from the tap. She stepped on a rolling step-stool to reach the coffee cups. She was beginning to move like an old lady, holding things with both hands.

Becca wandered back to the living room, over to the baby grand with its display of family photos. Doris had told her long ago the piano was their first purchase after the marriage and the move. It was a bribe meant to lure her to Mamaroneck. Becca had dreamed of lessons but then had to pretend not to want them, because her decision to stay in the city in her father's apartment meant, of course, that there would be no room or money for a piano, much less lessons.

It was a beautiful, shiny black piano. She had willed herself to hate it, the bourgeois piano. Now she ran a hand over the brocade seat of the bench. She remembered how it had left an imprint on the back of her legs the few times she did sit down to play.

She scanned the photos of Doris and Ben's discreet wedding, Ben's grown children and their children. There was one of her Bronx bubbe and zayde in black and white, another of them in color on a retirement cruise. The one obligatory shot of Becca at Hunter, in a cap and gown with a rolled diploma in her hand and Joycie by her side. Faded seventies film, all the blues washed away. Aaron's school photos, which she had dutifully mailed each year.

And then she came upon photos of Aaron she'd never seen, in teak frames. Aaron in his City College cap and gown, and several that were relatively recent, when his Nordic hair had finally developed enough heft to make a respectable beard. Becca stared at her son in these unfamiliar poses and unfamiliar clothes. A sweaty tank top stuck to his chest, showing muscles she'd never known, surrounded by dark-haired kids on a beach. Aaron in a sweatshirt, Aaron in a blazer. She had no idea Aaron owned a blazer. Her hand moved to her mouth as if to hold something back that wanted to pour forth. She began to cry, because this wasn't the house of a stranger after all.

It skips a generation, she thought. She knew this as a truism. All kinds of things are said to skip a generation, things that had nothing to do with her: alcoholism, the gift of gab. But was it possible that affection did the same?

She opened the bench now and found sheet music her mother had bought for her, bribe accessories. A couple of books for advanced beginners, a show-tune compilation with a nineteen-sixties-looking gold title on the cover, that fat typeface whose *S*s uncoiled and lay on their sides as if they were stoned. She dug deeper and found a stack of *Playbills*. Shows she hadn't thought of in years: "Pippin," "I'm Getting My Act Together and Taking It on the Road," "Loose Ends."

"Oh my God, Mom," she blurted. "When's the last time you looked in the piano bench?" Doris came out with rubber gloves on her hands. Becca fanned out the booklets, the familiar black-and-white and yellow covers, the slippery paper, the staple in the fold.

That was what they did together; the theater district was their demilitarized zone. They ate challah French toast at a diner on Broadway near the Brill Building, long gone. She worked at it a minute and even came up with the name: On Parade Diner. In the theater they set their pocketbooks in their laps and their forearms did a little dance so they wouldn't both land on the armrest at the same time, and they read their *Playbills* and the lights dimmed in the delicious slow way they did at the Helen Hayes or the Lunt-Fontane, and the hush spread through the orchestra (Doris always sprang for orchestra seats) and the velvet curtain parted, and for two and a half hours Becca moved out of her own life and into whatever lives were playing out on stage. If the play was good, she forgot all about her mother and in a way forgot about herself too. During intermission, the theater safely cradling them now, they leafed through their *Playbills* together. That guy who plays the son looks familiar, doesn't he? Did we see him in that Arthur Miller thing?

Once they had come out of a theater and found Jackie O. standing right in front of them. It was a muggy night and the headlights from the slow-moving traffic passed across her. Jackie's neck rose from her body like a pedestal custom-designed to support her head. Collarbones, eyeliner, the slight haze around her hair. And they waited until she passed and Doris whispered to Becca: "Did you see Jackie has the frizzies?" Yes, Becca had noticed it, and they giggled together, and then Becca said, "Well, thanks, Mom, it was great," and got on the IRT, while Doris got in a cab to go back to the hotel where Ben would be meeting her after his Yankees game or his meeting.

Doris was determined to remain immune. "I can't remember the last time we got into the city to see a show," she said, shaking her head and returning to the kitchen.

With her went another whiff of childhood, a clean green smell (mild and yet insistent) of not-quite-mint, not-quite-fruit. Becca stood in the doorway to investigate. It was Palmolive dish soap, standing like a huge plastic emerald on the counter. She had forgotten until now how she'd helped her mother do the dishes in the apartment. She had been allowed to squirt the soap into the sink. She wanted to make bubbles so she could fashion herself a beard and shave it with the blunt side of the vegetable peeler. But her mother had lost patience, was always on the verge of losing patience, so that Becca thought she must be a troublesome child indeed and after a while it was much easier to be troublesome than to try to be good and risk being called troublesome anyway. The prevailing memory of her childhood with her mother: trying to suck herself in. The prevailing memory of her adolescence: saying fuck it.

"I don't bite, you know," her mother said, and Becca almost jumped in the air.

So she came in and sat down on one of her mother's fiber-glass chairs, the kind that seemed as if it should swivel but didn't. Becca was tired from traveling with Carny, traveling with herself, holding herself together. What if she had gone to high school here, become a Westchester girl? "Need any help?" Becca asked.

"I have it under control."

"Ain't it the truth."

Doris held a stick of butter in her bony and veined hand. "You shut me out, Becca. You always have. And then you wonder why I protect myself."

"Whoa. What's the cause and what's the effect here? You were supposed to be the mother."

"For God's sake, Becca. I was twenty-three when you were born. I was human. And your father had his charms, but providing for a family was not among them, so, yes, I made a better life for myself and for you, but you thumbed your nose at it. Every time I pushed, you pushed back. And, might I add, you push hard. And you made your preferences very clear. I'm sure you understand when I say that I prefer not to be judged for my choices."

Becca picked a cuticle trying to pry it loose. But it bled. Doris was watching; Doris was always watching.

"God, I hated that. The way you always watched, waiting to pounce."

"You're a mother. I'm sure you know the impulse. It's really just the impulse to teach. Isn't that the job of a mother?"

"You abandoned me."

"No, Becca. If you replay it with that steel-trap memory of yours, you will know that it was you who abandoned me."

"You moved away, for Christ's sake."

"They weren't picking up the trash, Becca. Remember that? Remember the smell? Remember how all the trash bags had jagged holes from where the rats chewed through them? Remember how walls of the subway cars turned black from all the graffiti? Remember the track fires day after day?"

"Funny, what I remember is the energy. The art. The people."

"The junkies weaving down the street."

"I loved it. It was my home."

"We all make our choices, Becca. I chose not to live in squalor. And you know what? I'm happy with the choices I made. I feel safe."

And there it was, finally out like a splinter: the I told you so.

"I've never been able to overlook the things you overlook. You almost got killed and still you defend it."

"It's my home, Mom."

"You are not nailed to it like a signpost, Becca. People move. They start fresh."

Her mother scratched her head and Becca realized what looked odd about her hair: she was wearing a wig.

"You're not sick, are you?"

"Except for some stenosis and arthritis, I'm actually relatively healthy."

"Then why? Why put this synthetic thing on top of your head?"

"You're doing it again. That's one of the things you've never understood. You always did judge books by their covers."

"Gee, I wonder who taught me that."

Doris sighed deeply and set down the butter. "Look—no, I don't have cancer, knock on wood. Some women age with grace and others—the ones in my line—need a little help. I don't have your nice full face. I have these tiny little features and everything falling around them and this thinning hair, and I'm doing the best I can."

"Back it up. You're wishing you looked like me?"

"Well, yes, I suppose I am. You have the kind of face I always envied, the kind that doesn't need a lot of help. You have color in your cheeks and all that hair that comes from who knows where—your paternal grandmother, I suppose. Cammeyers."

"You don't have to say it like it's a virus. I loved him."

"Well, obviously I did too, Becca. But my history with the Cammeyers was different from yours. Your father had his charms, considerable ones, but he let me down in ways you can't even imagine. But you are absolutely right. I apologize."

The toaster oven dinged, and Becca grabbed an oven mitt.

They ate at the Formica table with the bottles of vitamins and calcium and prescription pills.

"How long are you planning to stay?" her mother asked. "Is this just a social visit?"

"Look, Mom. I came very close to dying the other day. Aaron is in Costa Rica. Joycie is in Arizona with Richard and Rose. Everyone in the Village is freaking out. I came to see you, okay?"

"If you had warned me, I would have had food in the house. I would have seen that Ben was up."

"That's one reason I didn't. I didn't want this to be a big formal thing. We can do the shopping together if you want. I can help you carry stuff."

Becca asked again about Ben.

"Well, I'm lucky and unlucky. He's not well, but he provided. I don't have to do much of the heavy lifting. Soon we're going to have to rethink the house. A lift on the steps, or else turn the TV room into a bedroom. It's not going to be pretty. Marry the distinguished older gentleman and this is what happens down the line. Of course, it's impossible to predict. Who would've thought I'd be the robust one?" Doris laughed at the thought and examined her nails.

And then Becca asked the bigger question. "So, I didn't know you and Aaron…" she began. "He's been here, it looks like."

"I'm his grandma, Becca. He's turned out to be quite a mensch, your Aaron."

For a little while time stopped pressing so hard. It was almost nice. She decided against asking about the carton with the wedding gown. They ate their poppy-seed bagels, which were chewy in a good way.

She could have placed a single phone call on her father's old Bell phone, dialed 914 and just said the word. Could have transferred out of Music and Art to the local high school and the scar would have healed decades ago, and she could have had a regular husband (because surely a husband was part of the package). And maybe Aaron would be home, and the years would be punctuated by Thanksgivings and seders eaten in dedicated dining rooms. She imagined herself pushing open the kitchen door with her rear end because her hands were holding the tray of stuffing or matzoh kugel. She would go straight to the oven, her mother's oven. She knew how it worked in normal families—the oven and the family. Things got hot and sometimes burned, but then they cooled down. You came back for more. Every fall and every spring. No matter what.

There was a commotion upstairs, and they both went running. Carny started barking.

"Shush, Carny," she said. "It's his house."

"Melva," called Doris. "The cleaning can wait. Come help."

"I've got it, Mom," said Becca.

At the top of the steps, Ben gripped the railing with both hands and slowly righted his disobedient feet, clad in huge black shoes with Velcro straps. He was still handsome, but now had old-man arms bent at the elbows. He looked at Becca for a second and she saw the terror tame itself into embarrassment and then sheepishness, the way he must once have collected himself to walk into his first board room. Getting older, she realized, meant seeing all the things your elders had managed to conceal before.

"So I wasn't dreaming," said Ben, making it down the stairs without mishap. "It's been way too long. I'm sure your mother is as happy to see you as I am."

He sat himself down on one of the sofas. She went over to greet him. He had missed a spot shaving, and a sliver of metallic hairs shone along his jaw. Wild eyebrows. Laws of nature gone awry, and Becca knew this was what her mother was holding at bay in herself, willing her body to behave like a lady. Melva finished her shift, got introduced, and said goodbye.

For a while they speculated on the bomber's motives and then Ben excused himself to make the long climb back upstairs and begin snoring like a lawnmower. She and her mother went to the backyard to walk Carny, who peed and pooped. Then they drank decaf and worked on the Sunday *Times* crossword puzzle in the kitchen.

"Eleven down," said Doris. "Dig, four letters, the second one possibly an *S*." They considered the word, verb and noun, literal and figurative. Neither of them could think of a word for dig, with or without *S*.

Becca said, "Have you ever almost died?"

Doris looked up slowly from her half-glasses. "I am not as dramatic as you, Becca. And life here in Mamaroneck, as I'm sure you've noticed, is fairly serene, and death tends to come with more warning. Would you like to tell me more about the Arch? All I know is what I learned on the ten o'clock news. I'm sure it's still very raw."

"I'll be okay," she said, though she wasn't sure it was true. "It's just, the thing is, I got off scot-free."

Doris sighed. "People pray to a lot of false gods, but one I've never understood is regret. Such an incredibly simple fact of life that the whole world pretends doesn't exist: we can't go back and change what's already happened. And yet people waste half their lives trying to. They can't predict the future either, but that never stopped them from trying."

"You sound very philosophical," said Becca.

"Well, as a matter of fact I took a philosophy class at Adult Ed last semester. But I would call it common sense."

Becca had to agree.

"Let's try to tackle the theme, shall we?" asked Doris, snapping the magazine crisply.

Domestic scene, somewhere on the spectrum between unbearable and okay.

When Becca and Carny said their goodbyes and headed out, a school bus pulled up next door and let out two little girls in tights and miniskirts. "Race you to the door," said one. "No fair," said the other, "you got a head start, Michaela," and the first said, "Didn't anyone ever tell you that life isn't fair?" and

Becca laughed out loud; Mamaroneck was full of philosophers today.

"Hey, can we pet your dog?" called the skinny one with the long curly hair. Carny consented. "His ears are soft," she said.

"Have you guys lived here a long time?" Becca asked. Strange not to know her own mother's neighbors.

"I've lived here since I was little, but Amree just moved in in second grade."

"Are they nice neighbors?" Becca asked, pointing to her mother's house.

"Yeah," said Michaela. "They have Kit-Kats for Halloween."

"Yum," said Becca. "One of my favorites."

"Me too," said Amree, who had beautiful straight black hair.

"Me three," said Michaela. "But I like Reese's better."

"What are you going to be for Halloween?" asked Becca.

"I don't know yet. Either Athena or Dumbledore," said Amree.

Michaela pointed to the Steinglass mailbox. "Sometimes we call them the Wine Glasses," she said, giggling behind her hand.

"Michaela!" said Amree.

"I don't like to be regular people," said Michaela. "I like to be scary things. Like monsters and ghouls. I like a lot of blood and guts. And fangs. I feel like having fangs this year."

"My brother wants to be a tape dispenser for Halloween," said Amree.

"Your brother is so weird." They shared a look.

"Actually, I'm Mrs. Steinglass's daughter," said Becca.

They didn't seem to care one way or the other whose daughter she might be.

A breeze knocked a pod from a sweet gum tree. The bright-red sumacs were trying to steal all the attention from the maples, the skinny leaves of a honey locust hung like fish skeletons. A mockingbird sang a borrowed song, and to herself she sang "Listen to the Mockingbird," a song that was on an ancient *Sing Along With Mitch* album her parents used to own.

This walk up her mother's lane suddenly felt like the sweetest gift the Earth could bestow. The sky was blue and the clouds cumulonimbus. The whole world was named so beautifully: cirrus, feldspar, Ursa Major and Minor. Becca was alive in Mamaroneck, Westchester, New York, U.S., planet Earth, Milky Way, as she and her friends used to write at the top of their homework. She was cutting it close with the train. She didn't dare run with her hip, but it turned out it was easy to favor one hip while skipping. Carny skipped too, looking up now and again as if to say, "Lead the way, chief."

It hit her in the lavatory on the train. She had peed before she left, but she and her mother had drunk so much decaf that she had to make a big to-do of asking the woman sitting next to her to keep an eye on Carny so she could pee again. In the mirror she saw what her mother had seen: her face was round and pink, not pinched like a Michaelman. A Cammeyer face, she thought. And then she realized her mother had been trying to tell her something about her father; Doris had protected her all this time. The train lurched and Becca swayed; it must have crossed back into Manhattan. She peed, flushed, and washed her hands in the non-potable water.

With or Without Pain

Lew's funeral was at the Italian funeral home on Bleecker Street, because it was the Village where Italians trumped Jews and because Lew happened to know the family. Her cousin Joycie, who hardly ever left her side that week, pulled her into the ladies' room and insisted on fixing her hair and putting on a tiny bit of makeup and murmuring soothing words. "You're going to be okay. You've got us. You'll get a juicy part. You'll meet a guy. You'll finish school, you'll go to college."

Joycie ushered her into the room with the stained glass and the wood paneling and wall-to-wall carpeting. The entire Village, it seemed, had already stepped through the door. Her mother was there with Ben, handsome and tall and with those graying temples that were considered so sexy then. He was definitely a catch, but Doris at least had the decency to refrain from touching him. Becca's friends from Music and Art were there in an unruly pack in the back with their Afros and their granny glasses, and seeing them helped.

Sheldon Glaberson gave a charming, loving eulogy and the chair of the community planning board spoke. The Lew who was conjured up in words was much more organized and purposeful than the real one. People flooded her afterward with their condolences, many with a similar gesture: a private smile and slight shake of the head, as if to say, Lew, Lew, what are we going to do about Lew?

It was a good story, his death. It happened at St. Vincent's Hospital, but not in the usual way. It was a Thursday night in the hospital's huge auditorium, where meetings were often held. As chair of some committee or another, he was on the stage. Becca was there, too, sitting off to the side; she was supposed to be following a local political issue for her U.S. government class and could get extra credit for attending. Lew was taking a motion from the floor or objecting or whatever he did; she was doodling on the brown-bag cover of her textbook. The house was packed, and tempers were rising. The other chair said to someone in the audience who'd stepped up to the podium to ask a question, "No need to have a heart attack; it's just zoning," and her father, who was never one for following instructions, promptly went into cardiac arrest. She watched the whole thing: the SOS call, the orderlies running down the long aisle with the stretcher, the attempt to defibrillate; everyone was too stunned to whisk her away.

After the funeral and reception, Becca told Joycie she was going to the ear-piercing place, the little store on Seventh Avenue South with the big sign that read "With or Without Pain."

"I don't get it," said Joycie. They had already gotten their ears pierced when they were thirteen.

"Here," said Becca, digging her fingernail as deep as she could get it into the hard cartilage near the top of her ear that almost no one pierced then. Joycie ran behind her on Bleecker Street.

"Becca, I don't think this is a smart idea. You just buried your father. You need time, and you definitely shouldn't go back to that apartment alone. Come to Queens with us. We can stop and pack you some stuff. If you still want to do it, I promise I'll come back in and hold your hand."

So Becca spent the night in Forest Hills among the Tudor apartment houses and the shrubs so green they almost hurt her eyes. The subway ran above ground as if it had nothing to hide, but to Becca Queens always seemed to be full of hidden things, a borough organized by Jews desperately seeking postwar order and stasis with a kosher butcher in every strip of stores.

Joycie's mother, her aunt Rivka, was Lew's much older sister. She and Uncle Sol had married late and had Joycie even later. And after Joycie they had another daughter named Sandra who lived in what they called a home in a place called Middle Village that they visited twice a week and whose name, when spoken, was spoken with a special hush. They kept kosher and had two sets of everything in their little kitchen, and were constantly getting up on stepstools and pulling out plates to get to other plates. They went to shul rather than temple. Joycie hadn't been bat mitzvahed because religious Jews didn't believe in it, but she spoke Hebrew and could chant it beautifully. Sol was skinny and had a tremor. Rivka always had a pocketbook over her forearm and a white cardigan over her shoulders, a shopping list in her hand, a Kleenex tucked in the sleeve. And she always served smoked whitefish because she thought Becca liked it, though what Becca actually liked was the look of the gold-leaf skin against the white flesh of the meat.

Aunt Rivka made up the day bed in the spare room that was to have been Sandra's, but Becca felt too numb to sleep. She knocked on Joycie's door.

"Joycie, you awake?" she whispered. Joycie's room, like the rest of the house, was Jewish, but hers was hippie-Jewish, with posters from folk concerts and one of those stylized embroidered hands someone had brought her from Israel. Joycie was a rebel in her own way, refusing to go to yeshiva, which her parents had taken hard though she danced in an Israeli folk-dancing group and she marched on Israel Independence Day.

"What's the matter, Bec? Miss your father?" She was wearing a worn-out nightgown with little blue flowers. Without her glasses she looked almost beautiful except that one eye turned in toward her nose.

"That's the trouble. I want to miss him, but it's like he's not gone yet. I can't make it be real, so I can't feel anything except confused."

Joycie shut her eyes to think this through. "Okay, here's what I think. I think you're in shock. I read a case study about it."

"But I feel normal. I notice all the same stuff I always notice. I'm alert. I'm talking to you, aren't I?"

"Shock is protective. People are actually kind of amazing. The numbness is there to protect you from feeling too much at once."

They sat quietly while Joycie thought some more.

"I know what. Tell me one thing about Uncle Lew—your father, one funny little thing."

Becca heard the subway screech outside as it slowed to a stop. She could hear the announcer call out but couldn't make out the words.

"I can't remember anything. It's all blank." She started to hyperventilate. The blankness was cold and seemed to have hands around her throat.

"Then I'll tell you something *I* remember about Uncle Lew. One time I slept over and he made us dinner—well, a TV dinner. The potholders were those ones we made at camp, but they'd gotten all grimy and disgusting. And he told us a story about the army that had something to do with giant blisters from his boots, and he looked around the room for something the right size and he picked up the potholder and said, 'Blisters this big!'"

"And I said," Becca added, "'that's bigger than your whole heel.'"

"And he said, 'My point exactly.' The blisters were so big they came up the sides. It became an expression around here: I've got a blister, a bee sting, mosquito bite the size of a potholder."

"Us too!" said Becca. "A zit the size of a potholder."

Her father's goofy expressions started to pour into Becca's mind. He used to sing do-wop songs but with Yiddish words. Rest your *keppe* on my shoulder. Instead of the "Duke of Earl" he would sing, "Milt, Milt, Milt, Milton Berle, Berle, Berle."

"The funeral was such phony-baloney," Becca said. "Sheldon was great, but the rest was like they were talking about someone I didn't know at all."

"I think maybe that's what happens. My other *bubbe*'s funeral was kind of like that, only I assumed I'd just missed knowing her the way they described her. I remembered her as a kind of stingy, mean old lady."

Becca felt prickles start in her eyes. A light went out on the street and now she could hardly see Joycie. But she knew she was there at the head of the bed and would stay until the crying was done. She went back to the stiff white sheets and slept without dreaming until eleven the next day, worrying her aunt and uncle.

Next day, just before the shivah at the Glabersons', the guy in the store planted his elbows on the glass counter.

"It's not your ear you want to hurt, you know," said Joycie.

"Why do you always have to find reasons? It's just a tiny hole in a useless part of my body and I feel like it," said Becca. "There's no reason."

"Becca, come on, we're already late," said Joycie. "Your mother must be plotzing. I'll come back in on Saturday and go with you. Promise."

The guy's eyes moved back and forth as if he had all the time in the world. "You girls need me, I'll be in the back."

Becca said to Joycie, "You sound like you're on Doris' side."

It was the only time she and Joycie ever got into a fight.

And Joycie, brilliant, reasonable Joycie, said, "First of all, that upsets me because I know how you feel about her right now. And you're just hurt and taking it out on me."

Becca called the guy back. "Here," she said, putting her thumbnail in the cartilage.

He took out his piercing kit. The alcohol on the cotton ball was wonderfully cold and smelled like a proper medical facility. The big hole puncher went in clean and quick, as if she were a plastic notebook.

"Do me again," she said, and dug her nail in right under the new hole. Joycie said, "Wait." But the guy looked into Becca's eyes and she stared right back.

"Your ear," he said with a shrug, and punched again. "Alcohol swab twice a day for the next week. Come back and I'll take out the studs and you can pick yourself out a pair or a coupla nice earrings from the assortment of singles over here." He unlocked the case and pulled out a piece of dog-eared cardboard with earrings poked through.

"What month were you born in?" he asked.

But she pointed to a tiny turquoise one in a silver setting like a miniature bottle cap. She thought she might choose an onyx for the other, in honor of her father.

"Going for that Santa Fe look. Come back in a week and it's yours," he said, returning the earrings to the case and locking it. In those days, people would steal phony birthstones.

She and Joycie finally made their way to Frieda's. The first time she had stayed at the Glabersons' townhouse was when she was in third grade and her parents took a rare vacation, a junket to Bermuda. How she had worshipped the Glaberson boys, Stuart and his big brother, Bennett. She could still call up the lavender sachet smell of the guest room. Stuey and Benny were working on a model sailing ship that they brought to the kitchen table after supper. And when she finished her home-work she sat with them and was sometimes given a task: to glue a tiny wooden rail into place or to stitch a sail to the mizzen mast. Everything she knew about sailing she had learned from these two strapping boys with their big hands, who were al-ways just ahead of her and always sweet with her. Becca hadn't known that a family could be so peaceful together.

She and Joycie milled around, accepting hugs from people she'd known all her life and some she'd never seen until today. Stuey and Benny came over with their wives and toddlers, and they called her Becky Thatcher, the nickname they had given her back then; the Glabersons were the only ones allowed to call her Becky. And as her eyes scanned the room, she half-reg-istered two separate flashy-looking women she didn't recognize, both of whom had sat in the funeral home quietly crying into hankies.

Doris wore a herringbone suit with an A-line skirt. She, Becca, wore an Indian print dress with sleeves that belled out and a sash that tied in the back and clunky brown shoes with a wedge. Doris looked her up and down in a feast of disapproval. Becca started counting to ten silently, but she got only to seven when her mother's eye landed on the ear, which was hot and throbbing and no doubt very red. Frieda sensed trouble and appeared with a tray of rugelach. Becca forgot all about the mysterious women, and about all the evenings her father was out at unspecified meetings.

Soon enough, her grief for her father grew and grew. She had to suck it in or it would knock her over. It was such a relief to hate her mother. She had to do everything in her power to avoid Westchester. Make herself so obnoxious her mother wouldn't have her.

She took a ceramics class in school that fall. The first assignment was coil pots and the second raku. She got As on both of those. Then they moved on to sculpture. They had to sculpt their own face or that of a loved one. Becca chose her father. The class met in the morning for a double period. She sat at a high table on a stool with four other students who were all making their own likeness, passing around a mirror like the ones in a beauty parlor, complaining about their features. Becca stared at her lump of clay. She punched it. She dug her elbows into it. She cursed it. She started with the mouth because Lew had been a talker. She couldn't remember what his lips looked like; what seventeen-year-old wants to look at her father's lips? What seventeen-year-old memorizes her father's face on the off-chance he'll die tomorrow? Round cheeks. That much she did know. But the rest was impossible to see clearly. In the end she made his hands. They'd once invented a game they called Alley Oop. You put a penny on top of each fingernail and then you flipped your hand and tried to catch the pennies as they fell. You got to keep any you caught. This way, said Lew, you'll never feel poor when you have money falling into your fist.

Taking Stock

Dear Joycie, *Becca wrote on a legal pad at the kitchen table*. It's Friday night and there's a full moon outside the living room window. I wish I could come visit you in Arizona, but there are hundreds of miles and dollars in the way, and I know your hands are full taking care of Rose. Oh, Joycie. I am the most self-centered woman in the world. I didn't even think to ask yet. How's Rose? How's Richard? Tell him I miss him, and his pancakes, Joycie. I keep calling you by name as if this were a poem, but it comforts me to say it. I'm a little crazy today, you may have noticed, and I don't know what to do. I had to cancel all my tours, and soon it's going to get cold. Soon all the leaves will fall and the old Chinese ladies will appear from nowhere or maybe Flushing to gather the ginkgo berries. And the pods from the locust trees will fall in the Westbeth courtyard, and the Jews will erect their sukkoth, and the crab apples will fall in St. Luke's garden (remember how Aaron used to love to gather them?!), and I am nearly broke, and I can't work because there are no tourists and there is no Washington Square, and as a result there is not much Becca.

Joycie, if you had to name one action that sums up your life, what would it be? Here's how I see you in your new suburban world: turning the wheel of a car with one hand while lowering the sun visor with the other, to push the button that opens the garage door.

Me? I'm just a girl in a walkup, forever rounding a landing on my way to the next flight of steps.

Ignore everything I just wrote. I remembered something you suggested once and I did it! I thought about someone else to get my mind off my own little woes. I pretended it was the early 1900s and I was a young widow who'd finished a twelve-hour shift in the sweatshop doing piecework, and then I had to corral my five children from where they were playing marbles in the street, and then I had to feed them, and then they fought about who got to work at the kitchen table and who was relegated to the floor. I spoke to them in Yiddish and they answered in English and I tried so hard to hear the words and grasp hold of them. I said, "Table, table, table" and "homework, homework, homework" to myself while I finished cleaning and was finally ready to brush out my hair and go to bed. And then I spoke to them in English, but it came out "clear your workhome off the toble" or somesuch, and the kids laughed their heads off, not in a nice way.

Then I snapped back to October 2006 and didn't hate it quite so much. You were right, as always. Maybe you're looking out your window at the full moon too. If we're sharing the same moon, we can't be too far apart, right?

When she sent her love to Joycie, Richard, and Rose, Becca took stock, which she hadn't had a chance to do since the power came back.

She took a deep breath, held it, and opened her tenement-sized fridge. She unwrapped the foil around the half a burrito from Monday's dinner. The tortilla was stiff as a Frisbee; some black beans rolled out of the end. She opened the milk and took a breath. It smelled strongly, for some reason, of sea scallops. She tossed it down the drain and the kitchen momentarily became a marina. The orange juice smelled like beer, and fizzed as she poured it down after the milk. The jelly would be fine and the salsa might make it through the week before a snowfall of mold would form across the top, and then she could skim it off. In the vegetable bin she cupped a bag of liquid lettuce that dripped brown goo. The celery gave way in her hand, the two carrots bent like Gumbys. There were a couple of apples in the fruit bin that she felt like kissing for their self-sufficiency. The one stick of butter was misshapen but usable.

Her belly rumbled. Sometimes she had cravings so strong she swore she could tell better than a blood test which nutrients her body lacked. She craved a cheese omelet. She pulled out an egg from the carton and wondered how to tell if an egg was spoiled. She pulled out the hunk of cheddar and went around all six sides with a paring knife cutting off the blue spots, but still the surface felt as sticky as mucilage. She went around again, leaving her with a cube not much bigger than a sample bite speared on a toothpick at Balducci's. She grabbed a second egg, cracked both into a bowl, and sniffed. No alarming smell. So she melted some butter and cooked them, tilting the pan and sliding the cooked part of the eggs aside to give the uncooked parts a turn in the heat, just as her bubbe had taught her, except that her bubbe put jelly in her omelets. Becca cut up her little cube of cheese, sprinkled it across the top and folded the omelet in half as expertly as she sealed letters of protest to the City Council. She refolded her napkin to hide the dirty sides, poured herself the last of the vino rosso, fed Carny, and ate her omelet, which perhaps tasted a little funky at first, but after a few bites funkiness seemed the normal condition.

In the bedroom she pulled off her sweats and stood, wearing only her hair. She heard her father: "Annual inventory, eh, *ketzelah?*" Once she had braided her hair like an Alpine maid, a girl with ecumenical ethnic tastes, Indian skirts wrapped around her hips, bits of embroidery blooming on the meadow of her denim, daisy blossoms everywhere. Daisies fashioned from seed beads that she had dropped onto the needle, letting them slide down the thin nylon thread, sticking the needle back in just so, so the line of beads gathered itself into a flower. Strands of daisies around her neck, her wrist, the slave bracelets they all made, joining ring to bracelet. Toe rings of hammered silver catching a thousand different bits of the sun. Girls in the park soaking in the sun, blouses loosened and shrugged off their brown shoulders, blond tips at the tail end of the braids, mementos of July to save for the winter, girls in class twirling the ends of their braids, idly sucking on them in the overheated chemistry classroom.

The guidance counselor in the straight skirt told Becca, "I have your best interests at heart," though it wasn't clear that this woman had a heart under her puckered cotton brassiere that made her breasts look like pine cones. No, Becca would be free, free, free, and would kiss the boys with the loveliest lips and lie down with them on the tape marks on the stage or on the old piers jutting into the Hudson, maybe one day on a bed if she could only find a safe one for a few hours.

She had given up the braids years ago when she looked in the mirror and first saw the lines around her eyes; she would be damned if she would cling to youth like her mother. And without the braids it was as if her whole body surrendered. She found she liked the padding and the anonymity that came with it. She liked all the hair. It kept her warm. She let it do what it pleased and she ate what she pleased and stopped when she felt like it and stopped thinking about what men might see. At a certain point all the men were gay anyway, and they loved her the way she was. And then so many of them died, and all the new men were young fathers, and they loved her too, or ignored her. Either way was okay by her.

At a certain point, she gave up mirrors too.

Now she looked straight into the mirror on the back of her door. Moonlight was coming through the windows and landing on her whole side, some parts familiar, some nearly unknown. She still had a shape and a waist, but there were places where flesh pooled and places where one part hung heavy onto the next, much of it lightly traced with iridescent stretch marks. What had she done with this body, the only one she had? Her pubic hair, which used to curl into corkscrews, was sparse and matted. The Viking used to pull it gently like springs, and she had taught him what became his favorite English word—*boing*. She didn't know the last time she had weighed herself. A silly theater girl in high school had said you had to take the pencil test to determine if you needed to wear a bra. But Becca had never bothered. She grabbed a pencil from her night table, lifted her breast and set it in. The pencil wasn't going anywhere.

When she was fifteen, she and her friend Raimundo, who answered only to Mundo, decided to go to junior prom, which was a subversive thing to do at the High School of Music & Art in those days. They insisted on calling it the "ruckus," and they decided to go formal—tux, gown, boutonniere, the whole works. They hung around school very late one day after rehearsal for *Li'l Abner*. And they snuck back in after the announcement came on the PA that all students were to leave the building. There was a women's wardrobe and an adjoining men's. Racks and racks and racks, all eras. The red Salvation Army suits that were used for *Major Barbara* and *Guys and Dolls*. Bavarian skirts with suspenders for the Von Trapp kids. Fringed suede vests for all the new God musicals.

"You'll be David Niven but with a touch of Vincent Price," Becca said. "A perfect white dinner jacket just begging for blood stains, fangs. We'll powder you up and make you very pale and handsome." He *was* handsome, too, in a way no one could see yet.

"I see you as a flapper with beaded fringe and a cigarette holder," said Mundo, though they both knew he was the one who wanted to be a flapper.

"Nuh-uh," she said. "Not this time. I was thinking more Myrna Loy meets the Wicked Witch. Sweeping the floor with lots of complicated details and one of those cold metal zippers on the side that I'll ask you to do up for me. I'll know it when I see it."

They rifled through a whole rack of dance costumes, heavy with beads. And sure enough, it was red, with huge forties shoulders, straight long sleeves, and narrow skirt, all perfectly glamorous except for the strange bunches of black lacquer cherries affixed on either side of the sweetheart neck.

She could wear anything in those days, or almost nothing. She slipped off her huaraches and untied her skirt, then climbed out of her leotard.

"Turn the other way, a lady is changing," she said.

"Don't change too much, dahling. I like you right off the shelf."

Carny meandered to the bedroom with a sock in his mouth, but the urge to fetch was vestigial in him. She scooped up his great length and plunked him on her bed. She rested her ear on his warm, short-haired belly. She could hear his heart pump and the food move through his digestive track. He sighed, settled into sleep, and began to dream. A rear paw twitched and his heart raced. Becca stayed there naked a long time, rubbing one of his soft ears. She began to cry, and her tears fell onto her hand. Carny woke up and licked the salt from her hand, and then fell back to sleep. She drifted to sleep herself and woke to a disturbance; music was playing somewhere. She looked out the back. It was Melora Ross in her glass-walled house, with her Pilates ball and her black leggings that belled out at the bottom and her little moisture-wicking T-shirt.

Saturday

Separation Issues

On Saturday afternoon Melora went to the office-office, and when she swung open the door, the only thing she could remember about why it had seemed like a good idea to come was that it had seemed like a worse idea to stay home alone in her mint townhouse on a desirable block.

The first thing that hit her was the nothingness, as if the power were still off. Ordinarily the office blazed with fluorescent tubes, and three or four different people and things hummed in different keys and at different tempos. Today a person could hear herself think, which wasn't a point in the office's favor. There were sweaters slumped on the backs of all the chairs, as if the rest of the realtors had been deflated and stuck in a closet until Monday.

She sat down in her swivel chair and dusted her computer screen with her sleeve. She rummaged through her drawers.

When the bell rang she practically leaped out of her chair to answer, having a crazy thought that it might be Niko come looking for her.

It was just a chubby boy of eleven or twelve in a soccer jersey with an open box full of M&M packages.

She looked down at him. "I don't suppose you're in the market for a townhouse on Washington Square."

"Excuse me, miss," he said. "I'm selling candy to buy new uniforms for my soccer team."

She motioned him in with a jerk of the head. He hadn't "ma'amed" her, at least.

"They're one-twenty-five a pack," he said. "The team gets a percentage. There's a—what-do-you-call-it?—markup, but that's how we make a profit. It's not unreasonable."

"I could use some protein. Do you have peanut under there or just regular?"

He nodded vigorously. "I even got a new kind, crunch. Here, they got buried. They're really good, if you like crunchy things."

His face was round and dark and sallow at the same time—the kind of kid you'd never notice in a crowd or a schoolyard. She asked him his name, which was Walter.

"Actually," said Walter, "I'm kind of lost."

"So am I, Walter, so am I."

"Excuse me, but I meant the regular kind of lost, like where's the subway to get me back to 145th Street?" He still had a sweet kid's voice; on the phone you might take him for a girl.

"You came here from Washington Heights? What the hell are you doing down here all by yourself?"

"Well, I was at that big pier with my team getting our pictures taken—you know how they do those pictures—" He feigned a dorky smile and held an imaginary soccer ball in front of him.

Melora laughed. Somewhere in a box or a drawer at home she had a slew of pictures of Cole in the same pose with the same dorky smile. Cole with teeth like Bugs Bunny, Cole with braces, Cole with a beautiful straight smile. This was the first thing that had struck her as funny in days, maybe weeks.

Walter fidgeted. "Maybe I should come back another time?"

She sighed herself down just as tears were starting to pool. "Give me one of each."

She fished through her purse for money. He smoothed out her bills and lined them up all the same way with his chubby fingers, and then tucked them into an envelope. As they completed their transaction, she noticed that he kept stopping to scratch at his straight black hair.

"Are you scratching your head because you're sweaty, Walter?"

"Uh, yeah," he said. "Me and a couple of my friends, we kicked the ball for a while after the picture."

"Do you have nits, Walter?"

He shrugged and then looked away.

"Walter, look at me. There's no shame in having lice. In fact, the little buggers prefer clean hair. You'd better sit down."

She was surprised when he sat obediently; someone had raised him well.

"I may as well do something useful to someone in this life. I used to pay people to do this work," she told him. "No, don't sit down. The light is rotten. Okay. Here's the plan. You and I are going to go in the backyard where there's some sun. Not only did I pay people to do this for my kid," she said as she fumbled with the back door, "but I once got a company to come into his elementary school and check all three hundred kids. I made my rich husband pay for it. I was very noble. I didn't think the staff or the teachers should waste their time picking nits. Then I made fun of the Orthodox Jewish ladies who came to do it, with their dowdy clothes. You know the funny thing, Walter? They didn't even have any hair!"

Now it was Walter's turn to laugh. "Yeah, I seen them up by my school," he said. "They dress kind of like old ladies. The girls, I mean." He blushed.

Melora usually avoided the backyard, one of those unreno-vated rectangles that old-timers thought were charming. Violet leaves ran amok out of every soft surface, and every hard one was slippery with lichen. She pulled up a pair of molded white plastic chairs, the kind that sprouted in such spaces like another invasive species, and shook out whatever organic matter had collected there. Sitting Walter down, she squinted at the sun to try to figure out the best position. She told herself to be systematic, and then she told herself to get on with it already. She dug through her purse for her reading glasses with the teal-blue frames that usually made her feel weighty and doctoral. Then she pulled out a comb and stood over Walter, thinking there must be a formula for dividing up the sphere of a head, but it no doubt involved pi and squares of things. Then she remembered you were supposed to put the nits on a piece of Scotch tape, and she ran in to fetch a dispenser.

"Okay, Walter," she said when she returned. "Let's suffocate the boogers. Your hair's short; it shouldn't take long, and then you get right on the A train; I'll show you where."

His hair was like a crop planted and tended by a tidy farmer. Her own hair was meant to look unkempt and half grown out, which with some people made her feel very together but with others made her feel unkempt and half grown out. She liked to tell herself it was the color of white chocolate, or incandescent light through a linen lampshade, or a tow-headed kid's summer hair. People occasionally told her she was beautiful, but she knew it was a B+ sort of beauty, the kind that squeaked you through.

At first Walter was a good patient, or client, or whatever you called a person with nits. "Open your hand," she said, and she pulled the pack of crunchy M&Ms out of her back pocket where she'd stashed it, tore it open with her teeth and poured him a pile.

"My mom—she's really busy," he said out of the blue. "She has two jobs, and all of us. And she says so far as she knows no one ever died from lice."

Melora felt stung by his lie.

He insisted that that was a long time ago, when he was little. Now she smiled, because she knew that the second lie was meant to cover the first, which was meant to cover his mother. There was a good name for lies like this—tiny, harmless lies told to avoid hurt feelings—but she couldn't think of it.

"I know you're supposed to slide them down the piece of hair. What do you call a piece of hair anyway?" she asked. "Piece isn't right. A leaf of hair, a stalk of hair?"

"Maybe like a strand?" offered Walter.

She cuffed him on the shoulder. "How come you're so smart?"

He smiled.

After a while he began to fidget.

"Do you have to pee, Walter?"

He peered at his big Casio watch. "I should go. I gotta go. I got a whole mess of homework."

Social lies—that was the term. A ripple of loneliness developed in the distance and began building power. If she wasn't careful, soon it would come crashing through the office and drown her.

"Not so fast, mister. Turn a little, okay? I think we got us something." She did, indeed, have something, something like a translucent sesame seed clinging to a strand of hair. She felt like a great discoverer. With care she slid it down Walter's hair and transferred it to the tape without dropping it in the lichen.

"Will you look at that—it's a tiny little egg sac with a tiny little bug inside," she said, holding the tape up to the sun.

She found three more near the first one.

"Isn't that cute? A whole nuclear family," she said. Then she asked where his family was from.

"Colombia. But they left when I was little. It wasn't a nice place. I got into Lab, the middle school, not the high school. It's pretty good."

"Whatever you do, Walter, don't be a lazy student. My son Cole was a lazy student. He knew he could get by on charm. He was spoiled. My husband was spoiled. We were all spoiled."

She suddenly missed the nineties. How easy and pleasant it had been to be a brat then! You could have a hissy fit any time if you just announced it first, like a fire drill. Being Cole's mom had given her a whole vocabulary for it. "I have separation issues," she'd say. Or, "I'm not good with impulse control" (or transitions or fine-motor skills). How she had loved those comforting books by those two doctors: *Your Six-Year-Old, Your Nine-Year-Old.* And what she wanted to know now was this: Where was the guidebook for *Your Forty-Eight-Year-Old?*

"Spoiled. Isn't that the worst word?" she continued. "Like someone closed us up in the vegetable bin and we got all mushy with blue fuzz growing on us."

Walter liked that one. He laughed heartily. He had the kind of face where every part crinkled up in the laugh. Even his ears seemed to be laughing.

"What's Walter in Spanish?"

"Ain't no Walter in Spanish. That was supposed to be the point. My brothers too: Eric, Kenny, and Jason."

"What's your favorite team, Walter? Man United? Juventas?"

"How come you know so much about soccer?"

"Oh, I'm just faking. My son used to play." She asked if he was a good student.

"I'm not so hot in math. I'm not crazy about numbers. They're kind of like my brothers—some are bigger and some are smaller, but they get on my nerves."

They chuckled together. Then they were quiet. For a minute the only sound in the Village was the crunching of M&Ms in Walter's mouth.

"I'm an only," Melora said after a while. "I did have this imaginary older brother with light brown hair that had gold shot through it; that was how I always described it to myself. I must have read it in a book. I think I had this imaginary brother mixed up in my head with the pony I was never going to get either."

She stopped to sigh and roll her neck from side to side in a yoga way, but she forgot to take an in-breath while doing it and had to start again. "But guess what, Walter? I got the pony. Yep, that was me—the girl with the pony. You wouldn't believe how nice people get when you're the girl with the pony. But I just went around with this sick feeling because it turned out that I didn't really want a pony."

He nodded his head. "I know what you mean. I had gerbils for a little while, but, man, was that a disaster."

She'd named the pony Max, and then it turned out that all the girls that year across Long Island were naming their pets Max. After a lot of muted arguments, her parents had sold Max to the owners of a stable nearby, the idea being that Melora could visit; but for years whenever they passed, Melora would turn her head away.

"So, you sell fancy apartments?" Walter asked. Melora had to stifle a laugh; it sounded like a kid's pickup line.

"Actually, Walter, people kind of sell them to each other. I just get to carry the keys around."

"My mom—you can never get a simple answer out of her.

Say, 'Ma, what's for supper?' and it's like she's teaching a class on the hours of the grocery store and the pros and cons of the one on 137th Street and the one on our corner. She'll give you a whole lesson on the side about how no one helps out and everyone has terrible eating habits and the kitchen gets all greasy and there's no money."

"She talks to you, at least. That may not be much, Walter, but it counts. There's effort in it."

He sighed like an old man who's seen too much.

Melora had worked her way around Walter's head, and now she parted the last section. He hummed softly. She was trying to suck the sugar off her M&Ms so she could relax with a mouth full of chocolate, but as usual she lost patience and crunched them at the worst moment, when the shell was all soft and bumpy.

"You know what my son Cole used to do?" she said. "At the playground, he used to introduce kids to each other. Jake, meet Alex, he would say. You two are both big Allan Sherman fans. Sometimes he would even bring over other moms and introduce them to me. I didn't even know how he knew them."

"That's kind of weird," Walter said.

"That's exactly what my husband and I told each other, back when we told each other things."

Melora worked extra hard on the last section of hair, but she didn't find a thing. "Okay, Walter," she said. "You're clean. Let's seal 'em up so they can't run away."

She put a piece of tape over the top, and then kneeled down beside him and held it up to the sun. They counted. There were only seven nits sealed inside, each with a little empty ring around it.

"Listen, let's get you home or you're going to have a whole semester's worth of lectures to listen to. You're supposed to wash everything you can wash. And whatever you can't wash you have to put in a plastic bag for two weeks to suffocate the shitheads."

Walter smiled; he knew she was teasing him. "Man, you

wouldn't last five minutes in my house. Every quarter you ever had would be in the special jar in the kitchen."

"Walter, do you tell little tiny lies a lot, the way you did before?"

"If you met my mom, you wouldn't even ask that question. And my brother Kenny—he's the oldest—one time he told me I'm a lousy liar, so I'm kind of afraid to. I think I'll get all sweaty and everyone will know right away."

She whispered in his ear, "They'll just think you have nits."

He smiled, and then told her about the MP3 player he was hoping to win if he sold another case of candy.

There was nothing left to do but walk back through the still office. Melora handed Walter his box and they went out the front door. The display photos of homes for sale rattled in the window.

Melora pointed Walter toward the subway station. The acoustics were different in the open air of the sidewalk, and her voice sounded shrill and unconvincing in her own ears.

"Uh, thanks," Walter said, looking down. "Thanks a lot."

"Oh, and I think you're supposed to stick your pillow in the dryer, high heat."

Walter nodded and turned to leave.

She waved goodbye. Walter would be a better son than Cole. He would be a better husband than Niko. She wanted to go home with him.

"Hey, Walter," she called. She was going to ask him when his next game at Pier 40 was, but thought better of it. Then she noticed she was still holding the Scotch tape with the nits. "I've got a souvenir for you."

He looked back, puzzled.

She waved the nits. "You could frame them—you know like how fishermen polyurethane the fish they catch and mount them on the wall?"

Walter smiled, but Melora could tell he had already moved on. He walked away slowly, with his feet splayed, as if carrying himself home was serious business.

Melora went home and signed up for two things that terrified her: the GRE and an introductory elementary education course at Hunter.

Projects

When Becca got up, her feet craved pavement. She wanted to swing her arms and walk away, away from the art books and the cupcake shops, someplace where the buildings weren't mortared with memories, where no one knew her, where no one felt they owned a little piece of her. She left Carny at home because she planned to walk long and hard. She left her cape at home and wore her black fleece like any anonymous middle-aged woman.

She walked like a soldier in a minefield, swerving west to avoid the pyre, then east to avoid Melora's house, west again to avoid Photojay's block, steering clear of the bank where she had nothing to deposit and nothing to withdraw, and the clinic where she was way overdue for a checkup. That left the West Village's raw river edge, up through the meat market where it could almost be the seventies. She walked up blessedly scuzzy blocks, bits of gristle greasing her soles, meat trucks unloading, the semipermanent camp of a homeless guy. She walked in search of the cussing longshoremen of her youth, the broken pavement, the malt liquor bottles. A rat slinked past looking both ways as if was doing a meth drop on the pier.

When she emerged she was in Chelsea, where the nonconformist streets of the Village uncoiled and stretched their limbs. Here you were fed north, up avenues, businesses all neatly lined on the road to midtown. The side streets were the harder-luck cousins of her streets, more motley and Victorian, the majority still unrenovated.

She found herself in the projects. The only things that meandered in Chelsea were the paths through the projects' lawns, and she took one and walked inland past playgrounds with faded fiberglass animals and big plastic tic-tac-toe games. Usually she walked in search of solidarity and conversation, but she walked today to unknow herself, she walked in search of nothingness amid postwar brick walls with windows full of complete strangers. Kids squealed, teenage boys smacked a blue handball. Abuelas with walkers sunned themselves on benches. On a mural, Stevie Wonder tossed his giant head to one side, dreadlocks flying in all directions with musical notes dropping off the ends. She wandered from one courtyard to the next until she had no idea where she was.

She walked by a little church with an upholstered door like a giant Naugahyde sofa. And because it was open and because Carny was not there to stop her, she wandered in like a tourist. It was just a neighborhood church with clashing palettes: saturated primary colors in the stained glass, the fleshy chiaroscuro of the paintings of Christ and the Madonna in gilded frames her father would have called "ungapotchka." Christ's bony chest was as pink as the ears of a Westie; the stigmata had a single drop of bright-red blood. She walked the periphery as if she were admiring the art. A plaster Virgin Mary stood in the apse like a lawn ornament, with too-regular folds in her light blue garment.

As long as she was in the church, she slid across a pew near the back and sat down. There were three old ladies ahead of her praying. Brass chandeliers, gold stars on the deep blue ceiling. She noticed how nice it was to have a big quiet room to walk into, a room that didn't seem to mind her sadness. She thought if she lit some candles for the victims it might help. They were a nickel apiece, and she fished change from her pocket and bought six from the woman at the front, who didn't speak English. *Seis*, she said, and then realized the woman was Polish or Russian. She held out the fingers of one hand and the thumb of the other, and the woman nodded and smiled. She handed Becca the candles and then placed her hand atop Becca's for a second, and then crossed herself, just the barest suggestion.

They were just like yahrzeit candles. There was a metal gadget for lighting them like the ones in chemistry lab. All she knew were the first two lines of the Kaddish, so she silently mouthed them as she waited for each wick to catch, and she recited the names—Jackie, Mary Anne, Connie, Laura, Wynnette, and Sheryl—and tried to call up an image of each face. Before long she was just another lady in black talking to God. She wished she had more change for the six widowed husbands. Soon there was a parade of faces. Her father's fidgety spirit, Ed growing old and splotchy, Camille so frail and thin, Mundo, the Viking. And now the rusty lid pried off the depression and Becca was ready to cry again. She sat back down in the pew and bowed her head and cried until both her knees were wet. No one disturbed her, and she understood the term sanctuary. The crying went through its phases, loose and wet and full of the conviction that the sadness would never end; she would always be a broken girl in a broken life going home to an empty tenement apartment. After a while her body dried, the crying became jerky and intermittent, and her throat tightened. After a while it began to feel less personal, more interesting. A house of worship, what a clever invention.

One of the old women suddenly marched up to the front and disappeared into the confession booth. A few minutes later the woman returned to her pew, and before she knew what she was doing, Becca went up too.

It was dim and hushed inside, the size of an old-law tenement hallway bathroom. It smelled of incense and Murphy's Oil. A cane partition, like the seat of a Breuer chair. She had no idea why she was here or what to say. She couldn't call a stranger Father; she couldn't call an action a sin. She couldn't ask forgiveness because she wasn't very good at offering it.

She was about to tiptoe back out when the screen slid open. "Well, welcome, then, my child," said a heavily accented voice. The voice was quiet for a moment, and then said, "Please relax. Perhaps it would help to breathe more slowly."

There was a sweetness in his voice, and he said what Joycie was always telling her. "That sounds very Buddhist," she found herself saying. She didn't know what to say next. What were her sins exactly? She was running away from Photojay, a man who was trying to be kind to her? She had gotten home safely when others had not?

"You are breathing. I can hear you. It is a very good thing to do. Try to savor it."

"I've never done this before," she said. "I'm not sure where to begin. Everything I know about confession comes from movies."

"Well, I am afraid I will disappoint you, because I am not Spencer Tracy," he said. "What is weighing most profoundly on your heart, my child?"

"I'm Jewish," she said, adding a tentative, very quiet "Father."

"And that is a heavy weight?" he asked. He was Polish, or maybe Russian. She could hear the smile in his voice.

"No, I wear my Judaism very lightly. It's about the Arch, Father. I'm the one who was leading the tour."

He sighed gently. "I don't suppose then that you are asking for a few Hail Marys and Our Fathers."

"I wouldn't know what to do with them if you offered."

"It has been a difficult week. It will continue to be a difficult time. Would it be helpful to talk about it?"

"You almost sound Yiddish, Father."

"Eastern Europe; we all sound alike, I'm told." Then he added, more thoughtfully, "You have a strong desire to make me something other than who I am."

"Is it easy for you? To know who you are? I seem to have lost the knack. My life has not turned out the way I had hoped and I can't seem to fix it."

"Maybe our task is not to fix our lives but merely to live them the best we are able."

"I'm in my fifties and I still work on the street. And now I've had to cancel all my tours."

"Employment is not my calling, I'm afraid. Unless you would like to do a shift in our soup kitchen."

"Of course. Silly me. You've made me feel very welcome. I didn't expect that. I actually have no idea what I expected. It feels surprisingly good to talk to a stranger."

"Maybe there's a reason this system has been around for a thousand years. Please feel welcome any time."

She half expected him to call her *ketzelah*. "I think this was a one-shot deal for me, Father, but thank you."

"Let me offer you this. I suppose it is all we have: go forth in peace and love, my child."

"Same to you, Father," she said.

She could hear him chuckle.

Becca gathered up her things and left. As she walked down Ninth Avenue, Chelsea's right angles seemed a little softer. The smell of frankincense lingered in her nose. Peace and love, she thought—the same words she used to write in bubbled letters in colored pencil on her paper-bag book cover during algebra class. She used to draw rings around the letters in rainbow colors until they covered half the surface of the book and grew completely abstract.

Lew piped up in her ear. "You could've just come to me, you know. I can advise. That Supak boy, a nice fellow. Look at how he adores you. You always were way too particular. I feared you would end up alone."

"What do you know, Dad? I was a teenager when you died."

"What can I say? I always was ahead of my time. But seriously, I get it about not wanting to join the club that would have you as a member. I'm the one who got your mother to the altar; they said it couldn't be done."

"And how did that work out for you, Dad?"

"There's a reason they call some people marriage material and other people heartbreakers, *ketzelah*."

"So if you don't want to get your heart broken, you go with the one who's too needy, the one who stands in your doorway with a bag of crullers?"

"I just want my little girl to be happy," he said, and disappeared like a plume from a steam pipe.

And then, out of the corner of her eye, she saw Jay across the street coming out of the post office. She panicked. She ducked into the hardware store by the lumber yard, the one that was laid out like a huge railroad flat, a long corridor with alcoves. She went toward the back and pretended to look at the samples of wood finishes.

She heard him call her name, and then he was standing in front of her.

"Refinishing?" he said, like an accusation. If things had gone differently, she would have told him about the funny Polish priest.

He wore a blue and orange scarf she didn't remember.

"Nice scarf," she said.

"My niece Jeannie gave it to me." He showed her where it said Syracuse University. "I don't really get the point of scarves, but anything for Jeannie."

Becca held up her plaid wool one. "This one," she said, "comes from Scotland. My aunt brought it back for me many years ago. Somehow the moths haven't gotten to it."

"Mine smells funny," said Jay. He held out one end.

"I'll take your word."

"No, smell. I want your opinion."

"I don't want to smell your scarf, Jay."

"You were hiding from me. Not just today."

A customer approached. "Don't mean to break this up," he said, gesturing to the shelf behind them, "but I'm shopping here."

"Oh, sorry," said Becca and Jay, in unison for a second, stepping aside to reveal the yellow cans of Minwax.

The man soon moved on. Becca stayed where she was but Jay came close. He put a hand up and leaned against the shelf, like a redneck cop in a movie. She saw things she hadn't noticed before. His pores. His thinning hair. There was a small hole in the armpit seam of his parka. If things had gone differently, she would have offered to stitch it up for him.

"One of us is going to have to look at the other eventually," he said.

"Just give me a little space," she said, and then she scrambled to explain, the litany of the commitment-wary. "I have to sort some things out. I'm confused. I'm not good at this."

"Show me one person who is." He looked her straight in the eyes.

"I've been on my own a very long time and I want to think long and hard before I step into something," she said.

"I'm not a land mine." He pointed to himself. She heard lenses rattling in his big pockets. "I'm just a guy."

She didn't reply. She just couldn't let him in again.

"Fine," he said, with a hard edge to his voice she hadn't heard before.

He walked away. She stood staring dumbly at all the products. Products that adhered to things, products that pried them apart, products to protect surfaces and skin and eyes from the other products. Products to make old things look new and new things old. Products to loosen clogs. Products to get to unreachable places and tight corners. Products that could stain, burn, spark, poison.

The bell on the front door clattered. Becca started to run after him, stopped, started again. She ran past the adhesives and stopped in the niche full of safety gloves.

When she got home old Mrs. Goldman was sitting on the floor of the vestibule.

"I tripped on that goddamned square of carpet. I told Carlos it was a hazard."

Becca helped her up. "Move your arms," she said, and then ordered her to move her legs.

When she ascertained that everything was in working order, she said, "Go forth in peace and love" and went upstairs to the sound of Mrs. Goldman's harrumph.

MENDING

When someone buzzed in the afternoon, Becca figured it was Ed or Mindy. But it was Melora, looking nervous and holding a bag of neatly folded clothes.

"Your super's wife let me in. I hope you don't mind."

"You're the second person this week who's appeared on my doorstep with a sack," Becca said, still wary. She could see from the way Melora was hesitating that she had something to ask that she wasn't sure she was ready to commit to. But then something caught her eye and she got distracted.

"Wow—that's a really nice locket," said Melora.

Becca, despite herself, was dying to show it off. And the locket was neutral territory. "Do you remember my neighbor Camille?"

"One of your old lady pals, right? The theatrical one."

"She's very, very old now. She gave it to me. Look—" Becca slid her thumbnail in and opened it up to show her Camille and Otto on the Jungfrau. Melora put the bag down and reached for the locket. The chain was just long enough that Melora didn't have to violate Becca's personal space to take it in her hand. Becca felt a tiny weight leave the back of her neck.

"It's beautiful. It looks Viennese. Art nouveau."

"Right you are. There's that Melora Ross eye."

Melora shifted her weight. Becca let her stew in the dim hall.

Carny waddled over and stepped off the stoop to nose Melora's shins.

Melora covered her mouth with both hands. "Tell me this isn't Carny," she said. "He was a baby…"

Carny got down on the cold tile floor and rolled on his back for Melora, did everything short of saying outright, I love you. Please love me back. Melora squatted to pat his belly.

"I'll be damned," she said. "I think he remembers me."

"Of course he remembers you," said Becca. "You're the one who let him lick the whipped cream. It was the highlight of his life."

"Oh God, I'd forgotten all about that. And I didn't *let* him exactly. I seem to remember the bowl tipped and he got into the whipped cream all by himself. So, anyway, I'm here for a reason. Hear me out." Melora sucked in her breath. "Teach me to sew." It was spoken like a command but it was a plea. "I have to stop spending money, and I thought maybe if I could hem and mend…" She held up the bag. "You know," said Melora. "Buy a woman clothes and she's dressed for a day but teach her to sew and she's dressed for a lifetime."

Becca laughed in spite of herself. "Ah, yes, who said that? Winston Churchill?"

"Margaret Mead," said Melora.

"Or was it George Washington Carver?"

"Jesus Christ."

"The man or the expression?"

The hinges creaked as Becca opened her door and let Melora Ross in.

"Oh, and this is a whatchamacallit—a quid pro quo," Melora said, pulling the stack of clothes out of the bag and plopping it in the middle of the sofa. "You already helped me with the koi so I know I'm pushing it. But I'm perfectly prepared to do something for you in return. Two somethings. I don't imagine you're in the market for a realtor, but I have other skills. You name it—yoga, weight training, fashion advice, horseback riding."

For all the focus on her quilt the other night, Becca had forgotten all about sewing, about how it soaked up unhappiness and nervous energy. She was already fetching the big basket she had inherited from her Michaelman grandmother, trying to think through her options on the way, but she was no tactician: an afternoon spent with Melora Ross might be more entertaining than one spent with her own thoughts, but would it come with strings like a night with Jay Supak?

When she got back from the bedroom, Melora was sitting next to the pile on the sofa, with Carny curled at her feet. Becca sat down on the other side, just as they had sat, in ancient times, on "their" bench in the Square with diaper bags between them and talked about everything. One muggy afternoon, Becca remembered, they had assessed their napping babies.

"Do you think he has the Viking's bone structure?" she had asked. "I always wanted cheekbones like Katharine Hepburn, and the Viking had them."

They decided it was far too soon to know. They moved on to Cole.

"He definitely has Niko's big fat eyelashes, that goes without saying," Becca said.

"I hope he doesn't swagger like Niko. I hope he gets Niko's brains but not his ethics. Do you think you can mix and match them or is it a package deal?"

Becca had argued, forcefully, as she did in those days, for free will, for creating one's own ethics. Melora had changed the subject.

"Where do you want to be in ten years?" she asked.

"In an elevator building. On the tenure track. You?"

"In an actual house that I sell to myself. With three or four more babies."

Now Becca pulled out a scrap of gingham, a needle and spool of thread, and a pair of small scissors, and moved the clothes to the side, the better to teach. How she loved to share knowledge.

"Ew," she said. "You smell like a bar. In Paris."

"Well, we aren't all saints like you. I like a cigarette now and again. It calms me down."

"I thought they were stimulants."

"Exactly," said Melora. "They do both at the same time. It's a beautiful thing. You should try it sometime. I bet you'd become an addict like this." She snapped her fingers.

"Not in a million years," said Becca. "Do you know how to tack?"

"Only on a sailboat."

"We're going to practice on gingham, just like I learned in socialist summer camp."

"Weren't they teaching you to overthrow the government?"

"They believed people should be useful citizens and have skills. We all learned to sew and cook *and* do Israeli folk dancing and civil disobedience."

Becca showed her how to stitch over and over into the same spot to anchor the thread, and then to take a nice even stitch inside each white square. Melora took off her shoes and wiggled her funny long toes on the coffee table.

"I get it—the gingham is like a ruler," said Melora. "Clever."

Becca pulled out a patchwork pillow cover that had been glaring at her from the basket for years, red and white in a traditional pattern called Robbing Peter to Pay Paul. They worked quietly on their respective projects. Sometimes she looked at the pattern and saw a series of overlapping circles jostling to fit a too-small space; sometimes she could let that go and see only the harmony of the bigger picture. Robbing Peter to pay Paul—she thought again of the way her mother had let slip her father's unfaithfulness. She thought of what it must have cost Doris to play the heavy all those decades; no wonder she had developed a stoop. Her father had betrayed her mother, and her mother had in turn protected Becca, had put up with Becca's years of scorn.

"Nobody's perfect," said the voice of Lew. Becca could practically hear the accompanying shrug that aimed to disarm. "Didn't I tell you from day one that they don't make 'em like your mudder anymore? Who could possibly live up to her standard?"

After a while Melora stirred. Becca was grateful for the distraction from the triangulation of her thoughts—bitter disappointment in her father, reluctant respect for Doris, her own all-consuming guilt.

"I'm about to run out of thread. Tell me what to do."

"Same thing as when you started. Tack."

"Cool. Symmetry."

"And don't bite off the thread. Use scissors."

Melora snipped off the thread and thrust the gingham at Becca. "How's my row, teach?"

"Not bad for a rank beginner with ADHD." She'd forgotten how much fun it was to tease Melora.

"This is kind of relaxing."

"So do me a favor. Next time instead of lighting a cigarette, hem."

"Is this the big secret of people who don't have addictions? They do stuff with their hands?"

"Pretty much."

"Do you think if you tried heroin you'd do it once or would you become an addict and stop working and not bother to eat and lose your lease and live in Tompkins Square and sell your body for the next fix?"

Becca smiled. "You've clearly thought this through."

"It's just, I mean—what if it's really worth it? What if it feels so much better than all the best things normal-people life has to offer? We're all going to die and be forgotten anyway."

What a relief to listen to the screwy contents of someone else's mind for a change. "Have you actually tried it?"

"I'm way too scared. I think Niko has—I mean, God, he hangs out with guys in metal bands. Okay, I'm ready for my next assignment. How about teaching me to sew on a button?"

"How have you gotten through half a century of life without knowing how to sew on a button?" Becca asked.

"There's this thing out there. Maybe you've heard of it: it's called the economy. People pay you to do what you're good at, you pay other people to do what they're good at. Everybody wins. At least that's the theory. It works better when there are two people to a household."

"Niko's still not back?"

"Let's not go there right now. I like sewing. Let's just sew."

They went through the pile—designers Becca didn't know, or knew only because their boutiques lined Bleecker or the side streets tucked into the Gansevoort meat market where once there had been secondhand stores or wholesalers. Becca's mother was a big believer in old-fashioned quality and had insisted Becca learn to recognize it, though Becca's interests had been elsewhere. Still, she knew the difference between a fully fashioned sweater and one with the sleeves sewn on by machine. The difference between real embossing and shiny raised lettering. The Gruyère and the domestic Swiss. Crystal that sang like Beverly Sills and Becca's tumblers, which came from a dusty old Mexican shop that had once been on Greenwich Avenue. They had a green Coke-bottle cast and a thousand imperfections, and more than once she had cut her lip on a popped bubble on the rim of one of them.

She and Melora rummaged through heavy cotton duck, handkerchief linen, some stretchy little exercise clothes. Jeans legs narrower than Becca's forearm, tops so loose and drapey that if she put one on she knew she would look like an armchair wearing a drop cloth. Melora pulled out a crisp cream-colored man-tailored shirt that was shy one mother-of-pearl button. They found two spares hidden in the satin label inside.

Becca got out her ancient tomato-shaped pincushion and had Melora thread her own needle. "Now tack," she commanded, and Melora said, "Aye aye, captain."

"So who came to your door with a sack?" Melora asked after a while, and Becca had never felt so relieved in all her life. She told her about Jay.

"Not that guy with the pockets? I thought you hated him."

She explained that she did and then she didn't and then she did again.

"Like the way boys are gross and then all of a sudden they aren't and then one day you wake up and they're gross again."

"Exactly," said Becca, "except that now he hates me. Everything this week is so concentrated. It felt like that after 9/11 too, right? Maybe it's always like that after a tragedy. Except when my father died and when the Viking left, it wasn't anything like that; it was just flat for a really long time."

Becca showed her how to catch the fabric while bringing the needle up through the holes in the button. Romance after so long had her completely confused, but having someone around to sort it all through with again came right back. Jay receded from view and friendship came to the fore. It seemed that the comparing of notes afterward might be the best part. She went back to her pillow. It felt great to move ahead on this one front, at least. She was about to tell Melora how grateful she was when Melora spoke.

"Speaking of your old lady pals, I sold Frieda Glaberson's house."

Becca swung around to face Melora. "What are you talking about?" she said. "I just saw her the other day. Frieda's not moving." She stretched out the word "moving" so it could fit her derision, confusion, and accusation. And she realized that while she had seen Frieda at the bonfire, she hadn't talked to her in weeks.

Melora picked up on the accusation and fired right back. "Well, tell that to my bank, which cashed the commission. Only commission I earned this year."

Standing up, still clutching her pillow cover, Becca managed to stab herself with a pin right in the pad of her thumb. She sucked the blood from the puncture and swore at the same time.

Melora knelt on the floor in front of her with a frenzy of old mothering instincts. "Here, show me. Let's wash it, and I'll get a Band-Aid."

She yanked her hand away. "What's the plan here? Kiss my boo-boo and make the pain go away?" Becca said, knowing she sounded like a petulant child; she just felt so hurt that Frieda hadn't told her, and disgusted that she'd welcomed the middle-man so deep into her life. Becca went to the bathroom and ran cold water on her finger.

She was the one who had introduced Melora to Frieda.

The boys were older by then; they'd moved on from the

baby swings. "The sixties are over," Melora had said from the sandbox when Becca tried to persuade her, for the third time, to attend a planning session at Frieda's for a big rally to protest the jail barge the city wanted to put in the Hudson.

"Ah, the favorite excuse of complacent baby boomers," said Becca.

"If this is how you entice someone into becoming an activist, no wonder all those people you're always working with are a hundred years old," said Melora. "Where do you even find these people—that one with the straight skirt up to her boobs and the one with the baritone who's really a man in disguise, I swear. If you're going to be smug and superior, just send my regrets to your precious Frieda Glaberson, high priestess of the meeting to plan the meeting for the meeting to plan the rally."

Becca pulled out her secret weapon. "You know that block of Perry Street with the Italianate houses you like so much, where you're always trying to peer into the parlors?" For all her fascination with exteriors, Becca had never worked up much enthusiasm for exposed brick or wide-plank floors, but Melora, she knew, lit up whenever she entered a parlor.

"This Frieda Glaberson person of yours lives in one of those? Why didn't you say so?"

"I buried the lede."

"Damn you, Becca. I'll go, but I'll laugh at you behind your backs all night, like a bunch of little Dutch boys with your fingers in the dikes. Mostly old arthritic fingers, I might add."

And Becca smiled, because Melora was way smarter than she gave herself credit for.

They left the boys with a fourteen-year-old girl they had found and kept secret from the other moms, because she actually liked to play Candyland and because (as Aaron had told Becca with great respect) she once kept a Hula-Hoop going for 117 spins.

They climbed Frieda's stoop, and while they waited for Frieda to come to the door, Melora opened the brass mail slot and made it talk.

"Greetings," she said in a robotic voice. "Do you come to protest? To leaflet? To rally? To picket? Are you deadly earnest? Are you holier than thou? If so, Aunt Frieda wants *you*!"

Becca elbowed her in the ribs. "Shut up. You should get on your knees and bow before these people. There wouldn't even *be* a Village if not for them."

And then Frieda came to the door, and Melora—nearly flat chested and a little wide in the hips, but lithe and leggy and always just this side of gawky—somehow condensed herself to fit Frieda's scale.

Frieda was fussing with a new plant on her windowsill. Melora walked over and fussed with her.

"Oh God," said Melora. "Don't ever plant a violet—they're like those brooms in *The Sorcerer's Apprentice*. They just keep reproducing."

Frieda was already leading Melora upstairs to her orchids, which Becca didn't even know she had. Becca stayed downstairs and let in one of the old ladies when the doorbell rang.

They watched Melora climb Frieda's stairs, ducking her head, while Frieda told her about the hand-turned posts of the banister.

"Who's the acolyte?" asked the woman. "She's adorable."

Now Melora came over to the bathroom and peeked in.

"Just checking that you're alive. Whoops, I guess that's not so funny, given everything." Melora walked away. "I'll get my stuff and let myself out," she called from the living room. "I got her a really good buyer, if that's any consolation," she called. "They totally get it about Frieda. We were even talking about calling whoever puts up historical brass plaques to put one up in her honor. I'll follow up to make sure it happens. I owe you a session…weight training, yoga, Pilates, you name it." Becca heard her front door open and close.

Everyone in the Village has an opinion, the way everyone in the south has a gun. It doesn't make any sense,
people keep saying. Islamic terrorists bombed the World
Trade Center, twice, because it was really big and it was
the house of money and the free market. Some say we kill
what we secretly wish for and can't have (and the mentally
ill have trouble with the concept of figurative language).
But what did the bomber/s know or care from hippies
singing about hearts of gold and leaving on jet planes and
rolling stones in Washington Square? Bullshit, say others.
This is the digital age, and knowledge is cheap and readily
available. Of course the bomber knew what Washington
Square represents.

The explosives were nothing special, nothing that left
a footprint or a black box. The kind of stuff used by
demolition crews, the kind that razed the Mother Cabrini
houses in Detroit, not so much fancier than the kind that
had leveled the hills of lower Manhattan in the nineteenth
century. No suspicious activity was reported that day.

What if the other shoe does not belong to a two-footed
monster? What if it's a millipede? It's so ridiculously
easy. At a certain point you really do have to rely on the
decency—or if not decency, at least laziness—of the
populace. It's when craziness meets up with ambition and
energy that people get killed.

There's little news as workers clear the rubble and inspect the buildings. The president of NYU, with its purple
logo depicting the Washington Square Arch and its campus fanning out in all directions from the Square, doesn't
look good. Parents of NYU students who've just paid the
first installment of the $60,000 annual tuition are sending

airfare to their kids. "I don't care," they reply to their children's protests, because eighteen-year-olds think they're immortal. "Get on the next plane home." Everyone has the same earworm pounding in their heads: Should I stay or should I go? They would Google the old Clash song, but there's no power.

The populace is getting educated about Adlai Stevenson, who, after failing to unseat incumbent president Dwight Eisenhower in 1956, gave a rally at the base of the Washington Square Arch; about Stanford White, who designed it; about hardware-store ingredients a determined and single-minded stranger can fashion into a pretty impressive bomb. Suspicion is centered on the hot-dog vendor. What New Yorker even sees a hot-dog vendor? It's like a farmer noticing a stone.

It will be death to tourism. Just kidding; it's the best thing ever to happen to tourism in the Village. Publicly Becca Cammeyer grieves. Privately she rejoices.

The mayor gave a press conference saying how much the city loves its tourists, how tourism makes the city what it is, how it's impossible to be a great metropolis without visitors, like the proverbial one hand clapping. The mayor has grown so eloquent, he's like Moses with an untangled tongue. He is suddenly governing in poetry, the man who usually had trouble getting his mouth around prose. The pundits are puzzled: is this the birth of a new phenomenon? Call it the Giuliani cure, except that messianic Giuliani pushed his luck too far with that bid for a third term. Everyone is watching this mayor for signs of overstepping.

All the NYU buildings and Judson Church, on the south side of the Square, were untouched but the Arch is a goner. They speculated that it was all the fillers the Parks conservators had injected to stabilize George during the renovation two years ago. Everyone was on a first name basis with Washington now, the poor overburdened man, the shy man with the wooden jaw and the unhappy face. A symbol now of—what exactly? It's hard to say until the perpetrator is identified. Please let it not be one of our own, the old-timers beg. The men who look almost like regular old men anywhere else, except for a touch of the mildly eccentric—a ring on the index finger, a beret, a pair of leather sandals hauled home from a Greek cobbler. What are we dealing with? It's unbearable not to know for so long. The evidence is so weirdly scanty. The perpetrator/s haven't left a note or a Web trail.

SUNDAY

THE GIRL WITH BRAIDS

The ground was covered with hay and surrounded by a real wooden fence like something out of a ranch, and inside were a couple of swaybacked black ponies. And the pony man. He was one of those characters from those days that straddled the late sixties and early seventies, a type the market could no longer bear—a huckster or a savior of wayward teenagers, depending on your point of view. These were the days when it was possible to be a slacker and yet run a business that could support you. The Village offered shoe stores that sold new moccasins and secondhand clothes for Halloween costumes, hardware stores with sewing notions, record stores that could feed a whole hippie family.

Becca remembered the whole Village smelling of patchouli, and most faces being half-covered by hair. Alterations of your God-given looks were limited to gobs of mascara, taming your hair by wrapping it around orange juice concentrate cans at night; you worked with what you had. The boys parted it far on the side and swept it across the front of their foreheads. The girls parted it in the middle and let it fall flat and heavy right past the tips of their eyelashes. You could see the shape of their ears through it.

The draftable ones floated down the sidewalk dirty and harmless and beatific, trying to smoke away the war, while the old Italian ladies in their lawn chairs shook their heads, perplexed, waiting for it all to pass.

Instead of saying goodbye, kids would stick out a hand and make a *V* for peace. In gym class one day they learned about trust falls. When Becca's turn came, she was nervous. The message was to trust your own, though the previous generation had sold out. But how to acquire the habit of trust? It was hard to keep her body straight, plank-like and yet let it fall, timber! But her classmates came through. She felt their fingertips on her back, let herself gently sway, lost track of which way she was facing and whose breath she felt in her hair. It didn't matter; for now she loved them all, would gladly kiss any one of them right on the lips. How sexy the world was. Even the dry trig teacher had genitals right behind the twill of his pants.

There on Washington Street, just a block inland from the Hudson, the pony man could be found in a cowboy hat and boots, wiping his sweat with a bandanna. He was missing a tooth on one side, Becca remembered, but so were a lot of people in the Village then. There might have been some kind of shack on the lot where he slept, but what she remembered was a collection of mismatched kitchen chairs that scraped through the hay to the dirt below.

He taught her to curry the ponies and to feed them carrots and chunks of yam from her hand. They were the most placid creatures in the Village. She had looked straight into their still brown eyes and they had looked right back without any demands being passed in either direction, and she had loved them for it. She hadn't even minded their big ancient-looking yellow teeth, which parted to reveal pink enormous tongues that bathed her like a warm washcloth.

She walked there after school, swinging the shoulder bag she'd made out of an old pair of Levi's, chemistry textbook and *Look Homeward, Angel* banging against her hip, and she sang a French lullaby she had learned in chorus about Maman, who's upstairs making cakes while Papa's downstairs making cocoa.

She wasn't supposed to walk through the Gansevoort meat market or along the waterfront on her way home from school, but it was the quickest route from the bus stop. Beware the butchers and the longshoremen, her mother said, rough men with blood and gristle and muscles and foul mouths, predators of schoolgirls in peasant blouses and hip-hugging jeans.

The divorce was finally done, and her mother was subletting in a big white brick building near Sixth Avenue, next stop Mamaroneck; Becca told Joycie that Mamaroneck was the

Lenape word for "snaring rich husband." Soon Becca would turn eighteen and be free to choose her own path. Every afternoon when she left the ponies she climbed the stairs and fished out the key that hung on a length of rawhide between her breasts and let herself in to her father's apartment in The Rebecca, which smelled of Barbasol and coffee cups.

Home in those days was a more makeshift, provisional thing. To Lew it was just a place where you read the paper, ate your supper, and slept. He would no more think of changing the furnishings than he would of redecorating a subway car or a deli. Modernism lived bright and big at MOMA, but the apartment was furnished tenement style, with old wooden dressers with brass pulls that rattled and drawers that swelled in July, cheap white shades that were always snapping out of reach, and an old GE fan that made a racket but didn't move much air. The pedestal sink in the bathroom had no storage space, just a porcelain lip; when she tried to set her toothbrush down, it fell in.

Mostly they managed just fine. They made a plan to take turns with the bedroom. Becca won the first coin toss and Lew let her stay. He knew how to cook three dishes: Swiss steak, Salisbury steak, and hamburgers, which he fried in a pan. So she learned to make lentil casseroles and curry and Spanish omelets, and they ate together early before he disappeared for his meetings and she did her homework and studied her lines and practiced guitar.

She took over the shopping, pretending to be an old Italian lady with a gold tooth and a string bag, and bought sausages at Faicco's, cheese at the latteria, sheets of ravioli on Grand Street. She pretended she was a chef at the CIA. Anything but a housewife.

They fought only when he came home crabby after a bad meeting. Liquor made him headachy and argumentative, and he would grumble about Doris the deserter.

Becca had friends in far worse shape. Some lived in old-law tenements with kitchen washtubs and for them a shower was a luxury experienced only once or twice—in a motel room on an overnight trip with the school glee club or a rare trip to the Jersey shore.

It was a hard time too. Becca had long assumed that the stage would be her rightful home. But the theater crowd sorted itself into factions and splintered: the Rogers and Hammerstein types vs. the Bread and Puppet types, renegades who didn't care if their stage was a proscenium or a campus lawn as long as they could open their mouths and get people to listen. Becca veered away from the posing, conniving theater girls and toward the great unwashed, the ones who were going to change the world, because from where she stood it sure could stand some improvements. But then she veered from them, too, because she loved the past that they liked to declare irrelevant. So she started to ally herself with an older generation, the women like Frieda and Camille with one foot in the Depression and the other in the sixties—willing to change the world and practical and unassuming enough to do it locally.

This was just before divorces got easy, when even in the free-love Village people felt sorry for you and whispered about you if your parents split up. She was shuttling between two one-bedroom apartments, neither of which really had room for her because, admittedly, she took up a lot of space then.

So she would get off the subway after school and run past the abandoned buildings to Washington Street, where the pony man would greet her with a tip of the dirty cowboy hat. He called everyone, even the ponies, "Chief," which annoyed some of the other vacant-lot kids who longed for a kind of attention he wasn't giving. But it pleased Becca, the way she also loved his habit of setting his fingertips on people's shoulders as if to steady them. And when little kids would come running with a nickel clutched in their fists, she would always be the one to greet them and let them choose a pony. She would hoist them up and lead them around slowly in a big circle, bits of fragrant hay catching in her huaraches.

One day when Becca had flunked a physics quiz and missed the last auditions for the spring show, *The Skin of Our Teeth*, she made her way to the lot, but the ponies and the pony man were gone. The wooden fence was being replaced by fresh plywood to seal off the lot. A bulldozer was leveling the shack, and the kitchen chairs were sitting on top of a curbside pile of trash. A bale of fresh chain link was lying on the ground, along with a construction sign ready to be wired to it. It bore the city seal and the name of Mayor Lindsay and comptroller Abe Beame, the man who became a symbol of the city's nadir and its long slog back, a man with all the charm of a zero on a balance sheet.

She marched over to the chain link and stomped on it, but it was more tensile than it appeared, and as she stepped off a jagged edge she caught her calf and tore a long slice of flesh. Blood began to flow down her leg and heel and into her sandal. She made a run for it, leaving bloody footprints on the sidewalk, the sticky, coagulating blood mixing with fresh liquid blood. She got to the corner of Bethune Street and stopped, out of breath, because she didn't know whose apartment to run to. In the end, she knocked on Frieda Glaberson's door. Frieda cleaned the wound and put on ointment and something she called a butterfly bandage so Becca wouldn't have to go to the emergency room and be stitched back together.

It Girl of 1983

For Melora it was always about the real estate more than the money (though of course it was about the money too). It was about the spaces and what you could do with them. When she arrived in the city right after college, she went on house tours and into little shops that sold the wares of Finnish designers and she grew wild with hunger. Could she even have said in those days—in her nubuck boots and her punked-out hair and the kohl around her pale eyes—what she craved? It didn't matter, the craving was all.

It was the way things were put together that turned her on. You could take an enclosure, any enclosure, from a purse at Charivari to a studio apartment in a white-brick building. And it could be horrible, but the city was full of people who knew how to make it fabulous. She didn't know herself how to make things fabulous. Her talent was knowing those who did. It was the age of the tastemaker, of curators, purveyors, and producers. Mary Boone, Dino de Laurentis, the Weinstein Brothers cutting their teeth at Miramax. And sure, they were all pretentious as hell, sure they were all doing impersonations of Sid and Nancy overlaid with Meg Ryan and the head curator of paintings at the Guggenheim. The trick was never to impersonate one thing at a time, but to make yourself into a collage.

She loved the sound of her wooden boot heels smacking the granite sidewalk of Greene Street or Crosby, her man's coat with the rolled-up cuffs slapping her Guatemalan leg warmers. She kicked aside the wrappers from all the Larmen Dosanko noodle shops, the papers pulled from monster muffins, bags from the cookie people: Mrs. Field, David, and Amos, who all used to be famous.

She and Niko didn't have all their stuff yet, but Manhattan was a treasure chest and they had the key, a plastic card they

handed to the cashier, who set it in a small satisfying machine
that embossed its raised account number onto a carbon-paper
receipt. There was a year—maybe 1983 or '84—when the balance was perfect, when SoHo opened its slender bangled arms
and said welcome. The triple-crème brie of Dean and Deluca
coursed through her bloodstream, and she slipped an old hatpin
she found in a secondhand shop in the Village through the la-
pel of her oversized blazer, and the moonstone caught the late
winter light off the East River and bounced it onto her cheek.

The lofts were alight with artists. The old beige buildings on
the 500 block of Broadway were fabulous, and one day when
a client canceled she stepped into the elevator of one of them
and pushed every button just for the pleasure of seeing the door
open: Helvetica type on glass, magenta paintings through the
doors, some crazy exhibit of Lucite porcupines, and that gallery
where you took your visiting relatives from Massapequa that
was just a room full of fresh dirt. The museum with the holo-
grams way down on Mercer. There was a store called 'Zona (the
clever post-collegiate names of things: 'rents, 'shrooms, 'burbs)
where she dreamed she lived amid the Aztec blankets and the
Swedish flatware. She couldn't get enough of the incongruities.
The tan of oak set against slashes of color. Plexiglass against
slate. Grandma crochet against army surplus.

She subscribed to everything, *Metropolis* and *Wallpaper* and
Blueprint. There was one magazine with three letters instead
of a name, on paper as thick as upholstery, and it didn't even
have articles. It was all pictures, saturated colors, with a smell of
paper-plant chemicals better than cologne, and the thing cost
something crazy like nine bucks, but she bought it every month,
counting out her bills with fingerless gloves or handing over the
magic card. Pickpockets were afoot, so you kept your money
deep in your pocket with your tokens.

The sound of money was beginning to be heard crinkling
throughout the land. It was starting to distract the artists in
their lofts with no doors. And the gay boys were waking up to
find their tan skin slashed with magenta.

She was in on the money. She had the best listings. Even the Upper West Side was fabulous then. Near Zabar's was a store called Pandemonium with black lights and a counter like a general store and behind it a wall of garment-dyed T-shirts in every overlapping color on the planet Earth, and the dressing room was just a curtain and a mirror in the rear. The shirts hugged her body, which warranted hugging because she had the things in demand then: long slim legs, broad shoulders. As long as there was a flat belly between the two, the rest didn't matter; cleavage was strictly for hookers. And when spring came she flung off the boots and the tweed coat and strutted through the streets. Who needed a park? It was all about the paper and the place and your fingers touching the goods. The only pixels were on Roy Lichtenstein's giant women with the worried faces. The cornices were falling and Mayor Koch was mayor and Pat Benatar was singing on MTV.

One day, roaming the cross streets of Tribeca not long after she and Niko bought the house, she fell in love with a bed. It was called a sleigh bed and it was the most beautiful thing she had ever seen. Everything else she looked at lacked sleighness but was also charged with her desire for it. Looking back later she feared she loved the bed more fiercely and more purely than she had ever loved Niko, ever loved anyone until Cole came, maybe in the same way she had loved her pony Max before her parents gave him to her and ruined the perfection of loving that was really made mostly of craving.

The bed was the color of chestnuts just like Max, dark brown and tan held in perfect tension so you could see through one to the other. The bed felt like chestnuts too, newly fallen from the tree in her parents' backyard in Nassau County in early fall when they were still cool and moist and she used to imagine leprechauns waxing and polishing each one with a tiny chamois cloth (one of the many things she never told anyone then, when it would brand her as weird, but told anyone who would listen now, because now weird was good).

The bed curved where all other beds lacked the imagination

to do anything but be perpendicular; it curved the way the Henry Moore sculptures in Damrosch Park curved. It was made of rosewood and cherry and it was carved by hand and with simple tools so that it wasn't fussy but it wasn't crude. Melora had to hold back from rubbing against it as she circled the showroom the three times she paid it visits.

She feared it was too big to go up their nineteenth-century steps. She made a special trip to Franklin Street with a heavy-duty measuring tape from work that sank like a rock in her pocket. She brought a notepad, one of those French ones with the graph paper that closed with a length of elastic riveted onto the back. She prepared in advance, remembering that length was followed by width and width by height. She even tried to measure the stairwell but couldn't figure out how or where.

In the showroom she took off her coat and set her bag down and crouched on the wide black planks of the floor. The saleswoman, who was really a set designer, was amused by Melora, and Melora got flustered because even the bed was hard to measure, which was one reason she loved it. The tape measure kept thundering and folding in on itself. She wrote down the dimensions, forcing herself to do it far more slowly than she usually did things. Then she walked home feeling a little closer to having the bed now that its biggest dimensions were written in her own handwriting. She walked up a forlorn stretch of Sixth Avenue, the tape measure banging her leg.

Niko was getting sick of the bed and he hadn't even seen it. He was raking in bucks. He'd signed two major acts, one a West Coast band he said was going to be even hotter than the Red Hot Chili Peppers, who were about to be hot. He was traveling with them all the time, ten-city tours and twenty-city tours and London and Tokyo. Melora's idea about the bed was all mixed up with her ideas about sex and making babies, which she was aching to do. Lots of babies. She pictured the bed on a Sunday morning, not a real Sunday morning but a made-up one full of babies and toddlers and all of them laughing and meandering around the bed and playing peekaboo in the covers. It would be toasty and they would all sing "Flee Fly Flo" and the "Name Game" and "John Jacob Jingleheimer Schmidt." And all the babies would have beautiful names, simple as a slab of slate; when you had a husband with a long Greek surname, you had to curate the names very carefully.

When Niko finally okayed the purchase of the bed pending her measurement of it, she made a deal with herself: she would hustle harder and do more homework and go to the community board general meeting every month and read *VillageWeek* cover to cover and make ten cold calls every Monday morning. She hustled home. She had work to do.

In the end the bed couldn't make the turn in the staircase from the parlor floor to the second floor. There was a recess in the landing wall known as a coffin turn, one of those crazy details that wasn't on the realtor test but that she'd learned years ago on a house tour. In the nineteenth century people died at home in their beds, and the builders took this fact into account. One of the many things she hated about the nineteenth century: people spent their whole short lives planning their death.

The delivery guys backed up, set the bed back down in the living room, mopped the sweat from their faces, hitched up their blue delivery-guy pants and tried a different angle. It wouldn't clear. The only saving grace was that Niko was on the West Coast.

Maybe the delivery guys weren't trying hard enough or weren't smart enough to find the right angle. She remembered her father making a furtive gesture occasionally when she was a kid, to maître d's and once to a ski instructor whose class was full and then suddenly not full. By now she had a wallet and she dug it from her purse. She rolled up two pairs of twenties and slipped them into each guy's hand.

So the guys hoisted it one more time with a pair of grunts, but their hearts weren't in it.

"Sorry, ma'am," one of them said.

"Fuck," she said. "What the fuck am I supposed to do now?"

She felt like a flamingo, way too tall and gangly and colorful and she swore her limbs were bending in the wrong direction as she tried to fit into a smaller and more sensible package.

And the other guy said, "Seems to me you got two possibilities. One: in through the window, if you've got a double window. I recommend piano movers with a crane."

When she made a face, the one full of questions and dismay that often made things happen, he said, "Try the *Yellow Pages*."

"What's the second possibility?" she asked.

"Cut off the feet," he replied. She didn't gasp. You always kill the thing you love the most. Was that an expression or had she just made it up?

She had them leave the bed upended in the living room, or rather in the living room and dining room because it was too big for one or the other.

She ate Chinese takeout upstairs on the old bed that night, because she couldn't bear to look at the sleigh bed and because Niko wasn't home to tell her not to eat on the bed. The chow fun noodles were stuck together and there were too many scallions.

She still felt queasy in the morning when she hauled out the *Yellow Pages* looking for piano movers. In the end she called the showroom and paid them a lot of money to take the bed away. When Niko came home she waited for him to ask about the bed, but he had other things on his mind, so she brought it up casually over dinner, saying only that she'd changed her mind.

The queasiness turned out to be pregnancy.

When she started bleeding and having pain, the obstetrician told her the embryo had implanted itself in the lining of her fallopian tube, and Melora cried because her own body turned out to be the one space she couldn't make fabulous. This happened in approximately one percent of pregnancies, and Melora, she said, was one of the lucky ones because her body aborted it quickly. She was still young, so very young, said the doctor in her SoHo office with the jutting wall and the little postmodern square cutouts and the Thomas the Tank Engine table. Melora put her hands on her belly, as flat as usual.

A year passed before she conceived again. The West Coast band's first album went gold but its second album didn't. Melora made a few sales but never made it into the top twenty of the firm. In her ninth month with Cole she dreamed one night that she was swimming in an ice-cold pool and woke up to realize her water had broken, and in the jumble of waking Niko, who, thank heaven, was home and fumbling for the phone, she remembered distinctly thinking, *It's a good thing I didn't buy the bed, because this would have ruined it.* Cole was born a week early the following morning. It was a Sunday, and the nurse at St. Vincent's set him on her lap in the bed and she sang "Cole, Cole, bo b'oil, banana fana fo f'oil." All the passageways inside her ached, even her throat. They never tried for another child.

Please, Mister D'Agostino

The reporters had stopped calling, Jay wasn't speaking to her, and she had seen her mother, so early Sunday morning Becca decided to hang the phone up once and for all.

It rang so soon after that she thought it was a fluke of the wiring. She said a skeptical hello.

"Get yourself over to D'Ags on Bethune right this minute," said the girlish voice. "I don't care if you're still in your jammies with your hair all mashed. I'm going to save your life."

"What the fu—, Melora," she said. There was a time when life had been like this, when the sun rose in the morning and she stirred her oatmeal on the stove and a call from Melora set the day sparkling and spinning, and she was nudging Aaron awake for an adventure with Auntie Melora and Cole.

She threw on clothes and unmashed her hair and went out, feeling she was doing the moonwalk over to Bethune Street— not sure whether her movements were taking her forward or backward. Unless Melora had found a bag of cash or the chair of the New School history department was holding a contract for a teaching post, Becca couldn't imagine any way that Melora could save her life.

She found her standing on the corner, a yoga mat in a bag slung over one shoulder, her big soft pocketbook over the other.

Unlike many Manhattan supermarkets, which were shoe-horned into residential buildings with cul-de-sacs and panhan-dles to work around the elevator shaft and lobby, D'Agostino's was spacious and well laid out. Becca loathed it. It was the kind of place where people like Melora spent their money. It had an overactive electronic door that always opened when she passed by on the sidewalk. She suspected it was programmed that way to lure people in.

Melora put a finger to her lips and tiptoed to the recessed

entrance with a grin on her face. Becca peeked inside past the Halloween decorations. It was dark, as if no one had told D'Ag's the power was back. "Here, take this," said Melora, handing her a big nylon tote that said Aveda. "We're going shopping."

Melora made a gentle pushing motion with the flat of her hand, and then tiptoed her fingers forward, a demonic smile on her face. The door was ever so slightly ajar.

It dawned on Becca that she was proposing they loot the store. Becca opened her mouth to state objections: it was eight in the morning; she had no money; she hated Melora. "You got me out of bed to steal?" said Becca. "You're sick. You want to be on *Eyewitness News* tonight, be my guest. I've had my day in the spotlight already." The six women flashed across her vision. She was learning to live with them like a cluster of floaters. She handed back the bag and started walking, wanting to go home and shower Melora Ross off her. She turned back and hissed, "And aside from being illegal, it's immoral."

"Let's just go in and take a peek. Tell me you never fanta-sized about winning one of those sweepstakes where you get to wander through a supermarket filling up your cart. We don't even have to take anything. We'll just pretend."

"How do you know alarms won't go off?"

"Duh. I go through other people's doors for a living. Alarms go off when you unlock the door or pick the lock, not when you walk through a door someone's left wide open."

"How do you know no one's inside?"

"It's a gamble. I've been standing here twenty minutes trying to look busy and not a soul has come or gone. If anyone were in there, they'd have a flashlight and I'd see the beam, right?"

Becca remembered. It was always like this with Melora, the chipping away, the seduction. If only she had eaten breakfast first and slept well enough to reason clearly.

Melora gave the door a gentle push. It opened right up. Becca slipped inside behind her. She pressed herself against the bit of unwindowed wall next to where they sometimes put out samples of fruit under a plexiglass dome: a cube of cantaloupe on a toothpick. On the rare occasions she came into this store, she always took two, on principle, to compensate for the crazy prices. Becca could smell Tom's toothpaste—fennel—drifting down from Melora's mouth, and she felt the way she always felt beside Melora: like a tree trunk.

"Doesn't sound like there's anyone here," Melora whispered.

"How do you know?" Becca whispered back. "There's a stock room downstairs. Once I took Aaron to pee in the bathroom down there. Maybe all the managers are having a meeting down there and it's just about to break up."

"When did you turn into such a nervous Nelly? Didn't you ever shoplift some little tchotchke when you were a kid?"

"That's beside the point entirely."

"Ooooh…that means you did! Tell me your story and I'll tell you mine while we take a little tour."

"Let's at least get away from the windows," Becca whispered. That was how they began tiptoeing down the produce aisle, with all the kitchen gadgets up above dangling from hooks.

Needing and wanting: how the borders ran together for most people. She had tamped down the wanting so successfully, for so long, that her frugality had cut ruts in her brain, right through the pleasure centers. It was kind of thrilling to be in an empty, unlit supermarket. But she had no desire to loot.

The Rebecca had replaced an earlier structure on the site. She had once gone to the Buildings Department and looked up the records. It had been a two-story frame dwelling, erected and owned by one Eliezer Wagner, merchant. Becca often imagined being his wife. Had she lived in the 1820s her needs would have been meager: a roof; a cooking fire and fuel to feed it; a frock, bonnet, and pair of sturdy shoes; some relatively clean water and a jug; a backyard garden; maybe a pig or a goat. That was her ideal. Not to grab like her mother or be a slave to fashion like Melora.

Becca had shoplifted from a long-gone deli on Hudson Street, twice, but she had no intention of giving Melora the satisfaction of knowing this. A pack of Juicy Fruit and a box of Good & Plenty. She could still smell the licorice and the wet cardboard from tilting the candy into her mouth. All the neighborhood kids had egged each other on. She knew even then it didn't make it right.

"Beads from the bead store," said Melora. "They were my starter drug. I went on to those tiny ceramic horses glued to a cardboard base. I swear it seemed like the local merchants were begging for it, putting all those shiny irresistible things right at a kid's finger height."

They were wandering up the carpeted aisle with the cleaning products and the paper goods. Becca had no dishwasher. She cleaned everything, including herself, with Dr. Bronner's peppermint soap, which she bought by the pint. She could make a roll of aluminum foil last for half a decade.

What she completely forgot was that where there are cleaning products, there is also one product she could not do without. She had to feed Carny. There had been a time when she bought him only wet food. Then she had begun adding dry food. Then she had gradually shifted the proportion of wet to dry. She had to mush the two together to get him to eat the dry. Morning and evening Carny gave her the baleful bloodshot eyes.

There was half an aisle of dog food staring at her, fancy new brands whose names she didn't even know how to pronounce. Premium versions of the old brands. Color-coded diets for puppies and overweight dogs and older dogs.

She looked in every direction, but a supermarket lets you see only what it wants you to see. She tried to listen harder, but once Melora stopped talking about the blond mane on her favorite horse, there was absolutely no sound, not even out on the street. The aisle was extremely well stocked—can nesting atop can, sacks of kibble stacked like sandbags.

The five-dollar bill in her pocket was starting to fray from her constant fingering. She ran her hand across a row of Purina cans, their paper labels smooth and taut against the aluminum.

She tried to think this through. She would buy the right number of cans and leave the money at the cash register with a note. Or she would write a check; she still had a little in her account. No, she wouldn't write a check. Then they would know she'd been here. She would ask Melora for a loan. No, she had a rule about not being beholden.

She aimed at the basic Purina and grabbed a can of beef, Carny's favorite. Not the overweight-dog formula or the older-dog formula. This had to stretch. She slipped it into the bag and slung the bag over her shoulder. Melora didn't notice.

She didn't feel bad. She felt great. She had to work quickly. She was so hungry and her cupboard so bare. This snooty store had been their enemy for so many years, gouging all her people, all the real Villagers on rent control.

She circled back to the previous aisle: oils, soups, tuna, ethnic, and Goya, glorious bean-bagged Goya products. Plastic sacks of black beans, white peas looking up at her with their single perfect eye, tiny orange lentils and burgundy kidney beans like semiprecious stones after a week in a tumbler. Versatile. Cheap as dirt. Life expectancy of decades. Every culture's cheap protein matched with every culture's cheap starch—kasha, bulgur, masa harina. So compact and concentrated. She always had a bowl of legumes softening on her counter. Just add good, free Croton water and a little seasoning. As long as there was Goya, she would survive.

She took only one of each. The happy motion of loading up a bag without first consulting a careful shopping list was like a hit of nicotine or pot. Yesterday's conversation about heroin, which had seemed irrelevant to her life just yesterday, came floating back. Her priorities flipped and now she wanted pantry goods, though she didn't have an actual pantry. She took a Hellmann's mayo. She took one of those nifty oversized juice boxes of chicken stock. Venturing to new aisles, she took Corn Chex because they had such a nice toasty flavor and the cut-rate market on Fourteenth Street where she usually shopped didn't stock them. She took a pack of pink, yellow, and purple sponges with long colorful lives ahead of them before they all turned the same muddy shade of gray. A can of pineapple juice.

She was just rounding the corner heading to the baking aisle when Melora finally appeared. "Oh, Jesus," whispered Melora. "You've got a weird gleam in your eye." Her gaze moved down to the bag, which Becca had set down on the floor. It had points sticking out in all directions. She could ward off a mugger with a single swing.

"You were right," said Becca. "You saved my life."

"Rebecca Naomi Cammeyer," Melora said, shaking her head in disbelief. "What I had in mind was maybe pinching a couple of Cadbury bars and getting the fuck out of here."

No one had called Becca by her full name in decades. She was flabbergasted that Melora had ever learned her middle name, much less remembered it. She had forgotten this about Melora. For a ditz, she paid attention.

"People like you don't loot, I don't care how much you may have it in for D'Ag's. I'm going back to my yuppie scum friends. At least they obey the law."

As Becca considered whether Melora was insulting or complimenting her, as she considered whether she, Becca, actually intended to walk out with a bag full of loot or was just play-acting, a tiny movement on the floor caught her eye. "Tell me you didn't just see something run across the—?" she asked.

The tiny movement, sensing or maybe smelling humans, turned and went the other way.

Melora stifled a scream when it was halfway out of her mouth. "Shit. Mouse." She started breathing, not slow and steady like yoga breaths, but quick and shallow, and Becca suddenly understood.

"You're doing Lamaze breaths! It's a mouse, Melora, not a breech birth."

"You're just as creeped out as I am and you know it."

And this, Becca now remembered, was the other thing about Melora. Melora always could see right through her.

They migrated up front toward the cash registers. Open space seemed suddenly safer than being squeezed in a dark aisle with a mouse. Here there was no food, just pictures of it on the cover of Rachael Ray's *Every Day* magazine. Who had a reliable system for knowing what was safe anymore, anyway?

"Hey," said Melora. "I just kind of screamed, didn't I? And no one appeared. That answers one question."

And now Becca could feel a shift in the atmosphere as they both let down their guard a little. She grabbed a shopping cart that had detached itself from its mates and went to throw the bag in. "Help me put this stuff back and let's get out of here," she said.

Melora grabbed the basket away. "I have a better idea. Hop in."

"You're insane," said Becca. "You know that, right?"

"I order you this minute."

Becca shook her head; she said, "No way."

"Afraid you can't do it, aren't you?" Melora made a stirrup of her hands. "Take off your shoe."

"No," said Becca, who had no idea if she could get herself in, let alone fit once she got there. "I'd say I'm more afraid of a store manager barging in and arresting us."

"Five more minutes. That's all I ask. This is a once-in-a-lifetime chance and I am not going to let you blow it."

"Damn you."

Every part of Melora wobbled as Becca leaned on her, making her wobble too, but the cart held steady as Becca hoisted herself in. D'Ag's had big suburban-sized plastic carts. It was surprisingly comfy inside.

"Go slow. I'm afraid I'll get nauseous. I get nauseous on swings."

"Aye aye, captain," Melora said, saluting as she wheeled Becca back to the Goya aisle. Though it pained her to let them go, Becca reached out and put all her packages back, smoothing out the bags.

"Bye bye, my lovely legumes," she said. She leaned out the other side of the basket and put back her mayo. An ancient jingle bubbled up in her and she sang about bringing out the Hellmann's and bringing out the best. Melora joined in.

Melora rounded the corner by the foil serving platters and the lightbulbs. She sped up a little on the straightaway of the cleaning aisle.

"Nauseous?" Melora asked.

Becca felt just fine. "Onward, mate," she commanded. Melora sped up. The bright jams went by in a blur. In the soda aisle Melora got a running start and stepped onto the rack at the bottom of the cart. She cried, "Up in the air, Junior Birdman!"

Becca joined in. "Who was Junior Birdman, anyway?" she asked in a lull in the laughing.

"I have no idea. I just know it's what you're supposed to say in circumstances like this."

"There are no circumstances like this," said Becca. "Proceed!"

"Please, Mister D'Agostino, move closer to meeee!" Melora sang, and this time Becca joined her; they were six years apart in age, they were miles apart in every other way, but they were both girls from the metropolitan area, and its theme songs were deep inside them.

The basket crashed into the dairy case, and once they examined it to make sure they'd done no damage, this struck them both as hilarious. Becca hadn't laughed like this in years. She had forgotten what glee felt like. She wished it could just keep coming, though her stomach muscles were cramping and her cheeks were sore and her eyes starting to tear. Every time she looked at Melora it started back up.

"C'mon," said Becca when she caught her breath. "Let's get out now while the getting is good." It took her a couple of tries, but she got herself out of the basket and started to wheel it back to the front. They passed the candy and Melora grabbed two Cadbury bars with almonds, possibly the smallest, shiniest things for sale in the whole store, and slid them deep into a compartment of her big pocketbook. Melora started to sing an old Raffi song, "Down by the Bay." Becca had forgotten all about it but the silly words came flooding back; once it had been Aaron's and Cole's favorite. The laughing tears turned to crying ones.

That's when they heard the voice, a very serious male voice with a light Caribbean accent.

"Ladies," said the man, who wore a blazer with a D'Agostino name pin, green and red and black. "You'll need to empty those bags right now and either return all the items to the shelves where you found them or pay for every item." He was standing by the display of autumn foods at the front of the aisle. He raised an index finger to a box of cornbread mix and pushed it from one side and then from the other until he got it perfectly aligned on the shelf. Becca glanced at Melora, who was bright red and shaking. Becca looked down at the carpet so she wouldn't start up laughing again. This fussy man could do whatever he liked with them. He might have grounds to arrest them, but right now it almost felt worth it.

He looked around nervously as if he were the one who had been looting. Melora seized on his distraction and held her purse wide open. He took a cursory look and didn't notice a thing.

"Here's what is going to happen. I am going to walk through the store with you and you're going to put everything back exactly where it belongs and you aren't going to say a word now or later to anyone. Understood?"

They both nodded.

Becca opened her bag. All that was left was the pack of sponges. She handed it to him, trying her damnedest to be serious. It weighed nothing. It cost a dollar nineteen.

"You don't sound sure. I want to be sure you will never say a word to anyone."

They said yes in unison.

"Now, get out of my store and don't come back."

And that was how Becca found herself in Abingdon Square in the bright morning sun, sitting on a park bench beside Melora Ross again, accepting a Cadbury bar. They each broke off one square of chocolate and let it melt in their mouths; they would save the rest for later.

A bomb: isn't that what sets all plots in motion these days? How cheesy. It used to be a mysterious empty-handed stranger was a sufficient plot device. For days everyone was bursting with questions. Why Washington Square and nowhere else? Why not the Yupper West Side? Tribeca? Is the bomber a terrorist? Is he young? Is he a he or a she or a pair or a collective? Someone homegrown or a messenger from a twisted Islamic sect whose satellite dishes glimmered in the Sahara and whose fiber optics were threaded through sand to bunkers?

Slowly answers trickled in.

It turns out everyone was kind of right and kind of wrong about the bomber, who was found dead in Montreal late last night, a suicide. He was an Iraqi national who'd been raised mostly in Canada. He was a nut job who'd read a mish-mash of American literature including Ayn Rand, Allen Ginsberg, and Saul Alinsky. He acted alone. He had a Queens affiliation. He leased a hot-dog cart in Washington Square. He had a vendor's license, and dark hair.

They found a notebook in which he wrote in narrow columns like verse, some in English, some in Arabic, script that sometimes trailed down the page and grew tendrils and leaves and sometimes an ear or a foot or a penis; another frustrated artist like Hitler and George W.

Pages are being published in the newspapers with more on the Web. He was a terrorist for the Internet age, a crowd-sourced terrorist, his head filled with comments and snippets, a collagist. It seemed even he was unsure what the Arch stood for, but he knew it stood for something that mattered to people, and maybe that was why he attacked it. He was obsessed with Columbine and other more obscure school shootings and he wanted in on the Wild West story of America. It had little, in the end, to do with Islam or Middle Eastern terrorism or virgins in heaven calling out to him. It had to do with a woman.

They had only one tiny piece of footage of the hot dog cart, taken on Monday afternoon by a tourist from Cambridge, England, who was shooting some folk singers and got him in the frame. The bomb, it appeared, was an elaborate suicide scheme for a man who was grandiose and insecure, like so many bombers, like so many humans. A man who just needed love and a creative outlet. A man with a poor sense of proportion, let alone right and wrong.

Who was he? He worked as an exterminator in Montreal, poisoning Canadian mice and cockroaches. A boy uprooted too many times by parents with a paranoid streak that was entirely understandable in swarthy people with Middle-Eastern accents in 2006. He took over the family business. Drove the white family van with the "Lay the Pests to Rest"/"Nuisibles? Non Plus" slogans inside jaunty quotation marks. When his father finally died of the heart condition that had him nearly bedridden for the last year and a half, he drove the van to New York. There were no other relatives in the old world or the new. There were no more checks or balances.

He was known as Bim, an unusual diminutive of Ibrahim. He had migraines, the kind with nausea and psychedelic lights. The hot dogs made him want to puke all the time. Like pink intestinal blockages. He reasoned: salt and fat were killing the populace already. He might as well kill them quickly; isn't it better to get pain over with fast?

There had been a bipolar girlfriend, whom he'd met in the outpatient waiting room at the McGill Medical Center where he went for his meds (during the rare periods when he went). She was (let's say for the sake of argument, for the sake of a coherent storyline) a cutter. She liked to let the drops of blood dry into balls like a line of mustard seeds so she could pry each one off with a fingernail and unstanch fresh blood. He had watched her amuse herself in the waiting room. Her mental illness was different from and yet similar to his—he forgot for long stretches that there was a body that trailed around below his brain.

Bim could have been cut off below the shoulders— that was how he felt, like a gigantic skull enclosing a brain that might otherwise burst, and then a bunch of appurtenances below of limited interest. Sometimes he would stare at his own brown hand as if it were a pigeon in the air shaft. Sometimes he raised his arm and bit his forearm just to feel the pain signal travel. He'd sit there with a mouth full of arm hair and flesh, smelling faintly of soap from the ninety-nine-cent store, and he dared his jaw to clamp down harder and harder, and he imagined figure skates and sled runners and the wood planes that sliced paper-thin layers of wood, and cheese slicers, and these images made his balls tighten and made squirts of blood pump toward his penis and he wondered if other men felt stirred in the same way.

Once he drew a lot of blood from the meaty part of his forearm. Once from the pale underside, which hurt more. He hadn't yet done lasting damage or produced a scar. He was in training to be braver. It was like calisthenics in the army.

The cutting girl had succeeded in her goal of obliteration. The drugs were a pale facsimile of what she yearned for. It happened, as it so often did, just when she was on the upswing. Just when her parents were cautiously optimistic. She's been holding down a job for four weeks, they said, their eyes bright with desperate hope. We ran into her boss at the mall and he said she's one of his best employees, always catches on fast.

When she offed herself—that was her preferred term,

Bim knew, because she used it, teased it, asked him questions built around it: *If you were to off yourself, just hypothetically, what method would you use?* She always had reports of others who had done it, in movies, books, in the tabloids. Maybe she had learned it from the tabloids).

In New York he lived in a squalid brick house in a neighborhood with no name in the wilds of Brooklyn. He had a bed in a room with three other beds and their occupants, and everyone tolerated different spices and cheap cuts of meat on the two-burner stove, and no one asked questions or offered answers.

MONDAY

KIN

Aaron was flying into JFK and Becca didn't want to miss a minute of the short visit he was squeezing in. She went down and sat shivering on the stoop way too early, yearning to feel a missing limb restored, sensation restored to skin that she thought was permanently numb. Her kin. Sometimes you needed to have kin nearby. The body she had nursed. His slightly uneven nostrils, his Viking-Ashkenazi hair.

The Viking was one of those products of his time who didn't believe in institutions, and she certainly had her doubts about marriage. She never pressed him. He left for Europe. There was a show in Berlin, a possible teaching gig. She gave him her blessing. Like an idiot. New Yorkers never go to the airport unless they have to, but she rode with him all the way to Kennedy on the train to the plane. They touched palms, lining up every finger as they stood in front of the big window watching the 747s take off. She shivered as he looked into her eyes. In the sunlight she could see the rays of yellow in his pale blue eyes, the shimmering reddish dots of his beard. He carried an old canvas rucksack with leather straps that curled up at the ends. In those days it was one of the ways to spot a European. She wanted to get down on the floor and beg him not to go, but that wasn't in the code. She had a bad feeling about the trip, though it was plain he loved her, plain they had something.

Or maybe he didn't love her, or loved her in some way she didn't understand, that didn't translate.

When she was a little girl she used to pretend the kitchen chairs were airplane seats and she'd close her eyes and grip the sides preparing for takeoff and imagine rising through the ceiling and through the tarpaper roof and flying with the pigeons above the city. It was one of the many things she'd told no one but him. She used to be so flattered by his interest. Then one day he surprised her with a huge painting of a chair at the top of a room breaking a hole through the ceiling. It was in a group show in SoHo. They called it a breakthrough, surreal and fantastic. She was the only one in the world who got it. The usual luminous whites and ivories, like whipped cream on butter on sour cream on mashed potatoes on vanilla ice cream, she had said to get a rise out of him. He promised the painting to her.

The Viking's boarding pass was in his back pocket. He wasn't wearing his Levi's. He was wearing some European brand. He gave her his brown felt hat.

"Write me," she said, taking care not to put a question on the end or to be too plaintive and emphatic and imply ownership.

"I will find the worst postcards in all of Europe. What's that funny word that means sentimental?"

"Corny."

"Only in the U.S. does emotion get mixed up with corn."

"Yes, I know. In Europe they feed it to the pigs. Sometimes we say 'cheesy' too."

She had to get back on the train and sit for an hour and a half. She stared at her reflection across the car, a sad hippie girl with braids dangling below the hat, which felt more precious than a Tiffany engagement diamond. He never went anywhere without that battered hat, with a brown ribbon and a tiny feather from a red and brown bird.

She was taking history classes then, some at Pace, some at the New School. She was refusing all help from her mother and Ben on principle, though now she couldn't remember quite what the principle was. She was working hard, waitressing and writing papers on Native American trade in the Pelhams, on Federalism, on the impact of dynamite on the development of lower Manhattan. She was in love with the city's history, so much more vibrant than the Cammeyers' and the Michaelmans'. She was playing her guitar in the Square on Saturdays. One day she was sitting on the rim of the fountain looking down at the frayed bottoms of all the bell-bottoms. She was picking out

chords to Leadbelly's "Goodnight Irene" when she felt the
strangest sensation rise up the middle of her body from deep
down, like a bubble, and the bubble was filled with nausea. She
waited for it to rise up her esophagus and terminate in a burp,
but it never did. It lodged between her stomach and her lungs.

The kernel of Aaron.

She wore the hat everywhere. When she sweated it smelled
faintly of the Viking's sweat. Then the smell faded. One day
she was riding the M11 and set it on her lap. She fell asleep and
missed her stop and when she got off she no longer had it; it
must have slipped onto the floor under her seat. She called the
MTA and even went to the lost and found at the depot, but the
hat never turned up. She went to the gallery where the flying
chair had hung, but a new exhibit had replaced it and the man
who ran the gallery wouldn't tell her anything because, he said,
she was no relation to the artist. She wanted to say, *But I'm his
muse; he told me himself.*

The Viking never knew. He had already left for Europe and
was supposed to come back in a month. What, really, were her
options? She could have told him, a boy with a six-month student visa and generations of expectations heaped on him. Or
she could do what she did, which was simple: front-load the
problem and hope it goes away later.

Peter—the hard one, the male member, the one who pe-
tered out and left her with a baby in her belly, one part Becca
and one part Viking. Every time the baby kicked or banged
its fists on the muscled lot line of her stomach, she imagined
the two sets of genes duking it out. She feared this baby and
adored it in advance, and cried because it would have no real
father or grandparents, but it would at least be rich in women.
Joycie organized the shower and was her Lamaze coach. Frieda
and Camille, still healthy and active then, were perfect aunties,
Frieda providing the crib and Camille the puppets.

When they finally cut her open to get the baby out, they
handed her a boy with white eyelashes and blond curls, and he
was like one of those shimmering theater fabrics that might be

hot pink if held one way but orange if held another. She gathered him to her and said, "Looks like you and me against the world." She called him Aaron because she liked the wide-open sound of it; most boys' names have a seal you have to break. Aaron because he spoke for his brother Moses, and Aaron because she read in the baby name book that it also means pregnancy. And Aaron because it was a name with a 2,000-year-old history.

The day she found out the Viking was dead and probably had been dead for a while, she thought, *More power to you.* There weren't a lot of guys like him around anymore. Their particular affectations had gone out of style. The ones who modeled themselves on the most dissipated antiheroes they could find. When you broke on through to the other side, you damaged your brain. Or it turned out there was no other side, just this planet with its usual pulls. She never did LSD with him. She held down the fort.

Goodbye is too good a word, babe, but he had never even said fare thee well.

The letter was in the mailbox on a Thursday when she was on her way to take Aaron to his afternoon cooperative playgroup. She noticed the stamps first, each with the impassive face of an unfamiliar queen above the word Sverige. At the bottom of the stoop she positioned Aaron in his umbrella stroller to face away from her, and she sat down to read the letter she had trained herself to stop wishing for and the one she trained herself to stop dreading. The handwriting was European, straight up and down, a seven with a slash through it and *P*s that made her think of soldiers in plumed hats. It was hard to believe the Viking's parents were real and not the cardboard cutouts he used to describe and occasionally paint before he smoothed them even further into nearly pure abstraction. The letter was very short.

Dear Miss Cammeyer,
We have found your name on an unmailed postcard among

the possessions of our son Peter. We do not know how well you knew our son. We are very unfortunate to tell you that he died in an auto accident in Germany.

Yours truly,

Mr. and Mrs. S. Malmqvist

She gave Aaron an extra hug when she dropped him off, though he was only two and wouldn't yet miss a father he didn't know he had and didn't know he was entitled to. She had an oral presentation to prepare but she ran to the library and pulled the big green guides to periodicals and sat in the crypt piecing together the death of her one great love, the father of her only son, at the perfect Christ-like age of thirty-three on the autobahn outside Berlin. She requested microfilm and scrolled through reels until her hand grew sore. She finally found one obit in a Swedish newspaper called *Dagens Nyheter*. It called him an abstract painter who had shown in Berlin and had work in the permanent collection of a regional museum in southern Sweden. It said he was survived by his parents, an uncle and aunt, and two cousins.

She leaned her head on the back of the library chair and closed her eyes and cried. If she had told him, he might have been more careful. He would have loved Aaron, would have given Aaron things she didn't have to give. She knew the name of the gallery in Germany. She knew the name of the town where his parents lived. She could have found him if she'd tried. She could have written or splurged on a long-distance call.

He might have become a kinder, more grounded Viking. They might have settled in together. He would have built the floor-to-ceiling bookcases with the sliding library ladder he had talked about. He would have helped carry the stroller down the steps sometimes; raising a child alone in a fifth-floor walkup bordered on the masochistic, as her mother liked to remind her. He might have become famous. She might have had time to keep up the acting or the singing or the activism. He could be sitting on the sofa tonight. They could have a TV and a good stereo. They could have traveled every other summer to Sweden, where Aaron would have played with the neighbor children. Oh, Lord. There were relatives. Maybe Aaron had some second cousins.

Aaron grew into an imaginative but fearful kid. Wouldn't sleep when he had a penny-sized hole in his window screen. "The bats will get in," he said. "Wolves." She bought a length of wire mesh and made patches—painstaking, finger-pricking work. Then he started calling her in to the bedroom in the mornings. "See?" he said, pointing to each smudge on the upper pane, where there was no screen. "Lick marks. Snout marks."

She said, "But we live on the fifth floor."

He said, "Wolves are agile. What's to stop them from climbing the fire escape? I bet they smell all your herbs growing out there."

He had the vocabulary of a professor and the staying power of a DA. She brought the herbs in to the kitchen table, where they withered. Still, he read everything about wolves in the library children's room after exhausting the library at school. Then he did a school report on the bubonic plague, and his attention turned to pigeon poop. He refused to set foot in Abingdon Square, despite the good black swings; pigeons roosted above in the sycamores, and the dark-green benches were light green and chalky with droppings.

As per the suggestion of the school psychologist, he drew giant corrals on construction paper, and labeled them—mammal, reptile, insect, bird—then filled them with all the scary animals.

"It didn't help, Mom. It made it worse. I just wanted to think of other stuff and draw other stuff."

So Becca had marched to his school to have a talk with the psychologist. There were two chairs facing the psychologist's desk. The woman moved the second one off to the side of her tiny office and made a point of telling Becca she could use it for her coat and bag. The husband chair.

The psychologist had said to give it a week or two before trying to assess the success of the corral exercise and of all the talks she and Aaron had been having during lunch period.

"It takes a little time to move on. I'm not a believer in big miracles, but I am a believer in small ones. Baby steps are all."

"Move on from what?" Becca asked.

The psychologist sputtered.

A Seven-Minute Vacation

In the morning Aaron neatened up the sofa where he'd slept and looked around the room. He was struck by how tightly packed her clutter was. Many books, all of them read, so their contents filled the living room and also her brain. Tchotchkes, mementos, photos. Of him mostly, and him and her. Her and him. Clay pots from Greenwich House Pottery. Drawings even, slowly sinking onto the bookcase, dusty where they buckled. When had he last made a drawing?

He called to the bedroom: "I'm just going out for a little while—stretch my legs."

"Sure," his mother said, coming out in her blue bathrobe, not sure at all.

She seemed older. Not in the face—she had one of those faces that weathered well. Lots of cheek, Polish peasant. How so then? Like one of those big wood porch chairs that sit low—what were they called?—left out for too many winters. Creaky, sinking into itself. A peg come loose on one side.

He took the old steps two by two. Dust bunnies stirred as if they wanted to stretch their legs too. Outside, few signs of week-old tragedy except for a slight hush. Like a minor holiday. He checked his watch: 8:10. Parents hustled little kids with big backpacks out the door. Grabbed their hands. He found himself heading east. He still liked the feel of a New York sidewalk under his shoes. Tenement, row house, row house, row house, restaurant. A new one since he'd been gone, but he couldn't remember the old one. Never one for that kind of detail.

He found himself at the site. No, that was disingenuous. Feet don't walk themselves. He maneuvered through a small crowd. Questions and statements and shaking of heads: Oh my God, it's so massive. Who the fuck would? Why the hell can't they? When in the name of God will?

He told his mother he was just stretching his legs and then he'd come home and they would have breakfast and catch up. But the park beckoned; it always had. And he needed to see it alone. Even alone her voice rang in his ears.

Funny how names stick. The Draft Riots. The General Slocum. The Triangle Shirtwaist. 9/11. Now the Arch. Where were you when the Arch came down? Funny word. Cats arch their backs, shoes have arch supports, heaven was supposed to be populated with archangels. The world was fucked up in a million ways but thinking about them all at once doesn't help the world and it doesn't help you.

He reached the front: no unauthorized entry beyond this point; shiny yellow caution, caution, caution. He decided to ration his looking. A superstition, but he wasn't sure what he was warding off. West side of the park first. Things were intact here. This was good. Why then was he disappointed? Had he come for a show, a shock? The enormous trees, the shabby lawns, the diagonal paths, the baby playground with the sandbox and the bucket swings like big black rubber diapers where his mother had retied his red sneakers and wiped his face with the damp washcloth she always carried in an ancient baggie, though all the other mothers had nifty containers of diaper wipes. All the other mothers—there was a time when he would have tried his luck with any of them. The concrete mounds. Other kids had woods and streams; he had mounds. His mother was queen and he was king when they stood atop the mounds and swept their arms out, declaring the Village their domain. Oedipal Aaron, they should have called him.

They were trying to tear down the mounds, she'd told him, when? A year ago? They (the other they, the good they) held rallies to save them. He moved to Costa Rica.

The sky was gray or white, hard to tell which. Nothing happening—that's the way it went. Most of the time nothing happened, and then a cataclysm, and then back to nothing.

He let his eyes go to the middle of the park, to the Arch and the fountain, saving the best for last—the best, meaning the worst, a glimpse of the damage from the bomb that missed his mother by a half-hour.

A week had passed, but the crater was still bad. Fluorescent orange netting making a huge pen. A pen full of slabs of white marble, but blackened like the back of a fireplace, facing this way and that. What was the expression? Willy nilly? Pell mell? So large; it's hard to remember the scale of things when you're away from them. A luxury, in a way—being near enough to the actual Square so he didn't have to reconstruct it in his mind, from his bad memory. In the crater, tubing and tangled wiring like roots of enormous trees. It threw off his sense of balance to look for the Arch and not find it, like being high and forgetting how to do a simple sum. In pieces on the ground. That was a lyric from a song. What song? Egg and dart motifs, a chunk of eagle wing, the uncanny words of Washington from the top of the Arch still readable: "the wise," "hand of God," and the one getting all the play in the papers: "to repair." He'd read about it on the plane. Oh God—he recognized a leg, in breeches. George Washington's femur and tibia and fibula, or was it tibula and fibia? A marble leg, but still. He started to sweat and thought he might vomit. No food in his stomach since the chicken burrito on the plane, soggy tortilla underneath. What kind of wuss was he? All he needed was to faint. He leaned on the police-blue sawhorse, but the wood was splintered and the legs wobbled as much as his.

Next the shrine, or shrines. Six separate ones run into one big one, big as the Macy's flower show. Every mum and carnation from every Korean deli in the Village. He could smell their perfume and the chemical burn from the bomb—the best smell and the worst, both going into his nostrils. His mother's photo of the women, enlarged and laminated (larger than life, large as death)—smiling, hefty, made up, definitely Southern; you'd want to call them ladies even if you never used the word.

The crowd around him—what brought them? Were they here for the women? He heard Southern accents; maybe all the city's South Carolinian expats were here in solidarity. Or were they here for the Square? Did they know the park the way he did, hold a proprietary lease on it from years spent within its borders, did they know the pebbly surface of the chess tables and the whispers of the dealers: smoke, smoke? How many had their first kiss here or threw their best friend from the granite ledge of the fountain accidentally-on-purpose? Oh Lord, what was the matter with him? You didn't have to pass an entrance exam to be entitled to grieve. But he wasn't grieving. He wasn't even sweating anymore. Nothing's happening for me today, he told himself. I am jet lagged. Some days are like this. You go to the white-hot center of tragedy but your heart remains cold. It's fear that does that, fear that insulates so well. Fear like asbestos that protects from the heat but makes tumors grow.

She always did have good comic timing, and never did work with much margin. She pushes the button on the tourist's camera. She leaves, a bomb explodes.

Why then could he not focus on the incredible good fortune? Why did he keep replaying the scene to match the way he thought the world worked? The smiling tourists in their make-up walk away and the queen of Washington Square makes some kind of insane supreme sacrifice, goes down with the ship while standing on the prow of the mound. What did this say about him? Was he one of those monsters like the celebrities who get interviewed periodically and let slip something no one is ever allowed to say: I kind of understand where Hitler was coming from, or I believe that now and then a woman deserves a slap to the face? One of the James Bonds said that. The sexy Scottish one, or was he Welch? No, that was Richard Burton. Not that he, Aaron, was a celebrity. Hardly. But his mother kind of was.

But she was home safe, sipping her coffee in the chrome and vinyl chair that belonged to the grandpa he never knew, like the father he never knew. No, he shouldn't go there, he wouldn't go there, it never helped to go there. He pivoted his thoughts back to her. Same old blue bathrobe. It could be on the National Register of historic bathrobes. Not quite safe—who would ever feel safe again?

The thing was, he did feel safe standing here outside the Square, because here he was, standing. It was hard to refute his standing, all parts in working order, his feet in their Costa Rican sneakers wide enough to support his vertical self. How odd the way humans can balance all day long on these small bases. How odd the way our arms hang down without our hands filling up with blood and popping from all the pressure. Amazing that we translate the gas of our thoughts into words that we push out of our mouths and that others seem to understand. Who came up with these systems?

A woman (not a lady) in rimless glasses walked by at the western corner and looked familiar. She nodded and he nodded. Math class? Day camp at the Fourteenth Street Y? He steered clear of nostalgia the way other sons tried to avoid their parents' diabetes. A whole industry out there, his generation reconnecting online when they'd barely had time to lose each other. He wasn't ready to bump into his former selves, too much like his current self. He knew all he could manage already, and there was no room to stuff more past into his present. Two exceptions: Camille, of course, and Frieda. He would go over to Frieda's. She would want to look at him and *qvell* and feed him rugelach, and there'd be Frieda-brand hell to pay if word got back that he was here and didn't come.

His mother made a living in this park, from this park. The Arch her base camp. Without this park, no living. Did that mean she would not live? And yet she did—live, that is, sipping her coffee, checking the clock on the stove, the wide 1960s clock with the radiating lines instead of numbers that amazingly still worked (but then it wouldn't have worked with the power out, would it?, though the stove ran on gas; he would figure that out later, after a nap). Just a quick walk and then they would have some breakfast and catch up.

He'd been gone so long, in Costa Rica that is, and had come in so late, so jet-lagged. Now he was exhausted in a wide-awake way in North America, under the overcast sky, here where his

native language was spoken, where he was not Ah-RONE or
AIR-en, but Aaron with a big dollop of a short *A*, the name
his mother had given him so he would always be first in line. At
the front of the barricades looking into the rubble-strewn park.
The South Bronx in the 1970s transplanted to the Village in—
in whatever name this wretched decade would end up going by
in the history books.

He'd been eighteen when the planes flew into the towers.
Now he was a couple of weeks shy of twenty-three and still
caught unaware. When would wisdom come? A thousand miles
away across seas and gulfs, and this park was still what he pictured when he pictured home. A strange thing about 9/11—it
happened to a place no one claimed and no one loved. No one
went there but tourists and employees. And somehow Villagers,
or at least he, had believed that conferred protection. He hadn't
realized it could happen in a neighborhood, on the grid.

The Washington Square Fountain. A bunch of jazz guys had
been jamming that muggy summer night of his first kiss, on
its ledge. Why did that night feel more real than this morning?
Which summer was it? Sometime in the Clinton era. Next to
him, the strap of the girl's yellow sundress kept slipping off
her shoulder, such a smooth shoulder, and each time she slid a
finger under the strap and slipped it back in place. Strap, slip,
slide: so many sexy *S* words. He made a pact: next time it slid,
he would slip it back. He waited, all the way through a loose
performance of some standard. The strap stayed put, right over
her small bundle of shoulder muscle and her collar bone like
a stroke of calligraphy and he thought he might sizzle and ex-
plode if he didn't touch her soon.

The musicians finished the song, lifting their guitars from
their sides to let the wood and the strings vibrate. He did remember the next song, a riff on "My Favorite Things," because one of the musicians said, "Barf, what do I look like,
Julie Andrews?" and another said, "Hey, man, it's the repertoire—gotta honor the repertoire." There was a stoned, home-
less-looking guy sitting beside Aaron on the ledge, and he was

having a grand time. "Oh yeah, those whiskers on kittens," he called, slapping his hands on his knees.

Finally, the strap slipped. Aaron stuck out his hand, surprised that it obeyed the signal from his brain. He slid his finger under and gently put it back. Her skin was warm and dewy with sweat. She turned to him and smiled. They hadn't begun the evening alone together. There had been a group, some private-school kids from Friends or maybe UNIS, but the others had trailed away. He thought of his old piggy bank, the way he used to turn it upside down to count the change, and slide all the pennies off to the side, leaving the quarters in the middle. She was a shiny new quarter. Her cheeks creased when she smiled, and he leaned over and kissed one of the creases.

Then her lips were right in front of his; it was only a question of eliminating the hazy air in between. He took that newly nimble finger and tilted her face toward him. He kissed her. Her name was Layla, and what was more astonishing, she kissed him back.

He was kissing the girl with the name of not just any ordinary song, but the longest and most beautiful in all of rock and roll, and when it came on the radio, back when everyone listened to the radio, all through the city in loading docks and Szechuan restaurants and drug stores he imagined everyone stopping the way he always did, taking a seven-minute vacation to hear the whole arc of a love affair.

The stoned guy said, "Go for it, man." He and Layla smiled in the middle of the kiss. He'd never thought about that—a smile and a kiss, two separate things happening at once. He could feel their lips part in unison, so effortless, and he had to admit there was a moment in the middle of the kiss when he considered this concept of actions that were usually separate happening at the same time, and standing now at the barricade he smiled because he remembered the first such example that came to him during the kiss: when you fart while swimming, the way the bubble rises up through your swimming trunks in such a cheerful, odorless, interesting way.

It was hard to find the fountain without the Arch to lead you there. His mother had once called the fountain the planet's out-ie belly button. He couldn't remember what the ledge looked like: granite or marble or concrete? The Parks Department had wanted to move it to make it line up with the Arch. Another evil plot by NYU, according to his mother. But now, no Arch and no fountain. A crater at the center of the center of the universe. There had been a huge block collection in his cooperative nursery school, and if you cooperated with your classmates you could make a giant arch if you knew the secret about placing the keystone at the top, which his mother had taught him. Would they be able to put the Arch back together, and would it be the kind of broken thing that grows stronger or the kind that's never quite the same?

He thought he heard someone call his name, tentatively, a young man's voice, a local voice—the short *A*. He turned to see a tall, thin boy—guy, man, dude—whatever name someone around his own age went by these days. Handsome in a hipster sort of way, black tousled hair and a couple of days' growth of beard, the sort that would somehow always remain a couple days' growth of beard. The energy that went into cultivating images here could power all of Central America. And then Aaron placed him.

"Cole?" he said, equally tentative. Confused, because Cole was the best friend, his first friend, the one he had pushed off the fountain.

His first friend, the prototype for friendship, not a school friend but a playground and sleepover friend, the friend who straddled the period between the baby playground and the unrenovated big-kid playground. Kids in Washington Square were still unrenovated then, too, brutal and primitive, organized onto sides like the tin soldiers at the Forbes Gallery—the working-class Italians, the striving Italians, the Jewish Jews from the Village Temple and the intellectual secular Jews from Little Red Schoolhouse, the private-school kids from north of the park with their nannies. If you had a best friend it was better; you could be your own platoon, the half-Jew with the Semitic face and the white Nordic eyelashes allied with the half-Jew with the Greek features—another mom in the playground once called them a black-and-white cookie, and then that became their signature. Aaron liked the chocolate and Cole liked the vanilla, so on the best days, when they walked home from Washington Square all cool from the sprinkler, they could sometimes talk their moms into buying them a cookie to split at Rocco's on Bleecker Street. Whenever he heard the term "sweet talk," that's what he saw; that's what he tasted.

And then puberty came, and the alliances shifted again, the kids splintering into a dozen schools and a hundred cliques and factions, each practically with its own national costume and dialect. By the end of elementary school he and Cole had been siphoned into universes so separate they rarely saw each other. But the mothers were part of the equation too. There had been bad blood. Can blood start out good and go bad?

"Oh God, I was just thinking about you and there you are. I just flew home from Costa Rica, but it's like the magical realism migrated up here. I haven't seen you since I packed up the Ninja Turtles." Where was all this blabber coming from? All those dry, silent hours of travel, it was like the words had backed up.

"Well, it's not so weird to see me here. I'm in law school." He gestured toward NYU. "I didn't land very far."

"Were you here when—?"

"I'm almost always here, but, no, I have an apartment in Astoria," said Cole. "My uncle's building. I was holed up there, studying." Aaron rewound, vaguely remembering a visit to Cole's grandma in Astoria.

"Nothing dramatic like your mom," Cole added. Aaron could feel questions wanting to emerge from Cole.

"Remember when we tried to catch a squirrel over there?" Aaron said. He pointed toward the mounds. "Jesus. It's all coming back. I never heard any news or anything about you, all these years."

"Well, our moms aren't exactly tight these days."

"Mothers," said Aaron, shaking his head.

"Tell me about it," said Cole. "My mom's a realtor now, and as you can imagine, she's not expecting a lot of commissions any time soon."

"Oh, of course. I forgot. I saw a banner with her name, walking over. I had to laugh. I'm sure you know how my mother feels about realtors." Everyone else called their mothers "my mom." He couldn't do it.

"You mean the blood-sucking parasites tearing the soul out of the Village?" asked Cole.

"You've read her placards," said Aaron, and they smiled. "I came all the way home from Costa Rica. You know about her and the tourists, right?"

"Aaron, she is kind of everywhere this week. How's she doing?"

It felt good, in a tethering sort of way after flying through the hemisphere, to be called by name by someone who knew him when he was, what, two? three? "And your father? Is he still here too?" Aaron asked.

"That's actually a harder question to answer than you might think. My dad is kind of AWOL and my mom is freaking out. I mean more than usual."

Aaron pictured the beautiful Melora dropping things and losing things. *Melora's having a little drama today*, his mother used to say. "Not because of this?"

"That's not clear either. Let's just say it coincided."

"Mine's making a big show of being stoic. Too big."

They stopped talking for a while and looked at the rubble. More pictures of his past: a production of *A Midsummer Night's Dream* staged on the mounds, his mother explaining to him that, yes, Puck was the disk you hit in hockey but also a character; mosquito bites; those special Good Humor bars with the toasted coconut coating.

"So you're off in—where did you say? Guatemala?"

An awkward moment—Costa Rica was nothing like Guatemala. Letting it go was more polite, but it also implied the conversation was almost over. "Costa Rica, actually. I'm teaching. English and math, which is pretty funny."

"So you're really doing one of those things everyone talks about doing. Is it as good as it sounds? It's got to be better than torts and contracts."

"Yeah," he said, "for the most part it is." He pictured his students at their desks looking up at him expectantly, his striped beach towel, the fellow teachers he had started to love.

Aaron tried to remember where Cole had disappeared to after their mothers stopped being friends, but got only the fuzziest picture. "You went to Little Red, right?"

"Yeah, and then a year of home-schooling and then York Prep, which finally took. So how is your mom doing?" Cole asked. "What a weird situation."

"My mother is not one to blame herself that I've ever noticed, so at least there's no survivor's guilt."

"Whereas mine blames everything on herself," said Cole. "She probably thinks this happened because she ordered too much takeout or—I don't know—had me vaccinated."

"As likely an explanation as any I've heard so far."

"Remember the Beluga whales at the aquarium?" asked Cole.

"Actually, what I remember is the endless ride on the D train. And the big mustard and ketchup pumps at Nathan's. I really wanted one of those."

Aaron checked his watch, calculating: better to be rude to Cole than rude to his mother. Cole had been the jumpy one when they were kids, but now he, Aaron, was the one who was hopped up.

"I promised my mother I'd be back for breakfast," he began. "I wasn't even supposed to walk this far."

"I'll walk you back. My first class isn't till eleven."

Aaron hated walking down the street with people. How could he explain, given that he was a sociable guy? It was the dance. Who leads and who follows and who determines the hierarchy. But Cole looked so genuinely—what was the word for the way his face moved forward and slightly up? Desirous.

Cole really wanted to walk with him. Cole even, for a second, placed a hand on his arm. He was half Greek, not so different from Central Americans. Funny the way people in warm climates touched while people in cold ones, who could have used the warmth, didn't.

He had tried to make his world simple. He stood in front of a class, standing on a concrete floor, and he taught the children to conjugate the verb "to be." In English there is only one form of being, he told them. Yes, we are rich in many ways, but we must make do with a single concept for things and people and conditions that exist right now and those that endure. It was supposed to be simpler: to give one name to all kinds of being, but it confused the kids and, frankly, it confused him. The jet-lagged *him* that was being right here, right now, with Cole—how was he the same as all the others? And yet if those selves were so different, why was it so hard to change when he tried, when he wanted to? The being he dragged around to different hemispheres. Was Ah-Rone, the jolly, pale English and math teacher, the same as Aaron, the son of Becca Cammeyer who almost died in Greenwich Village?

"Is it weird to be back after being so far away?" Cole asked.

Aaron nodded. "Pretty much everything is weird. It's weird to stay and watch things change; it's weird to come back and see the changes all at once. The village where I teach just got a frozen-yogurt franchise."

They walked silently for a while, past Sixth Avenue.

"Hey, happy almost birthday," said Cole.

He was about to say, *How the hell did you remember?* Then it came back: they shared a birthday. "I'd completely forgotten. Same to you. You think you don't remember anything, and I don't. At least not to pull out of my brain and say, here: this is a memory. But it's all in there somewhere when you don't go looking for it."

Over breakfast he would say to his mother: So, you'll never guess who I ran into on my little walk. She liked guessing games. Maybe he'd give her a clue. Three guesses and the first two don't count, as they used to say on the playground. What would the clue be? You loathe his mother. That would narrow it down a little. Unspoken codes. Topics to be avoided. The understanding that there were two kinds of people in the world: those who were part of the solution and those who were part of the problem. The boundary was shifty. The worst thing you could do was slip from solution to problem. That's what Cole's mother had done. It was like she'd died. The kind of death so horrible it's never mentioned but hangs over everything. He'd never been sure quite what she'd done to cross over. Just knew he couldn't be friends with Cole anymore.

Cole spoke. "Hey, could I stop by for a minute? Would she freak out?"

Aaron stopped walking to look at Cole's face. They were standing in front of the Sheridan Square viewing garden. Aaron needed to understand where this request was coming from. His mother wasn't famous-famous, meaning no one had ever used him to get to her. But maybe she *was* the woman of the hour. Like a celebrity chef. It was a creepy thought, someone sucking up to him for something his mother had, was, represented. But he looked into Cole's face and didn't see anything ugly there. Just shiny black stubble, tidy. Just a guy who had been his first friend in the world.

A volunteer with rubber garden gloves and a trowel and bucket was opening the gate of the viewing garden. The sun was trying to come out and not succeeding. He could see it through the clouds over the water towers of the big buildings to the east near the Square. Big, solid buildings. The Arch had been big and solid too.

"Hey," said Cole, running a hand in front of Aaron's face. "You in there?"

"Major jet lag," he explained. It was like a bog in his brain. No cranberries, just bog. What was Cole's motive and what would be his mother's response? People, guys especially, he noticed, always claimed to be good judges of character, but he thought they—people, guys—were full of it. You can judge character after a single meeting about as well as you can judge a moth as it flies past.

Bringing Cole up to his mother's was a very bad idea, he suspected. But then again, a buffer was always welcome when you're an only child with no father, nobody to make a triangle with. Just him and her, opposite ends of a tight wire. "Sure, come up and say hi quickly. Maybe it'll do her good to have company."

When they got to the building he climbed the stoop with Cole behind him and dug out the key his mother had given him and held the door open. "After you," he said in a joking way because it felt corny to be gallant. One of the million things he liked about Central America—you didn't have to put on your irony in the morning like you were putting on socks. You didn't even have to put a pronoun in front of your sentences. A simple verb did the job.

At the fifth-floor landing they both stopped to catch their breath. "You'd think everyone who lives on the fifth floor would be skinny and fit, but they're not," he said. Then he said, "Here goes nothing" and opened the door. "Hey, Mom?"

She was just where he thought she'd be, sitting at the table with her leg up on a chair and her hand wrapped around the coffee mug he'd made in pottery class, worrying like crazy. How did he know? By the way she didn't launch into a big "where have you been? I've been worried sick. All I asked was to sit and eat a bowl of cereal with you." The same way she saw right through him, which was why he hauled Cole up here, to put something in the way, a layer of lead to protect Superman from the Kryptonite. Not that he was Kryptonite. Not that she was Superman.

"You'll never guess who I ran into." Cole poked his head in.

"Hi, Becca," he said with a little wave. "Remember me?"

Becca stared. Of course she remembered. That was her business. The woman didn't own an eraser. She gave Aaron a look too quick for any other naked eye. A shriek only Aaron could hear.

"Oh, my lord," she said slowly, tightening her robe as if she were a person with vanity. One of the many old fears in Aaron's life: *What if a boob popped out?*

"Sorry to intrude, but I've been thinking about you so much. I keep telling everyone, 'I know her, or at least I used to know her.' I tell them about that day when you took us up to the stream at the north end of Central Park and let us dig and get filthy. We found crayfish and you let me bring one home on the subway, but my mom made me throw it out. That might have been my favorite day of my whole childhood."

"That was a very good day," she pronounced, nodding her head like Gertrude Stein. It was addictive: the approval of Becca Cammeyer. Cole was eating it up. Maybe that was why he'd come.

"Would you like a cup of coffee, Cole? It will have to be black. I haven't replaced the milk that went bad."

Cole, still standing in the doorway, shook his head no.

Aaron breathed, which it seemed he hadn't done in a while. Maybe one day he would get enough wisdom not to care whether each person in his life approved of each other one. But for now, another crisis averted. He could have kissed his mother and kissed Cole on his stubbled cheek. They looked at each other and both hesitated. He imagined his mother calling out with a "please send my regards to your parents" and almost broke out laughing. He needed a nap.

He saw Cole out into the hallway. They man-hugged and then Cole disappeared down the stairwell and Aaron went in to have a cup of black coffee and catch up with his mother, who loved him and whom he loved.

Some Time Later

Playdates

On Aaron's birthday Becca marched up the brownstone stoop, remembering when there had been no stoop, just a basement entrance from the years when the houses had all been broken up into rental units, remembering when Melora and Niko had restored it, piece by piece, the two of them and Cole living in one room at a time with great sheets of plastic taped everywhere while the contractors had made it all new again. Becca hadn't begrudged them the house; she had, in fact, been thrilled to be able to hoist herself and Aaron over the back wall for playdates and sleepovers. But the more the house came back together the more the friendship had split at the seams. Niko started going on longer tours and bringing in bigger money. And Becca remained exactly the same but somehow turned into a charity case. Cole was siphoned off to private school. The playdates grew less frequent and then stopped altogether. And now all these years later Melora stopped calling, and Becca feared they were splitting again.

She peered into the wavy glass at the perfect parlor, where the antiques and the modern canvases all balanced each other flawlessly. Intimacy was a skill that took practice. She was terrified. But the bomb had changed everything, outside and inside her, and she was determined not to change back. The bomb had split everyone open, and in a funny way it reminded her of the time in the hospital, the shell shock of birth. She took a deep breath and rang the bell.

Melora was barefoot and tousled, as usual. Becca stuck out a hand in a little wave. "I hope you don't mind me just dropping by," she said. Then, before Melora had time to say anything, she gave the speech she had prepared, which was the truth but not the whole truth. "I came because of the birthday boys. I miss Aaron so, and if I'm with you, strangely enough, I feel a little closer to him, because you guys are so tied up with him in my memory. But he's in Costa Rica, and I have no idea when I'll see him next."

"Well, if it's any consolation, Cole is about a half a mile away at NYU Law, and he might as well be in Costa Rica too." She motioned for Becca to come in. "I bought him a cupcake and told him to stop by anytime all day, but not a peep."

"You heard I saw him, right?" Becca said. Melora looked stricken. "Yeah, I know," said Becca. "Sons." She explained that Aaron had been in town and run into him in Zone A. Melora backed herself onto the sofa and patted the cushion for Becca to join her.

"I want to hear everything," Melora said. "But, hey, don't I owe you some personal training in exchange for the hemming?"

"Leave me alone. I live on the fifth floor. I carry groceries."

"And how's that going for you? Feeling strong and agile these days?"

"I didn't come here to be your project."

"But I want you to be my project. I've got it all figured out. I've got nothing but time. Let's do something constructive. Do you have any weights?"

"Where would I keep weights?"

"Just as I suspected." Melora ran to the closet and reappeared with the doughnut-shaped kind that slid onto a barbell. "This is brilliant. You just hold the rings. They don't take up any space. You can stick them under the bed. You still have that crazy Victorian bed?"

"Is this some kind of empty nest thing? What's with the crazy surge of energy?" She remembered this now, the way one conversation and activity always opened into another with Melora.

"Shut up. Put one of these in each of your hands and do this. Five times. You can tell me about Aaron while you're doing it."

The weights were cold and rough. She stuck her fingers into the hole and mimicked Melora's motion, raising one in each hand. It felt surprisingly good to hold actual, physical weight.

"No, no, it's not about swinging. It's about control. About working the muscle groups. We're going to go really easy around that hip of yours—don't think I haven't noticed, strengthen everything around the bad joint. Feel that in your biceps? You're making tiny little tears in the tissue that will heal. That's why you get sore. But when all those tears heal, the bones get much stronger. You're going to hurt like hell. I'll probably hear you cursing me across the backyard. It'll start tomorrow and get worse the next day. But then you won't hurt anymore. You'll start to feel so great you won't even hate me anymore. And you're going to look better too. I am not kidding. And whenever you feel like breaking open a bag of Kit Kats, you're going to pick these up instead."

"I don't hate you," Becca said. "I thought you hated me. I called. You didn't call me back."

Melora took a deep breath. "I put the house on the market."

Becca almost dropped the weights on the wide-planked floor. "What? Why?"

"Because it's way beyond my means. Because we never should've bought it in the first place. Because I dropped a vase full of marbles and all the marbles instantly rolled into the front corner of the parlor and as you know I was sure the whole foundation was cracked, and even though it turns out it wasn't and probably if I'd dropped a vase twenty years ago the same thing would have happened, things fall apart way quicker than I can get them fixed. Because I want a super like you. I have rental envy. I'm going to be a poor New York schmo in an apartment where someone else is paid to worry about the boiler. Oh—one more thing you should know that I wasn't quite ready to announce, which is why I didn't return your calls. Niko and I are separating. It hasn't been pretty."

"I'm so sorry, Melora," she said. It was the first time she'd called her by name since they resumed speaking to each other. Now she asked the essential *W* question: "Where?"

"I'll probably sublet for a month or two in Battery Park City."

"So you're staying in the city," Becca said, feeling desperate for Melora to say yes, trying not to let it show, because old habits rise up against new intentions and her habits had taught her that it was dangerous to let things show.

"After we split the proceeds and sock away money for our theoretical grandchildren, I'll have enough for a little apartment somewhere fringey. Not Fringe Festival fringey, just cheap. I don't know—Washington Heights, Crown Heights. Are there Heights in Queens?"

"Jackson. Foodie heaven."

"Well, on a teacher's salary that'll be about right."

"Teacher? Queens? If life weren't so upside down already, I'm not sure I'd believe a word you're saying."

And now Becca watched as Melora's shoulders crept up the way they always did when she was about to put herself down. Becca would have been willing to put money on the gist of Melora's next words. Becca held up a hand to stop her. "Don't even say it. You're about to tell me you wish you were clever enough to make this up."

Melora teared up and looked so sad and abandoned that Becca found herself doing something she had done many times as mother of Aaron but hardly ever to another adult. She put her hands on Melora's shoulders and looked her in the pale blue eyes and said, "Stop doing that. You don't have to do it. You're just about the smartest person I know."

Melora cried harder and then she reached out and put her hands on Becca's shoulders. "Okay, missy. My turn. What do I want to say to you? I guess the exact same thing, except that you're so busy selling everyone else short so no one else will notice you're terrified. Don't be so afraid of change. You don't want to get stuck in amber. I've been learning a little secret, the hard way: change is way scarier before you actually do it."

As they stood there holding each other's shoulders, all the things Becca had been dying to tell a friend in person came rushing forward: not just Aaron but her mother and her father and the Arch and the dead tourists and the fiasco with Photojay.

A decade's worth of news and gossip and disaster all packed into a couple of weeks. And then a key turned in the front door lock. Melora shook her head and smiled a big mother's smile.

"Well, what do you know, Cole's actually come for his cupcake!" she said.

Becca smiled back. Cole, after all, had once been the most important person in Aaron's life, which made him precious to her. She and Melora both craned their heads toward the door.

But it wasn't Cole. It was Niko. A more sallow Niko, with broader shoulders and still-black hair but less of it, and a rolling suitcase. Becca could almost see the dull afterglow of the fluorescents and smell the Naugahyde of whatever flight he'd been on. He wore a dark, well-fitted suit with a tie pulled loose. He looked like a man who just wanted to be home and wasn't sure where home was. The keys were dangling from his finger. He'd always been a tapper. He drummed on playground benches, on the handle of the stroller, on Cole's belly. They once talked about starting a drumming circle using baby bellies for the drums. Whatever was going on between Niko and Melora, her friendships with her friends' husbands were some of the best relationships with heterosexual males she'd ever had.

They saw him before he saw them, just a second or so, so they could watch themselves register on his face. He saw Melora first, and he all but stuck his hand out to her to be sniffed to prove that he was harmless.

Before Niko hit it big in the music business, Melora and Niko and toddler Cole lived over by the river in a rented alcove studio in a building that was kind of a townhouse but more of a dump. One year they made a Hanukah party. Becca cooked a brisket and brought it over in an old cast-iron casserole in the compartment under the stroller. She told Aaron he was the only boy in the city with a heated stroller. She and Melora and Niko and the boys—somehow the math worked out just right.

Niko made what he called his special Greek-style latkes served with a mix of pot cheese and feta, and Melora made green beans and honey cake. When they opened the door and leaned over Becca to kiss her without getting grease from their aprons on her, she felt a great rush of warmth and excitement in the air: we have created our own new people and now we are going to make ourselves a feast. The boys banged Duplos on the floor and chewed on dreidels. There were baby-proofing gizmos everywhere to keep them safe. The latkes were greasy and the brisket was burned on one side, but they blotted the oil and trimmed the meat and lit all the candles, though it was only the first night. Their lives stretched before them, long and straight and certain. They toasted to friendship.

Niko turned now toward her end of the sofa and slowly realized who he was looking at. He shook his head as if to clear the mirage.

"Hi, Niko," she said, as if twenty years hadn't passed since they last were in the same living room.

Niko smiled. "Have I walked into some distant century?" he asked.

Melora said nothing. Becca saw the anger on her face; clearly they still had arrangements to work out.

Niko said, "I heard you on the radio. I yelled 'I know her!' Or at least I used to. You must have felt strange with all this attention."

Melora didn't move for the longest time. She stared, hard. It was clear she held most of the cards. "This isn't a good time," she said. "I'm not sure I'm ready to hear whatever it is you want to say."

"Lor—don't make this bigger than it is. I'm just here to pick up those two boxes I stuck in the hall closet. I need them in the morning. I'll clear out. Promise."

Becca tried to get up to leave quietly. They both called out "no." She insisted. "You make me feel very wanted, but for all the wrong reasons. It seems to be my theme these days. Wish Cole happy birthday for me."

Melora put her hand to her ear in the universal "I'll call you" gesture, which they used to do to make fun of an officious mom they used to know. Becca trusted that she would.

LAYERS

The salon smelled of coconut and mango and an herb she couldn't place—cardamom? marjoram? She had passed this place a thousand times and not given it a thought, like all the other purveyors of luxury goods that might as well have hung a sign marked n/a.

"Yes?" said the young receptionist, her hair Moroccan-leather red and piled on one side of her face like something gift-wrapped. Tattoos of butterflies were scattered across her pale soft shoulders and arms. Becca caught a glimpse of herself in the mirror behind the butterfly girl's desk. Her hair looked like some coarse material prone to pilling—burlap, felt, home-spun. She reached out a hand to pat it down, the futile gesture of the frizzy haired.

"I have an appointment with Tatum," she said. "I haven't done this in a while. I haven't done this practically ever, to tell you the truth, except when my cousin got married in Forest Hills." The girl smiled that hybrid smile right between being charmed and 'who's the New York nut case?'

Under the herbal smell were acrid smells and burning smells. She felt the impulse to run. She had a rule: Never pay someone else to do tasks you can do yourself. She trimmed her hair a couple of times a year, and it always worked out fine. Why was she even here, in a place where she so clearly didn't belong? It was Melora's doing. Becca had told Melora she was going on a trip (to someplace else she didn't belong), and Melora had dug through her pocketbook and handed her a gift certificate and practically pushed her out the door. "This thing expires at the end of the month. I'll murderize you if you waste it."

Tatum turned out to be a boy, a skinny boy. He also had hair on one side of his head and a buzz cut on the other, as if sym-metry were the freakish thing. He wore a skinny tie and skinny pants, even skinny shoes. *So this was what people did with their days*, she thought. *This is why they never accomplished anything. This was why fashion had grown scary—all the good looks had been taken already.*

There was a protocol. He led her up some steps where, in a niche, a woman was applying makeup to a customer. "Free lesson today," she said, sweeping the woman's cheek with a fat brush. Becca felt she was in a bazaar in the East where it was essential to keep a tight hold on her money.

By the time they got upstairs, she and Tatum entered into some kind of understanding that involved him pretending she was an ordinary customer. He led her to a desk, where she was handed a smock and a big wooden hanger. In the dressing room she folded her top and stuffed it in her knapsack rather than put it on the hanger and relinquish it (to whom? where? why?). The smock was black and voluminous. There was a café too, and women waiting on padded seats with their ankles crossed. She took her place and considered bolting now while there was still time. The trouble with salons, she thought, as if she were any kind of expert, was that they wanted to turn you into someone else. But the real Becca would float back in a day or two.

She was led to the shampooing room. A new boy, named Holden, gently set her neck against the porcelain neck rest and tilted her head back. He adjusted the temperature until the water was almost but not quite too hot. She felt it slowly soak through her hair to her scalp, and it felt comforting. Now that she was warm and wet, she wanted to stay this way all day. She smelled the mango smell again, and then a squiggle of cold hit her warm head, but the warmth was pervasive enough to absorb the cold, and then his fingers massaged the shampoo into her hair. She could feel his hands work toward the ends. She could feel her hair acquiescing under his touch. He turned the water back on and began rinsing the shampoo out. He combed his fingers through her hair as if he knew it, could work with it, had been through couples therapy with it.

Holden gathered up the thick towel he'd set on her shoulders and pressed it to her head. He carefully dried her ears the way she dried Carny's after a bath, and he did an elaborate folding that resulted in the towel becoming a taut turban so she felt like a starlet in a William Wyler movie. He patted her on the back and said it was time to get a haircut.

She looked around to see what the other customers did with their things. In the chair with her bag stashed on the floor, she surveyed her face. Broad cheeks with a few broken capillaries, a face that belonged on a potato farm by day and dancing the tarantella in the town square on Saturday night. Next to her on one side was an old woman with beautiful white hair and on the other a young woman with a sour face. Tatum removed the towel and she felt a rush of cold. Then he began to play with her hair as if he needed his fingers to see. Her hair was forming corkscrews, silver and brown, coiling up around her face. She felt she should leave right now—it couldn't possibly get better.

"Tell me your dream for your hair," said Tatum, leaning in close and looking in the mirror with her.

"I don't spend a lot of time dreaming about my hair. I just trim it a couple of times a year."

"Come now. Every woman spends time dreaming about her hair. I don't believe you."

Becca realized he was right—the hours lost wishing it would behave better, wishing it would go back to the way it had been, remembering her mother brushing out the knots and braiding it before school. "Okay," she said. "I'd like you to cut it so it would curl instead of frizz, but I know that's not possible."

"Never underestimate Tatum." He said that it needed some layering, and that he could show her how to use some products that would make it behave, and he unfolded a fabric pouch and took out a pair of scissors. He began working in the back, combing her hair over and over and snipping. He worked quickly. The woman with the white hair on one side of her was telling her haircutter about her family's trip to the Galapagos. The sour woman on the other was discussing nail polish brands with her haircutter, and then they moved on to comparing notes about their boyfriends and a weakness for Entenmann's pound cake spread with Nutella. Becca loved the sound of the scissors in Tatum's hand, and the way he so expertly gathered a line of hair between his index and middle finger and snipped, letting it fall to the floor. When she trimmed her hair, she always seemed to grab too much at once and it would resist the scissors and she would have to saw at it. Someone else came by periodically with a large silent broom and swept up the fallen hair; what a great luxury it was to have someone else cleaning up her mess.

"Do you have plans for the holidays?" he asked. She nodded happily. Richard's mother was recovering nicely and he and Joycie were coming east for a week and they were going to cook together in Forest Hills. She skipped over the pending trip because she felt that she might puke every time she thought of it.

Tatum was working on the other side now, going straight down lines of her hair, and her face started to change before her eyes. He wasn't thinning out her hair so much as redirecting it like a traffic cop to flow in a more elegant pattern. Her face was suddenly lighter, softer. She looked at her features with interest, the way she looked at buildings, as an aesthetic and not just utilitarian object. Usually she saw others in her face. She tried to avoid catching glimpses of her mother, which was growing harder as the years passed. She searched for signs of Aaron. Now and then she caught her father's perplexed expression. She looked for history, for the Polish peasantry and the German Jews she came from, which might explain how she came to be. She tried to see what her tourists saw as she taught them and entertained them, but of course a face in repose in the mirror bears little resemblance to one lit up and in motion.

She saw cheekbones coaxed from hiding. She smiled, showing the slightly crooked front teeth that the Viking had once said were his favorite part of her face. She saw her neck, a part of her that she never gave a thought to. Her cheeks were rosy from the heat of the water. She slipped her hair behind her ears, the gesture of a playing girl. She knew she could never maintain it, that we all spring back to our default. But for the moment in the mango air she decided to believe in transformation.

A Box with a Black Bow

He held a little sign. Not even a sign. A piece of notebook paper bearing her name in Sharpie. She thought he would be ruddy. She pictured conference clothes, a suit with a raincoat folded over his arm, but that would be ridiculous here, with the sun bearing down through the skylights.

He wore a yellow sport shirt and he was tall and skinny and a little sunken. His face was long as well and it made her think of farm animals, of sheep or goats. She wanted to turn around and get back on the plane. But he called out tentatively, "Becca?"

He put a hand on his chest, a charming gesture (as if that was what had sunken his chest). "I'm Marc Kitchens," he said. Heavy southern accent, but not the fake-sounding kind.

"Becca Cammeyer," she said, idiotically, as if reading her own name off his hastily scrawled sign (signs would have been Jackie's province). Now what? Behind him, Katie Couric's huge pastel face smiled from a backlit billboard. The airport was sunny and petite after La Guardia.

"Did you check any luggage?"

Becca smiled at the thought. She turned to show him her Costa Rican bag and the small duffel she'd bought years ago at the Westbeth basement sale. "I'm a New Yorker," she said. "We're used to carrying what we need." The truth was her only suitcase had no wheels and was held together with duct tape, so she'd jammed everything into the duffel. She would need to borrow many things: an iron, a razor, shampoo. She reached up to slip her hair behind her ears, checking to be sure her new, improved hair was still there.

Marc started to laugh and stopped it short while it was in his throat.

"Oh God. I was going to make a joke about Jackie and her overpacking. My wife couldn't go to the gym without a suitcase."

He now put his hand lightly on Becca's shoulder to lead her out of the airport and into his life, what remained of it.

Outside it was as hot as August in the city, but otherwise nothing like the city. The airport had a lawn and trees. It had a fountain. They walked through a parking lot and then got into a car, a big one with low-slung seats and doors that closed quietly, as if with magnets. He put on a pair of Ray-Bans that had been sitting in the drink compartment. She hadn't thought to pack sunglasses; in New York in late fall the sun is always hiding behind a building, on one side of the street at a time. She put down the sun visor and still had to shade her eyes.

"Go into the glove compartment," said Marc. "There might be a spare pair in there." She spent so little time in cars she didn't know to push the latch down instead of in, and he had to help her. There was a pair of large Jackie O.–looking glasses; she realized they were Jackie K.'s glasses. It was too late to say no. They had a yellow tint that made the world softer and took away its glare.

"I'm afraid we're going to have to get through some ugly stuff to get out of here," said Marc. "Maybe you should close your eyes until I give the okay."

"Hey," she said, "the roads around La Guardia aren't exactly paradise." And then she remembered that he must have been dazed when he last traveled them. It wasn't even noon and she was exhausted from the effort.

After a while he said, "The area's had kind of a high-tech re-naissance lately, and the medical industry's booming. Used to be every guy you met was an engineer like me, but now everyone's a lab technician or a phlebotomist."

"Do you think people become phlebotomists just so they can say the name?"

This got a little smile out of him. "I have no doubt at all."

He had an easy way with the steering wheel. He glanced at his side-view and rearview mirrors. He turned on the CD player and Leonard Cohen started singing-growling. She did a double take and he caught her.

"You were expecting what, Willie Nelson? I thought I'd play against type." Now he got a smile out of her. They were even; maybe she could stop trying so hard.

She had let him talk her into staying at his house. She would have preferred a motel, but the flight was already eating up her earnings from the infernal legal proofreading, and if she had a motel room she would need a rental car as well, and she would have to find her way around somehow. She wasn't confident in a car; she'd never used a GPS.

The seats of his car were leather, firm padded channels of it. It had a stick shift. The car was wide but nearly silent. His hands on the wheel and his foot on the pedal made minute adjustments. "It was really good of you to make the trip," he said. "You didn't have to do it. People were great to us. Every step of the way. We don't blame New York. At least I don't."

"Oh, of course I came. I was the last to see them." The truth was that she came like an infant torn from its womb. "I hope I'm not too much trouble. I figured you're filled up to the brim already."

"You know, we never got a report back from our wives about the tour. They were really looking forward to it. They didn't really know anyone in New York, and you may have noticed, they're pretty friendly. Were."

He resumed after a minute. "It's weird. I keep thinking Jackie'll come and tell me about your tour. I had to lead the meeting that night at the Hilton, and I feel like that never happened either because I never got to report back."

It was as if he had set a box on the seat between them, a box with a large black bow, and he was desperate for her to open it, but just as desperate to save it for later. He was, she thought, imagining the box to be filled with stories that would bring Jackie back to him, new and fresh, for just a little while. Becca liked the plain way he spoke and wished he would teach her how to do it.

"There's some bottles of water in the back," he said. "I know I always get really dry on planes."

She realized she was terribly thirsty. She reached behind her and grabbed a bottle. It was one of those small ones with a sport cap. She was afraid she wouldn't know how it worked, but she managed to break the seal and drank it down in one go. She hoped the house wasn't too far because she couldn't possibly ask this poor man to find her a bathroom.

She asked about the trees with the dark waxy leaves, and he explained to her about magnolias, which it turned out were entirely different from what she had always understood to be magnolias in the north.

"In the city the Parks Department has taken to planting daffodils like maniacs," she told him. "Every March every little patch of dirt is filled with hundreds of them. It was nice the first couple of years, but everyone's starting to say enough with the daffodils already."

He smiled again while watching the road. She had found her mission: to do whatever it took to amuse Marc. It was wonderful when he smiled, like a ledger book full of red that she was trying to balance, a tiny bit at a time.

"It's gonna be Grand Central Station at the house, let me warn you. I'm actually glad. It helps a little, having people around."

"Tell me who so I don't put my foot in my mouth," she said. "I'm good at learning people fast." And then she gave him a piece of New York trivia. "Next time someone says Grand Central Station, you look all well informed and tell them that it's not a station, it's a terminal; there are no through trains. You can also tell them that the Hudson River isn't really a river; it's a tidal estuary. The water is brackish like the ocean."

"Thanks. I never knew either of those things. So here's a little primer. You'll meet our...my daughter Alexa, Lexie, who's beautiful just like her mom but even taller, like me." Here he had to stop and suck in his breath to master the impulse to cry. "Just like Jackie thirty years ago. Her husband, Tom, and their little boy, Trevor. My sister-in-law, Celeste, and her husband, Rory. They're the kind who have cats instead of kids—if you want to get in good with them, ask about the Persians. And Jackie's mom, Mae, who also looks like her but with pure white hair. She's with her second husband, Alan, who falls asleep."

The neighborhoods changed, as they do, to a land of strip malls to an area of new condo complexes, and finally, to a lavishly leafy suburban area. She had braced herself for gated communities, though she had never actually been inside one. She knew there might be pillars.

"We really are grateful to you," said Marc. "We feel like we have a celebrity among us. Have you lived in New York City all your life?"

"Born and bred Manhattanite. Hardly ever leave the city limits these days."

"Must seem pretty rinky-dink here."

"Actually, what it seems is really green. My eyes don't know what to do with all that green all at once." She was also noticing the cars, the way everything was organized for them, the crazy, inefficient way every building had to be surrounded by a field of asphalt to accommodate the cars.

How her mother had talked up towns! There are places people live that aren't noisy and crowded and dirty, she used to say, as if beginning a fairy tale, where you live in your own building called a house, and it has grass and trees all around it, on all four sides. And you can climb the trees and grow your own flowers in the earth. And you get from place to place in a car, which you keep in its own room called a garage. Becca, of course, already knew all this—the way she knew that Indians lived in long houses.

There was no gate, she was relieved to see. The houses were new, and pale, and very large, with mix-and-match architecture. All the porches had decorations: banners and wind chimes and spinning thingies that probably had a name. She welled up with fondness for the Yankee north, even for her mother's no-nonsense Mamaroneck.

"And here we are," he said, pressing a button as he pulled into a driveway of a house with a buff-colored brick façade and many eaves. The garage door opened. There was another car inside with a license plate that read ORGNIZR.

"Oh," she said. "Jackie's car."

"We used to joke about getting me a license plate that said SLOB. I was happy to let her organize all around me. I was her favorite project. We had a good arrangement. You have family?" he asked, a little embarrassed. "I'm sorry. I don't mean to pry. It's just I feel I know you, but I don't know a lot of particulars."

"It's okay," she said. "I'm a single mom. I have a grown son. Long story. My parents got divorced when I was a kid. I never quite caught on to marriage."

"I hear you."

She searched for something to get the spotlight off her, and an image of Jackie floated back to her. "Your wife made me do a funny thing," she said as he parked. "On the tour. I turned my body into a big map of New York. It worked really well. I plan to keep it in the act." She didn't tell him that she first had to spend the winter in a back office on lower Broadway proofing abstruse redlined documents.

He came around to open her door, which struck her as silly but kind of nice. "So this is that famous Southern hospitality I've been hearing about all my life." In reply, he made a grand gesture to lead her to the kitchen door.

She met the family and got everyone's name right except the stepfather-in-law, the one who napped. They walked around the house, sometimes like zombies, sometimes like ordinary bantering humans. Trevor the grandson got passed around and cooed at and cried onto. Three different neighbors had brought casseroles, and Becca leapt up with the three women left in the extended family to get dinner ready. The memorial wasn't until the next day. After she helped clean up, Becca retreated to the guest room to work on the eulogy she'd been asked to give.

The mourners had filled the lot and were parked on either side of the street and on the asphalt island not meant for parking.

There seemed to be a thousand Chevys in the parking lot wearing the same frown on their grills, all tsk-tsking as they tried to cool down in the hot rain. The magnolias were crying, the sweet gums dropping their weaponry for little girls to cut their tender feet on.

The umbrellas hadn't heard the dirge and tried to cheer them up with their polka dots and their Monets and even a map of the New York City subway system—oh God, Marc asked himself, who could be under that one?

He couldn't remember how he got there or in what car. He always noticed the car he was in. He was always the driver.

They entered the church the back way, past the gleaming stainless kitchen. The first person he saw inside was Trudy the kitchen lady, lit from behind like a diabetic Madonna. Trudy who had catered Lexie's communion, who received Jackie's famous eggplant casserole and Laura's famous sticky buns and on down the line (except for Sheryl, whose only famous recipe involved a punchbowl and a fifth of Jack Daniel's). He blundered right into Trudy like an airbag. Save me, oh Trudy, he thought.

This being alive—how dogged it was, how he hated it. He had always followed Jackie everywhere she went. Sometimes he'd followed her into the bathroom, though she always shooed him out and told him a lady needed her privacy.

The rain got heavier and noisier on the roof. He made it past the restrooms and the water cooler and reached the wood that marked the beginning of the sanctuary. He peeked in and saw lipstick and hairdos and much tailored suiting. It was hushed and yet very loud. Bodies in pews receding to the horizon. He was having trouble matching up faces and names, names and contexts—which one is the cleaning lady who had taken direction from Jackie for twenty years and which one the head of personnel at her office? His mechanic, his mailman, his across-the-street neighbor, his second cousin. Names bounced through his mind: Norm and Manuel and…

Someone was holding his arm. Someone was always holding his arm now and directing him, and he followed though he was tempted to fling the hand away with a violent motion that would terrify Lexie or his mother-in-law or the usher. It was a long way to the first pew. The wood was so dark and shiny. In the rain, the rose window had gone yellowish. The church was gasping for breath. The priest, Father Briggs, he recalled that name. He, Marc, was in the brig for a life sentence. There didn't seem to be much difference between a life and a death sentence.

He didn't see Becca. She was the only one he could bear to talk to, though one would think she'd be the hardest. Lexie was the hardest. He forced himself to glance at her. She was holding tight to Trevor, beautiful sad Lexie in her black dress with the square neckline. She reminded him of Jackie the day of the miscarriage when Lexie was two. He and Jackie had sat on the guest bed, where Becca was staying now. Why did they end up there? Maybe they had wandered in in search of neutral land, where no baby had begun and ended in the space of two months.

The organ played a muted chord. Mrs. Goethels, the choir director, once told them that Lexie had a lovely alto. Lovely alto. He remembered saying the phrase in the car on the way home that day and the way Jackie had grabbed his hand across the cassette tapes and squeezed it. Their daughter with the lovely alto and the square-necked dress and a column of air where her mother should be.

The column followed him everywhere. It walked beside him, it flitted around the audience, it filled up the cubic feet of the house. What was he going to do with all that house? Mrs. Goethels began a hymn. He couldn't remember the name but knew it had a line about cords that cannot be broken. People were still filing in through the vestibule in front. He heard someone say, the whole town is here, and someone else respond, and half the county. He wondered where they were putting all those umbrellas. He worried that someone would slip on the stone floor.

The men, his fellow widowers, had all arrived. He couldn't look at them. The kids and the grandkids, the aged parents. He had a desire to run back out the door and into whatever car brought him there.

His son-in-law, Tom, was going to speak. They'd asked all the family members who loved her but who had lives separate from her, because they could maybe hold it together. He wasn't ready for a eulogy. He'd been to these things. He knew how a person gets all tidied up in a small package and mailed away to nowhere. He wanted to set his hand on Jackie's warm waist, pull her stray hairs off his face. He wanted her to fix the back of his collar when he tied his tie. He wanted her propped up in bed reading a mystery so he could wish she would turn out the light and go to sleep.

All the bustling gradually died down, all the shaking out of raincoats stopped. Puddles formed on the floor. The organ moved on to "Be Not Afraid" and the choir suddenly sang. He hadn't even noticed the choir. They were in their blue satin robes with the white collars, and there was Mrs. Goethels moving her whole body the way she did. They were all opening their mouths wide. Some had their eyes closed. They sounded so pure, with no breathiness, just sound. He breathed. It helped a little. He thought maybe, for a minute, he could get through this with all these kids, if they just kept singing and Mrs. Goethels kept playing chords for the rest of his life.

Father Briggs came up to the dais. He was in blue too. He was holding his Bible. There was a white tasseled bookmark in it. Jackie called Post-Its the best invention of the twentieth century, but you couldn't put Post-Its in a Bible. She'd put one on his nose one time when he kept forgetting to call the accountant. Father Briggs put his hands on the sides of the dais. Marc had always admired his hands. They seemed like the hands of someone who worked in the soil sometimes. Marc didn't like being in the front where he couldn't see anyone. Lexie was on one side of him and Roger on the other. Roger was already blubbering, shaking up and down. Marc was afraid to put a hand on his knee or maybe his arm. He was afraid he would catch his crying.

Did a person ever run out of tears?

Father Briggs was hanging on to scripture for dear life. No one knew what to say. Marc couldn't get a toehold on any of it. Death be not. The valley of the. For he is thine. Rest for your servants, where there is neither sorrow nor. What did any of it have to do with a bomb in Washington Square? They would need the rituals of a more overtly violent culture for any kind of model to follow.

Finally Becca got up. She was wearing a long loose skirt and a jacket, not black but a dark print. Something about the cut told him she'd had this outfit for a while. She seemed ill at ease in her dress shoes even though they weren't very dressy. She kept pulling her jacket closer. She didn't have any notes. She adjusted the mike and introduced herself, though he was sure most of the audience knew who she was.

"I learned a long time ago that there is no right thing to say when someone you love dies," Becca said, "let alone when six friends die and leave a hole in a circle of friendship, a hole in a community, a hole in six families."

Marc felt like calling out hallelujah. Finally someone is talking about actual humans, about us.

"My work has to do with New York City history, so what I will do first is tell you a Manhattan story. In June of 1904, an excursion boat called the *General Slocum* set out from the East River in Manhattan," said Becca, with that forthright manner, that little bit of accent whose vowels were like a dollop of some starchy comfort food. She didn't speak loudly, but she made people want to listen. "There were about 1,300 passengers on board, mostly women and children who belonged to a German church on the East Side. They were heading to a picnic ground on Long Island, not too far away. It was their seventeenth annual Sunday school picnic." She paused to let them take in the scene, to wonder where she was going.

"Soon after the steamboat launched, it caught on fire and everything above water burned in about fifteen minutes. Over a thousand wives, mothers, and young children died instantly.

Many of the bodies washed up on the shore. Most of the families lived in a neighborhood in the East Village known then as *Kleindeutschland,* or little Germany. After the disaster, most of the men moved away and started their lives over."

It was a horrible story; how could he have never heard of this? But it was such a relief not to hear about Jesus Christ.

"Why do I mention the *General Slocum,* which is the smallest of footnotes to history? Because people bear unbearable sorrow. If it's any consolation—I know that's a phrase people use at funerals, and I suppose that sometimes there is consolation, as when someone very old dies, or someone whose life has been made unbearable by pain or disability. But I don't know if there's any consolation available now, or any that can be spun out of the situation. This is a small town, I know, some might say a provincial place. In fact, one of the women did say as much to me, on the tour. It's hard for me to recall accurately, but I believe it was Sheryl—your relative, your friend, maybe your coworker at the Chamber of Commerce." Becca had holed herself in the guest room the day before; clearly she had studied the dead wives' walking tour.

"And that, actually, is the consolation I'm offering. Take it if it helps: I now know Sheryl and Jackie and Wynnette and Laura and Mary Anne and Connie, and a piece of them will live in me for the rest of my life. And their loss has brought me here where I've never been before, here to all of you, and I am grateful for that."

Becca looked out into the room now, the first time she dared. The husbands were scattered in the first two rows with the remains of their families. "An event as horrible and unspeakable as this certainly forces you to think. And here's where my thinking has brought me: nothing is unspeakable. I could very easily have died that night, and your wives could have lived, and don't think I haven't thought a thousand times that it might have been better that way. I have fewer attachments and less family.

"I'm in a funny position as the last person to see them alive.

And very alive they were on their tour of the Village. I gave them a job to do, because when I was a student I noticed that kids were happier that way than if they were just passively receiving information. I sent them down Tenth Street on a treasure hunt, looking for a Federal-era house. For those who don't know New York, avenues run north-south and are very wide and bustling and mostly commercial, and the cross streets are narrow and mostly residential. And in the Village they're lined with little nineteenth-century red brick houses. Tenth Street between Fifth and Sixth Avenues is a particularly beautiful block. Well, your women fell in love with that block, same as I did when I was a kid. And they found the Federal house right away, and Wynnette pointed to the dormers, but she called them 'sticky-outy windows.'"

The audience laughed in recognition; Becca could hear the little hiccups where crying and laughing collided in their throats. The laughter went on longer than it should have, as if remembering her foibles could keep Wynnette's spirit alive for just an extra breath or two, one more round of chuckles. She caught a glimpse of Wynnette's husband, Rod, who, Marc had told her, came from the Ozarks and was trained originally as a civil engineer. Rod wiped his eyes with the back of his hand, trying to look nonchalant, like a gas station attendant cleaning a smudge off a windshield.

Becca resumed. If there was one thing she knew, it was when an audience was with her and when it wasn't. She and this group were one, at least for these few minutes, and it was the best feeling in the middle of the worst pain. And while she paused to let them all think about Wynnette, her father's ghostly voice, which hadn't been heard from since she arrived in the South, whispered in her ear, and what it said was quite surprising: "Ed Koch." All the dozens of times she had relived the tour, she had completely left him out of the story. "Oh—and I just remembered something funny," she said. "Ed Koch, the former mayor, came and chatted with us. So you should know that the six women—your wives, your daughters, your mothers, whatever relationship brought you here, to this—had at least a local celebrity sighting on their last night. The mayor flattered them, and they were tickled."

It felt so good to be in front of an audience again. Becca felt this was what she was born to do, but she didn't usually get to do it indoors, with a mike and an oak podium. The polyurethane was soft from the heat and she pressed her fingernails gently into it. She looked down at her skirt and hoped it didn't look too dowdy. She had prepared a whole speech about how tragedy can easily make people more hateful and more afraid, about how the women wouldn't want that. But she could tell none of that was needed now. It was time to wrap up.

"I knew them only for a tiny little while," said Becca, hearing the Southern slip into her voice as naturally as her skin turning pink from the South Carolina sun, "but from what I do know, I keep imagining—and maybe some of you are having a similar feeling—that they're back in the other room bustling around to get everything just right, making sure the caterers have everything they need. Jackie is pressing a check firmly into the caterer's hands. Sheryl is throwing back her head and laughing at some joke she's cracked, and Wynnette is maybe doing a little dance to entertain the others, and Laura is taking it all in quietly with those big eyes, and Connie doesn't like the way Mary Anne is setting the table and is going around after her and rearranging all the silverware."

When she headed back to her spot in the pew, hands reached out from every direction to give her a quick touch as if she were the statue at the Feast of San Gennaro.

"I think I'll turn in early," she said to the family that evening. She was feeling full in spirit and spent in body, and she thought the family might want some private time. Besides, it was so much easier to talk to a crowd, with a stage and a podium between them. She slipped off her shoes and lay down on the daybed with one of Jackie and Marc's photo albums, filled with old snapshots. Culottes, blazers with the sleeves rolled up.

Windswept hair, squinting eyes. Jackie and Marc and Lexie at Disneyland, the San Diego Zoo. She pulled a photo out of its plastic sleeve. The typed label on the back read: *Marc and Jackie and Alexa Kitchens, Kittyhawk, NC, 1996.*

Such a different life from hers. She and Aaron had schlepped to Jones Beach on the subway, the train, the bus, trudging through the parking lot, so vast Aaron used to believe he could see the curvature of the Earth on it. They had occasionally cadged an invitation to Fire Island for a weekend. They had gone to the Jersey shore, where the sand was dusty.

She leafed through shoulder pads and maternity leggings and wonders both natural and man-made. She saw Lexie's "sweet sixteen" and various graduations. Jackie was always easy to pick out because she was the tallest in the group and had the biggest smile. Funny how family photos never showed slamming doors or tax bills or the flu.

This room would become Marc's Fudgetown box. This was his fate: to look through the albums and never feel better, just open the wounds over and over. Turning the plastic pages compulsively, but never satisfying anything.

When the soft Southern voices in the great room gave way to footfalls on the carpeted stairs, flushing of toilets, water in pipes, she came out in her sweats to get a drink of water.

She was startled to see Marc sitting at the kitchen table with his head in his hands.

"Oh," she said. "Sorry. I was thirsty."

He insisted it was okay. He pulled a chair out for her. "Can I get you some—" he said, and then rummaged around to see what there was. "Decaf? OJ? Usually there's sweet tea in the fridge, but I don't know how to make it. I can tell you how a three-way catalytic converter works, but I can't make sweet tea."

In the end they had scotch. "To Sheryl with an *S*," she said, and they clinked glasses and each took a slug.

He put his head in his upraised fists and cried.

She was going home in the morning. The laptop on the kitchen counter was still open to Delta's website, with all those slots for places and dates and times, seat assignments, baggage fees. He would drive her back to the airport through the heat, and they would perhaps never see each other again or correspond regularly.

"Rod's really falling apart," he said. "The others are starting to lose patience. A bunch of Southern engineers mourning— not a pretty picture." He looked straight at her. "How do you stand it, living alone? And I'm not even living alone yet. I have a house full of relatives. Don't the evenings go on forever?"

"Think about a dog," said Becca. "A dog makes a lot of things tolerable." She pictured Carny, who was safe at home with Ed.

He shook his head. "We never had any pets. Jackie never wanted one. We were both working. I always kind of wanted a dog, to tell you the truth, but I can't. It would seem like such a—not betrayal." He struggled for the word. "A defeat. Like the whole time she was here there was this tight spring that held us in place just so. And now the spring's gone, and I'm back to where I used to be before her. That's it—that's what scares me. It'll be like she never existed, and I'll be the sorry kid I was before she came along and straightened me out, only this time I'm not a kid."

He did look like a middle-aged kid sitting there in his plaid shirt with his shoulders hunched up around his ears.

"I never had what you and Jackie had, so it's hard for me to imagine how it feels to lose it. But I am pretty seasoned at going without. I never thought of it as a skill quite, but maybe it is. Which is good news, because that means it's learnable."

She got an image of herself back in the Square, swinging her cape like Georgy Girl that evening. She tried to rearrange the scene like a playwright. "Can we buy you a cupcake?" they'd said, and she'd refused on principle. All the things she'd done in the name of principle. The women might be here now if she'd let them buy her a damned cupcake and she would be home with Carny's snout on her lap. Marc would be right here but he would be laughing while Jackie bustled around, tapping the last bits of salad out of the sink strainer, hanging the dish towel to dry over the handle of the oven. Marc would pull the trash out of the bin and take it to the garage, probably mock-complaining the whole way. Then up to bed to read for a while before falling asleep pressed together.

"I guess I should go pack up my stuff."

"That'll take at least a minute," he said, and a smile poked through the crying.

Her hand, all by itself, flew out and hit him lightly on the arm. "I was being polite. What I really meant is that you should go to bed. Lots of people are with you tonight and every night. Try to hold on to that just a little. You go on up; I'll get the lights."

And she turned off the kitchen light and was about to get the one in the hall, marveling at how fast she'd learned her way around this house, when Marc came back down.

His head motioned up the stairs. "I can't go up there. Just can't do it. I've been staying up as late as possible and falling asleep on the couch, but it's making me stiff and I hate waking up with the TV still on."

He sat back down and didn't say anything. She couldn't very well leave now but she didn't know what he wanted. She didn't think she had anything left to give anyone.

He finally spoke up. "My parents had the good grace to die before their lives got really miserable and limited, and I don't mean to be glib. They had a long and pretty decent marriage. They went within five months of each other. But Jackie. She was only fifty-eight, and she didn't seem to be even that. She had so much juice still in her. At least she was at Lexie's wedding and saw Trevor get born. Got to feed him rice cereal and hear him squeal with laughter. She called him the seagull. And I could see how it pained her to see that food get flung all over the kitchen, but—God bless her—she put up with it."

Becca sensed that some kind of floodgate was opening. He reminded her of Villagers, oddly enough—the way they collar you on the sidewalk and talk at you.

"I promised I wouldn't start this but I don't have the will-power. I thought I would be one of those silent widowers, a recluse, the kind who doesn't know to clip his own fingernails. But you know what? It doesn't matter if you're silent or if you can't shut up. You have a small window when you're allowed to be out of your head and after that—I don't know how long it lasts but I know I'm bumping up against the deadline."

"Well," said Becca, "I guess you build up a tolerance. My social network is more raggedy than yours. Everyone I know is already one kind of a mess or another."

Marc's eyebrows squeezed together the way she imagined they did when he was trying to figure something out.

"Not everything is engineered, Marc," she ventured. "Some things just don't benefit from analysis. As hard as you look, you can't figure out how they work because they don't make any sense or follow any logic."

"Having you around is just about the only thing that's made it more manageable."

Marc put a hand on her hand. It was dark in the kitchen. He hadn't turned on the overhead, only the fixture that hung over the table. His hand was warm. It covered hers completely. It bore a golden ring and colonies of dark hair above the knuckles. She was a sucker for a man's hand.

Help, Joycie, she thought. *What signal is he sending?*

She ventured a look into his face, but it didn't clear up the question; he didn't seem to know either.

She had an idea. "Do you have any cards?" she asked. When Aaron was young she had always carried a deck in her bag, for emergencies.

"Of course. In the drawer marked 'cards, decks of,'" he said. He came back and tossed a deck on the table. "You're on. Rummy 500? Want a lemon bar? Every woman left in this town brought lemon bars."

"I hear they go great with scotch," she said, and dealt them each a hand from the brand-new deck.

For a little while the only trouble in the world was the

whereabouts of the king of diamonds. Then, he got up and turned on the radio. A Bach fugue came on. "You've got to be kidding," she said.

"What, you don't think this will cheer me up?"

"Let's find something completely unevocative. We need some really dumb music. Dumb and happy." She flipped through the radio dial until she came upon the Bee Gees in the middle of "Staying Alive."

He had to clamp his mouth to keep scotch and lemon bar from spurting out with his laughter. He went over and turned it up.

"Hey, you can't do that," she whispered loudly. "We'll wake everyone up."

"Mae passed out Ambiens. Nothing's going to wake anyone for at least the next four hours."

They played quietly while Billy Joel and the Temptations came and went. Then another wave came over Marc. He put his face in his hands. He covered his eyes. "A lifetime of never crying in front of anyone and now I'm Niagara Falls."

"It's not a falls," she said. "It's a tidal estuary."

He burst out laughing. She joined him. They both nearly choked on lemon bars. The spurts of laughter were wonderful, but they dissipated so fast. She couldn't possibly dole out enough to carry him to safety.

They finished two games in silent concentration. She started to deal a third. "Mind if we don't finish this round?" he asked. "I can't concentrate. I keep starting things and then when I'm in the middle of them I can't remember the point. Sometimes I can't remember the rules. Jackie was the one who read the booklets. She was always unfolding things and spreading them out on the table to study. And I'm supposed to be the engineer.

"I actually thought the other day in the middle of having my teeth cleaned—I kept the appointment she'd made me—the dentist told me he wanted to give me a fluoride treatment, and I couldn't remember what that meant. I said the word to myself and knew it was familiar. And you know what I thought, what

I actually thought? Maybe this is Alzheimer's. And the idea actually seemed appealing, at least for a split second. Maybe I can forget everything I know."

"First of all," said Becca, "I cry in public all the time. I did it in front of a bunch of tourists in the middle of a tour not long ago. Made an utter ass of myself. All it means is that you have feelings. Why are guys so scared of feelings? Don't answer that. I know why." And then she had another idea: she gave him a job to do. "Tell me a story about Jackie and you. One that no one told at the service."

He thought for a second and then launched right in. "Well, if there's one thing you know about her it's that she liked to plan. When Lexie was around eight, I guess—I can never remember what happened when unless I can link it to the new car models for that year. Anyhow, she wanted to go to Epcot to see the animatronics. I kind of planted the idea. I thought they were very exciting. So we decided to drive down over spring break, us and every other family in the downstate. And we got into the mother of all traffic jams. Times like that I always wondered if it would be better or worse if Lexie had a sibling. You have the fantasy of them entertaining each other in the backseat, but of course all our friends complained about the bickering. Bickering was never our family's problem."

Marc's whole posture changed. His shoulders went back down and his head rose up as if it didn't weigh quite as much.

"So Jackie decides we're going to get off the highway and see the sights of the first town we happen upon. I ask, what if there are no sights, and she's utterly confident. She promises she'll find us a sight. That's something I loved and hated about her, depending on my mood. She was fearless. She never worried, at least not about the things I worry about.

"So I pull off an exit, and it takes us onto another highway, but an old county road sort of affair, and she tells me to turn left even though my instincts tell me to turn right. It's the kind of road with nothing much on it, a body shop, a Baptist church, I don't know what all. And Lexie spills apple juice all over her shirt and is on the verge of a meltdown. We're in tobacco country. Have you ever seen a tobacco barn?"

Becca shook her head. She had seen so little; Manhattanites think they're so worldly, but she was the ultimate provincial.

"They look like a regular barn except there's all these openings between the boards so the tobacco can dry. They basically look like a badly made barn left to fall apart. Lexie's always been fascinated by them, I suppose because she's used to living here where everything's brand new.

"Anyway, we hear sirens up ahead and next thing we know we come upon a barn that's on fire. Every inch is brilliant orange. There's a fire truck and the firefighters are just starting to spray it. It's fantastic to look at, all that white water and those orange flames. So I pull over and we get out.

"We're a good safe distance away on a little gravel road. We can feel the heat on our faces and hear the crackling, and the whoosh from the hose and the hissing from the steam. And at one point I remember looking over at my girls and they looked so beautiful in the glow. I worry that it's going to give Lexie bad dreams, but it's just so damned interesting none of us can stop looking. Every few minutes there's a huge settling as a post gets burned enough to fall. And we hear this tremendous crackling as it hits everything it's attached to and breaks it. I put my arms around my girls, my tall girls, and I think about the world's fierceness and beauty, and I can feel Jackie's side through her jacket, and I run my hand through Lexie's thick straight hair that seems like it's been poured out of her head. I'm just happy we're together and we're safe. I like knowing that I'm keeping my girls safe. That's what my whole career's been based on: keeping people safe. I'm holding on to both of them and I guess we're waiting for the building to collapse. One side comes down first but the other stays up for a really long time. We all take off our jackets. We still have a long drive but we don't move."

Becca could tell he was almost talked out; sleep would come now and carry him safely to morning.

"It was just a barn full of tobacco; it smelled like someone had lit a million cigars all at once. No one was in it and we were watching, just tourists passing through. And eventually I shifted on my feet and we all got back in the car and back on the county road and back on the highway. The worst of the traffic was over. It got cloudy and then a few drops of rain fell, and Lexie said, 'That's good for the fire, right, Daddy?' And I said, 'It's the best possible thing.' We drove into Orlando at sunset and the next morning we went to Epcot."

Becca put her hand on his. He went upstairs to bed and she stayed down and turned out the lights.

Not Just Any Loot

There was a package crammed into her mailbox, soft like a small item of clothing, badly wrapped in brown paper with yards of packing tape. He'd written on the back: *read letter first.* She pressed it to her chest and carried it upstairs.

She passed Ed on the steps and waved it at him. "Lookie what I got."

"Oooh, loot," he said.

"Not just any loot. Costa Rica loot."

She sat on the horsehair chair and set it on her lap. Aaron's handwriting was never sure which way it wanted to slant. Like West Fourth Street, he had said once, cracking her up. Maybe you are your mother's son after all, she had thought but held back from saying.

Dear Mom, she read, *Here in paradise it turns out things aren't so simple.* Her heart sank. When you're a mother, sometimes the world tilts toward you and sometimes away. All is right or all is wrong, and you're always extrapolating from clues. Same old Aaron, always standing on the outside, weighing in with disapproval. She read on.

> They say they have no military and that all the money goes to education, but they sure fooled me. We've got hardly any books and we're ridiculously understaffed.

His tone began to brighten, and she with it.

> You should see me managing a class of forty-seven. I make that face you used to make, that one that always shamed me into behaving. It works. Just stare them down and make them understand it's silly to waste time when the world is so interesting.

New paragraph: *I don't know when I'll be coming to New York.* Now she was a linguist on the prowl for meaning. He said "to

New York" rather than "home." But he didn't say he *wouldn't* be coming. The last visit had been so short. There had been so little time to talk.

She put her hand over the bottom of the page. They always wrote each other funny PSs. She wanted to save it.

I have news, he wrote. This was unheard of. Aaron didn't make announcements, not this most loving child, more loving than she could have wished for, but who was equally adept at turning away, Aaron who was always leaving, even when he was present, the most lost kid in the Washington Square playground, Aaron who cupped his hand around his math homework because it was none of her business, as if she might cheat off him, Aaron who was always running off to join other families, Catholic families from Our Lady of Pompei with so many kids he could burrow among them and avoid scrutiny. Overworked, negligent parents—that was his idea of a good home life. Households full of males.

I'm committed through this year but I'm not sure about next year, she read, and her heart sank deeper. *Plus,* she read, *there's something else. I met someone.*

Becca started to smile and started to cry. She was overjoyed; it was high time. She was nervous. The name popped out before she read the next sentence: *Ana.* She loved Ana already and feared her; Anas with one *N* came from somewhere else far away. They were likely to be Catholic.

> Her name is Ana and she's great. I knew it right away. She's the 'specials' teacher, which means music and art and library, such as it is. The first time I saw her in action, she had the kids put drops of watercolor on paper and blow on them through a straw to their hearts' content. How cool is that? When the paint dried they outlined the blobs with black ink until they started to suggest things or just were interesting shapes. They were fantastic. They're still hanging in the halls.
>
> If I stay next year I think I'll be very ready to make a move. Maybe even stateside, as they say. I thought that the

better my Spanish got the less I would miss the States, but
the opposite thing seems to be happening.

She's from Copenhagen. That's right, a Viking. Speaks
perfect English.

Aaron with his crazy blond Swedish-Ashkenazi features.
When he'd gone off to Central America, his hair was the dark-
est it had ever been. Now it was bleached by the sun. His summer head, she used to call it, only even more so now, bleached
pale, curly. His yellow-brown eyes. "Blood of my blood," she
said aloud, shaking her head with wonder. She took her cupped
hand off the bottom of the letter.

> PS. I caught a wave for you like you asked. I held it in my
> fist for a while but then I set it free. It drifted out to sea to
> join its friends. And then a seagull pooped on it and it got
> mad and rose up and made a chalky whitecap. And then
> an oil rig came chugging along and its pointy prow just
> missed the wave. And then the wave floated on its back
> for a year or two, which in its self-published memoir it said
> was the happiest time of its life. And then we fell out of
> touch. For all I know it's approaching far Rockaway right
> now, and if you run, you might be able to catch the A train
> in time to jump into it and make a big splash. Except that
> it's winter, so it might be a pretty cold splash and you'd
> have to ride all the way back shivering with your hair wet.
> So on second thought, stay home and let my wave crash
> onto shore in peace.

> PPS. Her mom is Danish, but her dad is a Jewish guy from
> Skokie. So you can take a breath now. And open your pres-
> ent.

She was already picturing the T-shirt with his school's logo,
which she would wear proudly though she looked terrible in a
T-shirt. There was a little more writing:

> I remembered you saying you loved these. I was never sure
> what one was so I asked around. You'll be happy to know
> it was made by a collective of women run by women.

It was a white cotton peasant blouse, long sleeves, gathered at the neck, ties with tassels on the ends and hand-stitched embroidery with bright reds and purples and blues.

She pulled off her sweatshirt and put it on. She carefully arranged Camille's locket. The cotton was stiff but would soften with time. She ran a hand over the cottony bumps of the embroidery. She had a rule about never wearing the handiwork of strangers but she would make an exception.